## The Final Hours of Muriel Hinchcliffe

Claire Parkin was born and brought up in a village just outside Cardiff and graduated from King's College London with an MA in nineteenth-century English and American literature. She worked as a journalist on women's general-interest magazines for many years, writing for *Essentials*, *Woman & Home* and *Candis*, where she was known for being able to turn her hand to pretty much anything – from interviewing boxing champions and war correspondents to learning how to pole dance and the correct way to iron a shirt. Other career highlights include taste-testing eight varieties of mince pie during an August heatwave, begging Victoria Beckham to donate a dress to a charity raffle and visiting six second-hand car dealerships in one afternoon, in a bid to expose sexism in the motoring industry.

CLAIRE PARKIN

# The Final Hours of Muriel Hinchcliffe

PAN BOOKS

First published 2024 by Macmillan

This paperback edition first published 2025 by Pan Books
an imprint of Pan Macmillan
The Smithson, 6 Briset Street, London EC1M 5NR
*EU representative:* Macmillan Publishers Ireland Ltd, 1st Floor,
The Liffey Trust Centre, 117–126 Sheriff Street Upper,
Dublin 1, D01 YC43
Associated companies throughout the world
www.panmacmillan.com

ISBN 978-1-0350-2847-4

1 3 5 7 9 8 6 4 2

A CIP catalogue record for this book is available from the British Library.

Typeset by Palimpsest Book Production Ltd, Falkirk, Stirlingshire
Printed and bound by CPI Group (UK) Ltd, Croydon, CR0 4YY

MIX
Paper | Supporting
responsible forestry
FSC
www.fsc.org
FSC® C116313

Visit **www.panmacmillan.com** to read more about all our books
and to buy them. You will also find features, author interviews and
news of any author events, and you can sign up for e-newsletters
so that you're always first to hear about our new releases.

*For R, who made everything possible,
and H & E, who make everything even better*

Oft have I heard that grief softens the mind
And makes it fearful and degenerate,
Think therefore on revenge and cease to weep.
— Queen Margaret, *Second Part of King Henry VI*
WILLIAM SHAKESPEARE


Life's not fair, is it? Some of us drink champagne in
the fast lane, and some of us eat our sandwiches by
the loose chippings on the A597.

VICTORIA WOOD

# Monday, 24 June 2019

## *Evening*

# A death is announced

Now that I think about it, it wasn't so much Muriel telling me she was going to die – it was more that she gave her death an actual date and time that unnerved me so much. I am well acquainted with Muriel's prophecies, unfailingly vague and melodramatic, invariably relating to her health or safety – a whispered *Ruth! You MUSTN'T leave me alone tonight, I felt the Angel of Death's icy palm caress my cheek during* EastEnders . . . that sort of thing. Yes, I am very familiar with Muriel's predictions, which, by now, I am able to predict myself, because they occur – without exception – when I have plans to go out for the evening.

But that was the other curious thing. I had no such plans for tonight. I was a free agent, anticipating the familiar, comforting ups and downs of a night in with Muriel: a cup or two of chamomile tea, a game of Scrabble, a furious row. It had been an unseasonably cool, wet June and I was sick to the back teeth with the relentless grey of it all, with everything feeling so damp and claggy – inside and out. It would have been so pleasant (had things not taken the turn that they did) to have curled up in my usual armchair next to the electric fire, having finally persuaded Muriel to switch the blasted thing on.

As it was, when she made her declaration, I was on my knees

scouring the dry skin from her heels, while she reclined in her wheelchair, the soles of her feet raised with the aid of a heavily embroidered velvet cushion – a crimson, pom-pom-edged monstrosity that even I consider prehistoric (and I am just as old as Muriel; only fifteen seconds separate our forays into the world, seventy-six years ago). Her feet were an absolute sight and I felt deeply ashamed of my lack of care because I am Muriel's carer, as well as lifelong friend and confidante. There is no one but me to look after her, and the crusted skin, ram's-horn nails and cheesy fungal infection burgeoning between her toes betrayed the shabby, neglectful creature I truly am.

What else do I remember? I know we were listening to *The Archers*. Or rather, Muriel was listening as I scrubbed away with a pumice stone, dipping it intermittently into a bowl of soapy water, while she frowned and shushed me. I don't recall what I was thinking, though I did notice the sun's glare spot-lighting the greasy fingerprints on the bay window, which caused me to cast a more critical eye than usual over the rest of the room before wishing I hadn't because . . . oh God – the mess! Dirty dishes (at least three days' worth) stacked on the hostess trolley at Muriel's side, mounds of *OK!* and *Hello!* magazines spewing over the seats and arms of two brown-leather, button-back sofas, crusty ferns and parlour palms sulking over the rims of their chinoiserie planters, and deep layers of dust blanketing absolutely *everything* – bookshelves, table nests, dado rails, the TV set and a teak cabinet displaying a collection of curios acquired during Muriel's lifetime: her grandfather's leech jar, a maiden aunt's wooden leg, two glass asthma inhalers left behind by Harvey, and a stuffed ginger tomcat that had, in fairness, belonged to my mother.

The state of the room – and I hold my hand up to this – is in no small part down to my domestic ineptitude. But I'm not the only one at fault here. The elephant in this house is Muriel, or rather Muriel's short arms, deep pockets, and downright pig-headed refusal to put a penny towards renovating the place. Edwardian houses, I often tell her, do not look after themselves, Moo. They need love, care, attention, money – money, they need money! And she'll always reply with some nonsense or other about how all her pennies are spoken for in taking care of me. As though I'm the one who needs looking after!

Then I remember thinking I should probably get up and shut the curtains, because the evening light had taken on the garish quality that occurs when the sun sits behind a layer of thin, black cloud, which is always a trigger for one of my 'heads'. It often portends thunder too, which neither Muriel nor I much care for (Muriel says it's down to suppressed memories of wartime bombing raids – and she might be on to something there – but she also believes in water-dowsing and colonic irrigation. So who knows?). The wind was getting up too – the quickening that one experiences just before a storm – and, across the road, Number 73's hanging baskets were swaying rather violently, scattering spent petunia heads all over the place.

I opened my mouth to say, 'Best batten down the hatches, Moo, we're in for a rumble of thunder, I think,' because *The Archers*' exit tune was playing and I knew it would be safe to speak, without the risk of more shushing. But then I felt Muriel's body stiffen, which was odd because her condition means she can barely move a muscle from the chest down. Yet there she sat, erect and unyielding – as though someone had shoved a broom up the back of her kaftan – speaking in a gruff, clipped tone, so very different from her genteel lisp that I instinctively looked over my shoulder, fully expecting to see an intruder standing in the doorway behind me.

'In exactly seventy-two hours,' she said, 'I am going to die.'

The pumice stone slipped from my grip, falling into the bowl with a resounding plop. I let it lie there for a moment and looked up at Muriel's face.

Her eyes were tightly shut, jaw jutting forward slightly. She had rearranged her features into a pinched sneer – a deeply unsettling expression I hadn't seen before – and yet she still looked beautiful. It is remarkable, I remember thinking, that women blessed with such stereotypical good looks (platinum hair, smooth pink skin, button nose, wide blue eyes) can be excused so very much in life, however badly they behave. I, however, was blessed with a face only a mother could love, and even my own mother struggled at times with that.

I plucked the pumice from the bowl and resumed my scrubbing, swiftly running through a limited list of options in my head. A dismissive 'Don't be so bloody silly' would be heartless *and* reckless (Muriel can be quite the sting in the tail if provoked). Say nothing? Well, that would be even worse. I know from bitter experience that ignoring one of Muriel's cries for attention leads to days of The Silent Treatment and the threat of a telephone call to her solicitor, Mr Tonks.

In the end, I said, 'I'm so sorry, Moo.'

That seemed the safest response. With Muriel, when in doubt, I always offer an apology. Even if I've no idea what I'm apologizing for.

Her eyes snapped open. 'Yes, well.' She sighed, face and

body relaxing at last. 'I suppose it can't be helped. Now. Chess? Ludo?' Her lips twitched. 'Scrabble?'

I struggled to my feet. 'Let me clear up first. Oh, blast and buggeration!'

Muriel arched an eyebrow at me.

'Sorry,' I said, rubbing my thigh. My tights, I realized, had laddered down one leg, all the way from gusset to ankle. Brand new they were – fresh on that morning – and pricey support tights because of my varicose veins. It's all right for you, Muriel Hinchcliffe, I thought, you with your collection of slinky black stockings that never ladder at all because you never do a bloody thing!

And then I felt appalled with myself, because Muriel's condition means she can't do a bloody thing at all and never will again. I, on the other hand, still have a body that works perfectly well – a squat, solid, functioning body that Muriel would surely exchange her fame and beauty for in a heartbeat.

Shut up, I told myself. Shut up, put up, and count your many blessings.

'My knees,' I muttered, 'playing up again.'

Blessing Number One: My knees might be giving way, but at least I have a roof over my head.

'You should lose some weight, dear,' Muriel said.

Blessing Number Two: I eat and drink very well. Far too well, in fact.

'I do try, Moo, but at our age, it's not that easy—'

'Pffffft!'

She dismissed me with an imperious waft of her arm, draped in the pink and red silk swirls of her favourite Pucci kaftan – one of several purchased forty years ago from a bijou boutique just off the King's Road. It still fits Muriel perfectly well, in spite of her years of industrial boozing, and I couldn't help staring enviously at the lustrous folds concealing the slender legs that I knew hung uselessly, aimlessly, underneath.

Oh, Muriel. Only someone as stunning and stylish as you could make a wheelchair look like a fashion accessory!

I was with her when she bought that kaftan. With *my* husband Harvey's money, of course.

Blessing Number Three:

There is no Blessing Number Three.

# Four hours later

Something very odd just happened.

I have been asked to go out. With a man!

Who would have thought such a thing? Not me, certainly not after the first few hours of the evening, which had not been promising at all. I was not in the happiest frame of mind because Muriel's prediction had really shaken me, and, after finishing off her feet, I took much longer than usual to do the washing-up. I needed the solitude, you see, and I love being in the kitchen; it's my favourite room in the house. In fact, the kitchen is the only room I can truly call my own, for Muriel never goes in there. She has no problem at all visiting my bedroom when I am asleep – I often wake to find her next to me, staring down from her wheelchair – because she needs to know exactly where I am, all hours of the day and night. Muriel's vulnerability frightens her so, and I excuse her intrusions because I know they come from a place of fear, and who hasn't felt fearful at times?

But this evening . . . well. Things just got to me a little more than usual, and I spent ages scrubbing away at the pots and pans, even the clean ones, cursing Muriel the whole time for refusing to buy a dishwasher. Things had turned very dark outside – it was raining heavily by now – and thunder, just as I'd predicted, was grumbling away in the distance. Nevertheless, I was able, for a short time at least, to push Muriel's announcement to the back of my mind, reasoning that her uncharacteristic precision – her assigning an actual date and hour to her death – was nothing more than her playing silly buggers, and since she'd have sensed that she'd got a rise out of me, I had better get used to the idea of her doing it again.

With this in mind, I thought I'd kill a few more hours cleaning the cooker top, dismantling each one of the gas burners, and scouring the grouting between every single wall tile. And then I decided to get stuck into the floor tiles too, which I knew would keep me occupied well into the early hours. This is a very large kitchen, stretching across much of the rear of the house, and would extend a little further were it not for the study directly next to it that was converted from the original scullery (and where a woman of my position would have slept when the house was first built, or so Muriel once told me during a particularly heated game of Ludo).

I love the kitchen because it is mine, not because it is in any way beautiful, although it really ought to be. A generously proportioned room like this should exude bright and airy elegance, but instead it is rammed with heavy oak units and beige laminate worktops from the early 1980s, with a hotch-potch of dated appliances squeezed into the few available spaces: a Baby Belling cooker here, a waste-disposal unit over there, a twin-tub washer one side of the cellar door, a chest freezer on the other. Languishing under the window is the original, blackened range, a magnificent contraption that has not been used in decades – and what a shame, I thought, as I beavered away, what a wicked, criminal waste of such a fine piece of machinery!

I don't know how long I'd been cleaning for when Muriel came to find me. I was on my hands and knees with my back to her, of course: debased, defeated, *derrière* exposed and ripe for a kicking. Just how she likes me.

'RUTH!'

'Oh!' I exclaimed. 'I thought you were asleep!'

She was wedged – slanted, half in shadow – up against the architrave, because the kitchen is the only doorway Muriel's wheelchair can't get through. Much of the house has been remodelled over the years, with Muriel's mobility always in mind: doorways have been widened, while a stairlift gives her access between the ground and first floors. But the kitchen has always defeated us. I have tried to find a builder willing to widen the kitchen door, or remove the dividing kitchen and hall wall completely (I believe such open-plan designs are very fashionable in this area of north London). But the wall is a supporting structure and, as I must repeatedly explain to Muriel, removing such a vital component could jeopardize the stability of the entire building.

'You BITCH!' she shrieked.

'For God's sake, Moo, can't you see I'm cleaning?'

'Liar! You've been avoiding me.'

'I have not!'

'You have! You don't want to play Scrabble!'

'Moo . . .'

'Don't you Moo me. You haven't touched that floor in years! You're . . . you're neglectful! And dishonest. And abusive.'

'But I've never laid a finger on you!'

She had me now, or so she thought, because she was poking at that bouffant hairdo of hers with skinny, overexcited fingers, preening, in anticipation of her usual *coup de théâtre*.

And there it was –

'I am going to telephone Mr Tonks,' she announced. 'I am going to telephone Mr Tonks and tell him to change my will. You will not,' she added haughtily, 'inherit this house after all, Ruth Donne!'

I sighed.

I have been in this situation many times before. I know The Script inside out – every word, each pause, the steps it invariably follows:

1. Muriel and I have a furious row.

2. If I do not grovel or show enough contrition, Muriel threatens me with Mr Tonks, and wheels herself into her study.

3. I trot behind her, pleading for mercy.

4. Muriel reaches her desk, picks up the telephone – a black Bakelite model, probably worth quite a few quid these days – and holds the receiver up to her ear in a most dramatic fashion. (It is the only telephone in the house, because Muriel detests technology. She will not allow mobile phones or the internet either, but we do own a fax machine – a remnant from Muriel's writing days – which she leaves permanently switched on, 'just in case'.)

5. I count to three – giving Muriel time to dial the first few digits. And then I burst into tears.

6. That always does the trick. 'Oh, Roo!' she'll cry, replacing the handset. 'Dear, poor Roo. Of course I won't telephone Mr Tonks. Now, give me a cuddle, you silly old thing!'

7. We kiss and make up. I'll make some tea and we'll have a game of Scrabble, which Muriel will win.

Not so tonight.

'No,' I said.

'No? What on earth do you mean, no?'

'No, you will not telephone Mr Tonks.'

We stared at each other for quite some time. A rumble of thunder shook the house – or perhaps it was a Tube train running beneath us? – and I saw a cloud of doubt pass over Muriel's face, then actual fear as her eyes widened and her lower lip began to tremble. I believe she thought I meant her physical harm, so decided to do the decent thing and put her out of her misery.

I reached down into the cupboard under the sink.

'No, you will not use the telephone to contact Mr Tonks,' I said, slamming it onto the draining board with a gratifying *ping*. 'Because I have unplugged it, and I have it here.'

I fled the house by the back door, a barrage of Muriel's choicest threats and insults booming in my ears, a Tesco Bag for Life in hand containing my emergency supplies: a tube of Pringles, the dregs of one of Muriel's many bottles of Tanqueray, and twenty Silk Cut. I hurried towards the shed at the bottom of the garden, wading through the sopping grass in stockinged feet, my thighs wrestling against the confines of my too-tight skirt.

The rain was falling more gently now, and the worst of the thunder and lightning had passed, which was something, I suppose. But that didn't do much to ease my gloom. It was only late evening – nine o'clock or thereabouts – but might just as well have been the early hours of the morning, or the end of bloody time, for that matter, for it was so overcast, and the weather so foul that the neighbouring gardens were completely deserted, and I felt like the loneliest woman in the world. I paused in the centre of the lawn and looked back up at the house, one of a terrace of identical red-brick villas – but our windows were dark and lifeless, while the surrounding houses flickered and glowed with television sets and lamplight. I could hear faint singing and laughter, too, from several houses down, and someone – a child, I expect – playing the trumpet, badly.

The shed was warm enough and dry, though a little too cobwebby for my liking. I unfolded a deckchair, unscrewed the Tanqueray, lit the first of many cigarettes, and sat back, trying to understand the failure I'd become, and how: an Oxford-educated journalist, reliant on her best friend's charity, half dreading, half hoping for the day that best friend finally died.

Such a shabby, shameful way to live.

I have known Muriel all my life. People often say they have known someone all their life when, in truth, they have only known them since they were at school together. Moo and I, however, have literally known each other since the day we were born, 22 March 1943, at St Hilda's Maternity Hospital, Hampstead, where our mothers bonded over the shared traumas of shaved vulvas, enemas, and labouring in a basement room, while the air-raid sirens howled outside. I was the first to appear, a screaming, livid, ten-pound bruiser, complete with a head of jet-black curls. Muriel made her appearance a fashionable fifteen seconds later, looking just like a little doll and barely making a sound.

'Which was most considerate of her,' my mother once said, 'because you were making an absolute racket, Ruth. You even drowned out the all-clear siren. Matron was furious – we had no idea the raid was over and were on tenterhooks for hours.'

Our mothers remained friends in spite (or perhaps because) of their many differences. Mine was a short, squat, no-nonsense thoroughbred, the sole issue of an aristocratic family fallen on hard times, dragging her lineage further into the mire by falling in love with a cash-strapped vicar. 'It wasn't the plan,' my mother once said. 'Not what my parents had in mind for me at all, and my father was very disappointed at the time. But I married for love, Ruth. What on earth else was I supposed to do?'

I could tell, though, when I saw her eyes flitting from her own frayed hems to Muriel's mother's fur-trimmed necklines, that she sometimes wished she'd done something else entirely. I really couldn't blame her. My father, a kind but distant man, was already married himself – to God – which naturally put Mother's nose out of joint, constantly having to play second fiddle to The Man Upstairs. As for me, I was neither Father's third nor fourth fiddle, but rather an amusing pet that elicited the occasional affectionate pat on the head. My memories of him are sketchy and always viewed from an odd perspective: gazing up at his wobbling jowls, while he sermonizes furiously from the confines of his pulpit, or watching his diminutive figure glide ever altar-wards, until all I can see is a bald pink head atop a long black cassock.

Muriel's parents were what my parents called New Money.

Her father wasn't a Man of the Cloth, like mine: he was a Man of Means. I could never tell from the tone of my mother's voice whether this was a good or bad thing, but Muriel's mother wasn't happy at all. Oh no, for all her wealth and beauty, my mother wouldn't swap places with her for the world!

'Why not?' I remember asking (I must have been about twelve at the time). 'Muriel's mother is incredibly pretty,' I added. 'Stinking rich, wears lovely clothes, and lives in the biggest house in Hampstead. And her husband is handsome and wears nice suits. Besides, Muriel's mother never gets cross.'

*Unlike you.* I didn't actually utter those words, but then I didn't need to.

'I don't get cross!'

'I think you do.'

'Well,' my mother sniffed, 'she gets sad.'

I couldn't argue with that. Muriel's mother always looked on the edge of a nervous breakdown: all pursed lips, fluttering lashes and sucked-in cheeks, though I'd assumed these were fashionable affectations – the better to set off her pillbox hats, nipped-waist suits, and darkly rouged lips.

'She gets sad,' my mother said, 'because . . .'

'Because?'

'She didn't marry for love.' My mother smiled unpleasantly. 'And neither did her husband.'

No wonder Muriel spent so much time at our house. Back then, I couldn't understand why – why she, living in that white stucco mansion, poised by a lake on the Heath, like a Gainsborough dream, would want to spend a single second in our cramped, Victorian rectory, just off the Finchley Road.

But Muriel loved staying with us and my mother loved having her there. Most of all, I suspect, my mother loved the fact that Muriel's mother was always three sheets to the wind and oblivious to the absence of her only, extraordinarily pretty daughter.

I cared, though. I cared that I had to give up my bed for Muriel and sleep on a mattress on the floor. I cared that I had to let Muriel share my toys and allow her to win the games we played, because she had such a terrible time at home. And I cared when my mother spent hours – so it seemed – brushing Muriel's white-blonde hair, oohing, ahhing, and gasping over its lustre and perfection:

'Look! Muriel lets me brush her hair without any fussing or fighting!'

Muriel, stifling a giggle, arched an eyebrow at me.

'Muriel has smooth, straight hair,' I observed. 'And mine is thick and wiry. I fuss and fight when you brush it, Mother, because it really hurts!'

'It's true,' Muriel said. 'Roo's hair is impossible to brush because it's so thick and lovely. I wish I had hair like that, Auntie Vi. It's just like yours, you know.'

And my mother, clutching the hairbrush to her breast, beamed, as though the Lord Jesus Christ himself had descended from heaven to bless her.

Muriel winked at me.

In those days, she pretty much always backed me up.


I must have been making a lot of noise in the shed, because the next thing I knew, Joanna, from next door, was shining a torch through the window.

'Ruth? Ruthie? Are you all right in there? Elliott said he could hear someone crying!'

I took a final sip of gin, extinguished my fag against the rim of the bottle, reluctantly rose from my deckchair, and padded outside.

Joanna had evidently dressed in a hurry, because she was wearing a grubby white bathrobe and a pair of dark blue Crocs. The crown of her bobbed hair stood up in damp, platinum tufts, and she was absent-mindedly rubbing at a graze on her elbow. I realized she must have vaulted over the garden fence to 'rescue' me and, judging by the soap encrusting the right-hand side of her face, had abruptly abandoned her evening ablutions to do so.

'Elliott,' she continued, peering at me with that permanently pained expression of hers, 'was looking for something in the summer house, and said someone was locked in your shed and sounded distressed!'

'Summer house?'

Joanna motioned to her own shed on the other side of the lawn, its door ajar and light bulb blazing, illuminating at its core a large, scruffy ginger cat propped against the foot of a steel chimenea, one leg raised aloft and vigorously washing its undercarriage. There was no sign of Elliott, Joanna's lodger and 'handyman' since her barrister husband ran away with his clerk, though the air, which should have been fresh and clear following the purifying effects of a storm, smelt very strongly indeed of marijuana.

I gulped and wiped my nose with the back of my hand. 'It's Moo. You know. We had another row.' The cat stopped licking itself for a moment, assessing me quizzically through narrowed amber eyes.

'Oh, Ruth . . .' Joanna placed her hands on her hips, cocking her head to one side, preparing to address me in that schoolmarmish way of hers that has become more frequent and pronounced since her youngest fled to a university at the other end of the country.

I knew it was coming, and there it was –

'Who's caring for the carer, hmm?' she said.

I smiled weakly. 'Well, no one, I'm afraid.'

'You're a marvel, Ruth. An absolute saint. I don't know how you do it.'

'Needs must.' I sighed.

'But you *must* look after yourself – get some respite! It's all very well taking care of Muriel, but what about taking care of Ruthie, hmmm? Who's looking out for you?'

At this, the cat rose, sashayed out of the shed, padded across the lawn, and inelegantly clambered over the fence, before landing and rolling onto its back at my feet, revealing an off-white, underfed abdomen. I took my cue from Joanna, who was sensibly ignoring the creature, and chose to do likewise, despite a lifelong weakness for ginger toms – of both the human and feline variety.

'You've hurt your arm,' I said. 'I do hope you haven't injured yourself on my account.'

'Oh!' Joanna waggled a finger playfully. 'Now that's typical of you, Ruth, always deflecting attention from your own crisis by worrying about somebody else! I'm fine, I really am. I cleared that fence, no trouble at all. It's the yoga and Pilates, you see, keeps me fit and flexible. You should seriously consider it. Yoga is terribly good for stress.'

'A holiday would be even better,' I said. 'If only I could get someone to stay with Moo for a while, or just pop in a few times a day.'

'She's still not speaking to her family, then?'

'I'm afraid not.'

Joanna nodded sympathetically. 'I suppose it's difficult after what happened with her son . . . people do blame each other, don't they?' She cleared her throat. 'Poor Muriel. You just can't unsee something like that, however many years it's been. How many years has it been?'

'Twenty-three,' I replied. 'And two months. And three days.'

'Understandable, really,' Joanna was musing, 'why she is the way she is.'

I shrugged and spread the palms of my hands. A gesture of something, I didn't know what.

Joanna spoke more lightly. 'Have you tried a carers agency?'

'Well, I can't afford that,' I said, 'and I can hardly expect Moo to pay – she doesn't like strangers in the house.'

'Oh, dear.' Joanna stared thoughtfully down at her Crocs. 'Ruth?'

'Hmmm?'

'Well, I have a proposition! I hope you don't think I'm being interfering or presumptuous . . .'

My heart started beating a little faster. 'No,' I said. 'Of course not!'

'Well, my father's staying for a few days – he's only a couple of years older than you – and I know he'd love to have someone to have a natter with and help him put the world to rights. I think Elliott's driving him a bit crackers, to be honest – bit of a personality clash, I'm afraid. He'd adore your company, though, Ruth! Why don't you go out together tomorrow night? It would do you both the world of good!'

Not quite what I was hoping for.

'A couple of hours,' Joanna was saying. 'Muriel can cope by herself for a couple of hours, surely?'

'Well, yes. I think so. But you could always pop in and say hello to her?' I suggested brightly.

'Oh, I'd love to, but no can do. Book club, I'm afraid, with the mums from Henry's old primary school. Always a bugger to get us together in the same place at the same time, so I really can't cry off. Another time, yes?'

'Please.'

'So, tomorrow night. I'll tell Daddy to knock for you around eight.'

The cat stopped writhing at my feet and gave an approving yowl.

'What's his name?' I asked, finally caving and stooping down to stroke the beast. But I lost my footing as I did so, and grabbed Joanna's arm instead.

'Lawrence,' she replied, steadying me. 'Gosh, I think you need to go to bed, Ruth.'

'Lawrence? He looks more like an Orlando to me. You know, like the kiddies' book from years ago – *Orlando the Marmalade Cat*!'

'Marmalade?'

'Well, he was orange, wasn't he? Or ginger, you might say.'

'But my father is bald, completely bald!' Joanna frowned. 'No one's ever called him Orlando. He's always been Lawrence.' She leant forward and sniffed me. 'Oh, Ruth, have you been drinking again?'

I shook my head. 'Not really. Well, just a sip,' I said. 'The remnants of Moo's gin. Speaking of Moo, I'd better get back to her.' I nodded at the cat. 'And get my friend something to eat. Tinned pilchards, I think. We have a cellar full of the things. Oh – regarding your father, Joanna. Baldness I can just about tolerate. But does he still have all his own teeth?'

'Do you know,' Joanna muttered, gently removing my hand from her sleeve, flexing her fingers and steeling herself for a return vault over the garden fence, 'I have absolutely no idea.'

# Midnight

I fed the cat outside, by the back door, because Muriel would never allow him in the house – not in a million years. She is such a jealous, possessive creature! That said, I'm not entirely sure that I'd allow Puss in the house either. On closer inspection, he was a mangy-looking thing that probably had fleas, poor sod.

'What's better than pilchards, Puss? A saucer of tinned red salmon, Moo's favourite, that's what, you little lost soul who nobody loves. Now, you can't come in, but what do you say to spending the night in the shed?' I ran a hand over his bony spine, a sickening mixture of pity and disgust rising in my chest as I did so.

Puss sniffed at the saucer, his ginger- and white-hooped tail bristling at the distant bark of an urban fox. He wasn't remotely interested in the food I'd put down for him, but crouched down with his back to it, head disappearing briefly in a face-engulfing yawn.

'I'm knackered too,' I said, tickling under his chin, 'but I can't face bed just yet. I'll have to check on the Princess of Darkness first, and she's had plenty of time to think up an exceptionally cruel and unusual punishment. Muriel Hinchcliffe is evil,' I added, too loudly, not caring whether Moo or Joanna, or the tone-deaf trumpeter several doors down heard me. 'And I am good, Puss. Isn't that right?'

The cat cocked his head to one side, as if to say, *Oh, Ruth. You and I both know that's not entirely true, is it?* and, buckling beneath the weight of my petting, flattened himself onto his belly and slithered away from me, into the night.

I gave in to Muriel, of course. I apologized first.

After saying goodnight to Puss, I returned to the kitchen, peeled off my tights and stuffed them into the pocket of my skirt. Muriel wasn't where I'd left her, thank God – the thought of her jammed in a doorway for hours while I cried myself stupid in the shed like an unhinged garden gnome made me feel quite sick with shame. But then where the hell was she? What had Muriel been doing all this time? Something seismic had occurred between us – that much was certain. We had entered uncharted territory, Moo and I, and by veering from The Script during our argument, I had given her permission to do so too. But wasn't it Moo who strayed first, by saying she'd be dead and gone in seventy-two hours? Surely it was all her fault, everything that had happened this evening; Muriel's fault for not being her usual daft, vague self!

And I was no longer my usual self, I knew, as I steered Muriel's downstairs wheelchair away from the bannisters, steeling myself for the ascent towards the rosy light emanating from under her bedroom door. I climbed upwards, gripping the bannisters and stairlift track with slippery fingers, acknowledging as I did so that the house, too, seemed different tonight. The gold-embossed wallpaper and deep-pile carpets felt oddly insubstantial beneath my touch and tread, while the hall, staircase, and landing seemed more capacious than ever before, as though the house was holding its breath, waiting for something to happen.

I heard a cough from Muriel's room. That was it, my cue, my signal that she was alive and, if not well, at least in a position to communicate that I was expected to go to her. And God, was I glad to hear it. Because I'd imagined all manner of dreadful scenarios – the consequences of my wicked neglect – a freshly expired Moo, sitting upright in bed, her face fixed with a dead-fish stare; a collapsed Moo, spelling out RUTH IS A BASTARD in Scrabble tiles on the floor at her side . . .

As it was, I was relieved to find no such thing. Moo was still dressed and sitting in her upstairs wheelchair, which she had positioned pointedly next to her bed. With a face blank of any emotion and her little white hands folded neatly on her lap, she was the very picture of the uncomplaining patient meekly awaiting the return of the wayward, neglectful carer. She had, however, managed to unfasten her chignon, leaving strands of hair hanging limply over her shoulders; turned down her bedspread, revealing a large yellow stain burgeoning from the centre of her under-sheet; removed her make-up with cotton wool balls, scattering the little white puffs – now bruised with the remnants of black mascara – all over her Persian rug; and taken a white satin nightie and matching bed jacket from her chest of drawers, folded them neatly, and placed them on her plump pink eiderdown, crowning the pile with an artfully placed pair of plastic pants.

'I am ready,' she announced stoically, 'for my bed now.'

'Super,' I said, unscrewing a jar of ointment. 'Would you like me to cream your buttocks for you first?'

'No. Thank you.'

'I'll help you out of your kaftan then, and into your nightie.'

'I'd rather you didn't.'

I carefully returned the jar of ointment to its place on Muriel's dressing table.

'What would you like me to do, Moo?' I asked quietly. 'You know how you struggle to get into bed without my help.'

She looked up from her folded hands and glared at me. 'I would like you to stop being such a bitch!' she said. And then she started to cry.

I sat down on the bed and sighed.

I had never known Muriel like this before – a shuddering, blubbering wreck. I stared down at my muddy toes and wriggled them awkwardly. This was a victory all right, but a grubby one.

'You're being downright cruel,' Muriel sobbed, 'and it scares me when you behave like this, because I need you, Roo! Without you, I can't do anything any more. I can barely get on the commode by myself. And I'm getting worse! I'm a great big baby, that's what I am. And I know I'm terrible to live with, and I know I sometimes say bad things . . .'

This, too, was a new development. Was Moo showing remorse? Was she actually going to apologize to me?

'Well,' I said, attempting to grease the apology along a little. 'We all say things when we're upset. I've said some terrible things to you, but I always say sorry after.'

'You've done some terrible things too,' she choked. 'You un-un-plugged my telephone!'

'I did,' I said. 'I'm sorry. I'll put it back in the study first thing, I promise.'

There.

I did it. I gave in. I said sorry first.

And in my mind's eye, I could see my mother clapping and cheering: *Well done, Ruth – excellent show! You're stronger than Muriel – you've done the right thing. You had to let her win, because she must be first sometimes. Surely you can see that now?*

Muriel smiled brightly, the tears – and embryonic apology – gone for good. 'That's better, isn't it? Now we can be friends again!'

'We're always friends, Moo.' I rose from the bed. 'Let me help you with your nightie.'

# One hour later

We are lying in bed together, Moo and I. She wanted me to stay with her a little while, just until she fell asleep. It was hard for me to say no, and so I said nothing at all.

Moo's double bed has four oak posts and a carved headboard featuring entwined roses, ivy leaves, and overweight gambolling cherubs. It also has a lumpy mattress, with body-sized indentations on both sides. Mine (in the room across the landing) is a modest single divan and considerably more comfortable. But I was so exhausted after all the evening's ups and downs that it seemed the right thing to do somehow, to crawl under the bedclothes beside her.

I took her hand in my own and held it up to my face. Her fingers were soft and cool, and smelt very strongly of Pond's Cold Cream.

'Tell me a story,' she said.

'Me? You're the romantic novelist!'

'I'm too tired, Roo. I can't make up stories any more.'

'Well, what sort of story would you like?'

'A happy one. About being young.'

'Oh . . .' The room was dark, my head woozy, and my brain stubborn and terribly slow. I scissored my calves against Moo's flannel under-sheet and tried to come up with something.

'Once upon a time . . .' I ventured. 'A long time ago. Before everything happened . . .' I was drifting off a bit.

'Yes?'

'There were two little girls. Born on the same day. They grew up together.'

'Us!'

'Well, yes. Us, if you like. And the two little girls became young women – vibrant, exciting young women. One was clever, but not so beautiful; one was beautiful, but not so bright. And yet, together they were something. They really were quite something.'

'Oh, we were, weren't we, Roo? Everyone wanted to be with us. Everyone wanted to be our friend!'

'The two girls,' I went on dreamily, 'didn't go to the same school, but were just like sisters anyway.'

Moo's voice cooled. 'I don't want to think about school,' she said. 'I didn't like it there one bit. Start the story later.'

That was understandable. For Moo, the experience of secondary school was not a happy one: packed off as a boarder, aged thirteen, just one month after the death of her mother from an overdose of sleeping pills, her father keen as mustard to move his mistress into the family home. Moo wasn't bullied as such, but she had few friends, and was desperately lonely. Her thrice-weekly term-time letters I left unopened for days, because I was too busy, you see – too engrossed with the social and intellectual thrills of my highly selective grammar school to notice the subtle distress calls issued, on pale-pink paper, from Bellevue Ladies' College, somewhere on the south coast:

*Daddy is annoyed with me because he had to send a whole new uniform. My old one is too big for me, I have lost a lot of weight.*

\*

*I keep getting headaches, Roo, really terrible headaches. Please don't be cross with me, but do you think I might have a brain tumour?*

\*

*Dear Roo, I was so happy to receive your letter! Today, I actually managed to eat my supper – and keep it down!*

\*

*I keep thinking that everyone back home is dying. Or already dead.*

'When we were sixteen,' I said. 'I'll start the story there.'

'No, not then either. You completely disappeared up your own backside when you were sitting your O levels.'

I smiled. 'Did I now?'

'You were insufferable. Such an intellectual snob. Still are.'

'Well, you were an insufferable airhead. Still are.'

I could feel her shaking next to me, laughing silently.

'Start the story at Jimmy Graham's twenty-first birthday party,' she said. 'You came down from Oxford for it. Such a happy night! Remember what I wore?'

I did. 'That little black velvet dress,' I said, 'with a feather boa draped around your neck. And you were carrying a ridiculously long cigarette holder, even though you'd never smoked in your life. You were very full of yourself because you'd landed your first modelling job, promoting hostess trolleys at Selfridges, and the local husbands kept turning up asking for 'demonstrations' and slipping you their telephone numbers. You were on cloud nine that night, and so was I, because . . .'

'Because?'

I was going to say, *Because Harvey told me he loved me. After just three weeks of pursuing and wooing him, he was already wholly, utterly mine.*

'Because the Cuban Missile Crisis was over,' I said, 'and we were all so relieved – remember? We even danced a conga round the room. Jimmy took off all his clothes in the name of peace and tried to get the rest of us to do the same, but I was having none of it, because I was wearing that beige trouser suit and thought I looked the bee's knees. Elegant androgyny was the look I was aiming for – very ahead of my time, so I thought – but you fell about, the moment you saw me. The world's shortest, fattest sergeant major was how you said I looked.'

Moo, who had been humming Little Eva's 'The Loco-Motion' – the tune that was playing as we danced the conga that evening – squealed with laughter.

'What a cow I was! I was very jealous, actually, that you could carry off something so hideous. I'd have *died* if I'd had to wear something like that.'

*Died.*

Moo's mattress seemed to give way, plunging me downwards, just for a second. I grabbed her hand.

'Moo?'

'Hmmmm?'

'Do you really think you're going to die?'

'What?'

'Tonight. During *The Archers*. When you said you were going to die.'

'Oh, that,' she said drowsily. 'Well, we're all going to die some time, aren't we? In the midst of life we are in death, or whatever it is that it says in the Bible. You tell me. You're the vicar's daughter.'

'But it doesn't say anything about dropping dead in seventy-two hours' time. You were very exact, Moo.'

'Was I? How very unlike me.'

'Yes, it was.'

'Oh, well. I don't remember.' She yawned. 'I'm tired, Roo. Tell me more of the story.'

'I'm tired too,' I said. 'I want to go to sleep.'

'Finish it quickly, then.'

'Well, the two girls. They grew up. And then they got married.' I paused. 'To the same man, one after the other. The end.'

I waited for a response, but none was forthcoming. Muriel must have fallen asleep, because all I could hear was the soft, rhythmic hiss of her breathing.

Tuesday, 25 June 2019

# The morning after

I woke early, around 6.30, roused by the bloody racket of the refuse collection going on outside. Moo, snoring away at my side, seemed oblivious to the dragging of bins and sharp yells of the council workers, which led me to wonder if she was now going deaf, and whether this latest affliction might actually work to my advantage.

My head, though – God, my head! It felt so woozy and my mouth bone dry. I was still dressed too, save for the tights that I had removed by the kitchen door the previous evening. I uncoiled them from my skirt pocket, regarding the filthy, laddered legs in disgust and dismay. Such behaviour – at my age! I'd completely lost the plot. Brawling with my oldest friend, drinking her gin, and chain-smoking like a navvy. My chest was tight, my sinuses hurt, and my stomach was hollow with the cold suspicion that I had said or done something utterly unforgivable.

But what? I had unplugged Muriel's telephone. I had refused to follow The Script. That was it, nothing more. I had not slapped or screamed at her, I had not pushed her down the stairs. I had, in fact, remained remarkably calm in the face of extreme provocation, so hurrah to me for that. There was nothing obvious to trouble my conscience at all, so why did I feel so unsettled?

I got out of bed, lumbered out of the bedroom and across the landing towards the bathroom, pausing at the top of the bannisters to squint down the stairs. I wanted to check whether I had shut and locked the vestibule door before bed, as I customarily do.

And, of course, I had.

I could not remember doing so, but I had.

I also could not remember upending Muriel's wheelchair in the middle of the hall floor in a fit of pique. But, apparently, I had.

And there was something so brutal about the positioning of the chair – its spindly wheels pointing pathetically upwards, exposing the black, flimsy underbelly of the PVC seat – that I felt compelled to turn it the right way up as quickly as possible.

It struck me that now was as good a time as ever to use the stairlift to make my descent (I have not dared use it before; Moo expressly forbids it), but it took a few seconds before I registered that the seat of the stairlift was not by my side – that it wasn't, in fact, at first-floor level at all, as it must have been for Muriel to travel upstairs to her room.

No, the stairlift seat was below me. At ground level.

Had I, in my guilt-ridden clumsiness the evening before, pressed the controls without realizing as I made my way towards Muriel's room, thus releasing the seat to make an unmanned descent? I mulled over the possibility as I hobbled down to the hallway, hauled Moo's wheelchair back to its upright position, and made my inaugural ascent. By the time the stairlift and I had reached the landing, I'd reasoned that yes, this was the only sensible explanation and, thus satisfied, made my way to the loo.

I didn't pee much, but remained on the seat for quite some time, because the bathroom was cool and, if not particularly clean, at least the suite and tiles are white and easy on the ageing eye. Then I cleaned my teeth, splashed my face with water, and briefly considered showering and washing my hair. But my hair is cropped so short these days that a little talc rubbed into my scalp is quite sufficient for removing dirt and grease, though I did rinse my feet because they were filthy, and stripped off my blouse and skirt to give my 'pits and bits' a quick flannel-down.

I returned to my room in a much happier mood. The sun was shining, which made a nice change, and I was back in the land of the lucid at last, capable of reasoning that however questionable my behaviour the night before, it had been worth it, in a funny sort of way. A big up-and-downer always clears the air between Moo and me.

My bedroom is smaller than Moo's, but still larger than average. It is not as lavishly decorated as hers – you will find no chaise longue, Persian rug, satin eiderdown or chandelier in this room, but you will find simple comfort and, I like to think, a degree of taste and practicality. I used to be a messy little devil – a collector and chronicler of all manner of things (or hoarder, as Moo would say), but I lost several journals and photographs when Moo had the house deep-cleaned and redecorated twenty or so years ago now, and the heartbreak and upset it caused (never mind the unholy row with the decorators, who denied all knowledge, of course) made me clean up my act. I now live a much simpler life, favouring what I understand is known as 'Scandinavian style': muted paintwork, light wooden furniture, clever storage systems, and bright, airy spaces. Sometimes, I wonder whether I was born a half-century too soon. All my life, I have felt off-kilter, out of time.

I returned to Moo at eight o'clock. She was sitting up and beaming at me, the antics of the previous evening apparently forgotten.

'Roo!' she exclaimed. 'Do you know, I really fancy poached eggs on toast!'

'Do you now?' I said. 'Well, you'll have to get up for it first. Come on, I'll help you into your chair.'

'Can't I have breakfast in bed?'

'It's a slippery slope,' I said, gently tugging at her eiderdown. 'One day it'll be breakfast in bed, then lunch, then supper, then all day, every day, in bed.'

'Sounds bliss,' she murmured.

'It's giving up,' I said, 'and we're not having that, now, are we? Here, put your arm around my neck.'

It's a good thing I am strong and sturdy and Moo so incredibly light, because moving her around the place does take its toll on my back and legs.

'There, now! You're back in your chair,' I said.

'I need the loo,' Moo snapped. 'You should have put me on the commode first!'

'Well, why the bloody hell didn't you say so?'

She pouted. 'Well, you usually do put me on the commode first. And I didn't like to argue.'

I stared over her head out of the window. Across the road, Mrs Number 73 was picking up spent petunia heads from her front path and stuffing them into her wheelie bin. She is a slim, well-turned-out (as they all tend to be around here) woman of Far-Eastern appearance (Muriel says that she is Thai – a mail-order bride, perhaps?), and I usually see her with a baby clamped to her cashmere-clad breast. But the baby, I realized today, was no longer a baby at all, but a strapping great toddler, waddling beside his mother in a pair of Bob-the-Builder trainer pants, mimicking her actions, a fierce determination etched into his podgy, petulant face.

I looked down at Moo and sighed. 'Come on, then,' I said.

We breakfasted at opposite ends of the Regency dining table, salvaged from Moo's family home after her father dropped dead from a heart attack triggered, so my mother said, by excessive jiggery-pokery with a high-class call girl. We assisted with the smash-and-grab, Harvey and I, pitching up at Heath House in a clapped-out hire van early one morning when we knew Drusilla, Moo's stepmother, was at a party out of town. We took the table and matching chairs, a radiogram, a Persian rug, two silver candlesticks, a case of claret, and Drusilla's cat – a large ginger tom answering to the name of Lord Cedric Bristlerump. Such daring, such unshakeable self-righteousness the three of us had, aged twenty-one!

'Losing Lord Cedric,' Moo observed at the time, 'will hurt Drusilla most of all, more than losing Daddy, I think, because she only loved Daddy for his money. I'm not a cat person, though, Roo. Could you and Harvey take him for me, please?'

So, I gave Lord Cedric Bristlerump to my mother, who rechristened the cat Fred and treated him like a prince for the rest of his days. She needed something to cosset, you see, now that Moo was too old for cosseting, and my own father had inconsiderately suffered a fatal stroke six months before.

'Which is just as well,' my mother said, with tears in her

eyes, 'because he would have been appalled at the three of you, stealing from Drusilla like that. And I don't care how you justify it – in the eyes of the law, what you did was wrong.'

'But in the eyes of God,' I replied, 'what Drusilla did was even worse! She stole Moo's father, driving her mother to drink, and the pox-riddled bastard left nothing at all for Moo in his will. She was his only child, for heaven's sake! How would that go down, do you honestly think, in the eyes of Daddy and the good Lord?'

And I found myself this morning wondering what the eyes of Daddy and the good Lord would make of the three of us now: Harvey deceased, Moo diseased, and me disenfranchised. I glanced across the table at Moo, who was happily chewing on a slice of toast, and nearly said something to that effect, but ate my muesli in silence instead, and pretended to read *The Guardian*.

Moo was already dressed for the day in a cream silk blouse and linen slacks, but her hair still required brushing and styling, and she needed a manicure too.

'Up or down?' I asked.

'Hmm?'

'Your hair.' I folded my newspaper. 'Up or down? Chignon? Plait? A Gibson twist?'

She thought for a moment. 'Down,' she said, nibbling daintily on a piece of crust. 'Swept off my face, with my black velvet hairband.'

'I'll go upstairs and get it,' I said.

After the previous evening's upset, the house seemed its usual self again, as – thank God – did I. I wouldn't go as far as to say that I flew up the stairs to Muriel's room, gay as a lark, but I did feel very much brighter than I had for some time – I might even have been humming a tune. It was the first decent morning we'd had in weeks (I have always been sensitive to the weather) and the morning sun was beaming through the front door's stained-glass panels, scattering rainbow shards of light over the hall walls and ceiling. I was quite the optimist, for once, imagining, I'm ashamed to admit, how I would decorate the house should it ever come into my possession. I can't help having such thoughts from time to time, but I always remind myself that I would have to endure the loss of Moo to claim my prize, and then all visions of Farrow & Ball paint colour charts swiftly disintegrate into a pit of self-disgust and despair.

And I was wrestling my way out of this pit on my return to the dining room, feeling very cross with myself – I didn't want to put a dampener on what had been, until then, a fairly pleasant morning. But Moo had vanished. She had evidently mobilized her wheelchair and was cooing to me from the living room, across the hall. I doubled back on myself, scuttling over the parquet floor in my slippers, and was passing the study when I realized that the fax machine was in operation, droning away to itself, while spewing forth a sheet of paper.

I stopped, struggling to quell my mounting excitement. Who could it be, I wondered? Moo's old agent, a journalist, or PR guru perhaps? Whoever it was, it might be an excellent development for Moo, who was once considered one of the greatest romantic novelists of her generation. Sadly, she has not penned a book in over twenty years, and people these days do lose interest if one is out of the public eye for more than a nanosecond. Consequently, Muriel Hinchcliffe (MBE) has been out of print and agentless for quite some time (though I understand from Joanna-Next-Door that her books are available second-hand on the internet, for the princely sum of 10p).

But Moo is nothing if not hopeful. She believes vehemently that a Muriel Hinchcliffe revival is not just a certainty, but imminent.

'The BBC have serialized *Poldark* again,' she told me, several years ago. 'It's only a matter of time before they dramatize *The Camelford Chronicles* too! Now who,' she mused, 'do you suppose would play Lady Loretta Delabole? Or Captain Latchley?' And we spent a fun few hours debating the attributes (or otherwise) of various Hollywood luminaries, many of whom were, in fact, dead, or at least well past their use-by date.

However, Moo has been rather less hopeful of late. She rarely talks about *The Camelford Chronicles* at all, and when she does mention her work it is with a sense of sadness, regret almost.

Though regretful of what? I wish I knew. Not of writing the books in the first place – of that I am certain. Churning out (albeit lowbrow) fiction gave Moo a sense of purpose and pleasure (not to mention a sizeable income) during a particularly bleak time in her life. Regret that her illness prevented her from penning more than five novels? I doubt it. Moo's hands and brain have remained mercifully free from disease (thank God), and while her ceasing to write did coincide with the onset of her symptoms (a plethora of neurological maladies that baffled all but one of the Harley Street doctors she consulted), Moo's illness is not the cause of her writer's block. Because I believe it is writer's block that afflicts her – she simply cannot write any more. 'The words aren't there,' she told me once. 'They're all used up. Gone, for good.'

Yes, Moo has abandoned hope, pretty much. She allowed it to return – briefly – a year or so ago, when a journalist from *The Sunday Herald* pitched up one afternoon, wanting to interview her for its arts magazine. Moo believed – we both did, actually – that this would lead to Great Things, or at the very least *The Camelford Chronicles*' long overdue return to bookstores. But the journalist – a rather sniffy middle-aged woman, called Kate Porter – had a deeply unpleasant manner, Moo said, and 'a thoroughly aggressive interview technique'. When Moo telephoned the newspaper to complain, the article was spiked.

That was the final straw, I think.

Which is why, when I heard – then saw – the fax machine grinding into action, I think I actually said out loud: 'Oh, it must be a miracle!' A national newspaper requesting an interview? The BBC wanting to set out its terms?

I sneaked into the study (I always feel guilty entering it, because while the kitchen is my domain, the study is unconditionally Moo's), which is a small claustrophobic room with red velvet curtains at the single sash window, leaving the dark oak desk and bookshelves in permanent shadow. It has a lingering smell of stale roast dinners too – owing, I suppose, to the kitchen next door – and of beeswax polish, even though I have not dusted the room in years.

The fax machine is on Moo's desk, directly beneath the window, where a leggy climbing rose blocks much of the residual light. I crept towards it, holding my breath lest Moo hear me and catch me out, because it always feels like a violation, touching the objects on her desk. Though I always touch them anyway: tracing the pads of my fingers over the smooth black contours of the Bakelite telephone, fluttering the tips of my nails against the typewriter keys, cradling the photo of Harvey bouncing a red-haired baby boy on his lap.

I rarely look at the other photographs, the ones that cover the study walls, though when I do, I am always struck by the colourful life that Moo has led. Here, in the alcove by the window, is a portrait (circa 1969) of a miniskirted Moo perched on Michael Caine's lap (photographed by Terence Donovan for *The Sunday Times*, no less). On the opposite wall is a windswept Harvey steadying himself on the Blackpool promenade, shaking hands with Tony Benn (Labour Party conference, 1973), next to a paparazzi shot of Moo and Harvey at their engagement party, exiting Annabel's nightclub, wearing matching trouser suits.

There is only one photo of me. September 1981. I am holding hands with a scowling boy dressed in shorts, blazer, and an overlarge straw boater. He is clutching a one-eyed teddy bear, while I stand side-on to the camera, entreating him to smile at the lens, even though I know his heart is breaking. For mine was breaking too.

Anyway, I plucked the fax from the machine, and must have gasped out loud, because the words on the page made no sense at all. They made perfect grammatical sense, of course, but I could not process their meaning at first because they were not what I expected; the words were not supposed to be like this – threatening, accusatory, utterly vile:

I know exactly what you did and now I'm going to make you pay

That was it. Nothing else. No name, no company heading or address. The rest of the sheet was completely, brutally blank.

I must have been in the study for quite a long time, because Muriel came to find me.

'There you are!' she exclaimed from the doorway. 'What on earth have you been doing in here?'

'Nothing!' I said. 'I've not been doing anything!'

She eyed me slyly. 'Then what is that in your hand?'

'This,' I said, thrusting the sheet at her face, 'just came out of the fax machine. Do you know anything about it, Moo? Is this your idea of a joke?'

I didn't mean to accuse her. Now, with a calmer, more rational head on my shoulders, I know it would have been impossible for Moo to have sent the fax. But I was frightened, and when I am scared I get angry, as do we all.

'What,' I said, jabbing the words with my fingers, 'is the meaning of this, Moo?'

'I have no idea,' she said flatly. 'You tell me, Roo.'

'What?'

'Well, I couldn't possibly have sent it.'

'Neither could I!'

'Is it addressed to anyone?'

I stared at the fax, flipped it over, and examined the other side. 'No.'

'So it may be a wrong number.'

'Well, yes,' I said. 'I suppose it very well could be a wrong number. I hadn't thought of that.'

'There's something here.' She pointed at a series of blurred digits at the bottom of the page. 'The fax number of the sender. I believe some fax machines are connected to the telephone line. I suggest you call it, Ruth, so you can direct your accusations at the actual perpetrator.' She glared at me. 'Go on then!'

'Go on then what?'

'Dial the number!'

'Why me? It's your fax machine. And as you never tire of reminding me, it's your bloody telephone!'

She pursed her lips, picked up the receiver, and started to dial. 'All right,' she said, 'I will. I'm not scared.'

'Neither am I!'

'Of course not, dear.'

There was a pause while Muriel clamped the receiver to her ear. And then she winced, wafting it through the air towards me, so that I could hear the high-pitched whir for myself.

'Fax machine,' I said shakily. 'It probably sent this stupid message to us by accident. A wrong number.'

'That would be the most sensible explanation.'

She replaced the receiver with one hand, tossing the fax at me with the other. I tried to catch it, but my hands were shaking so much that the paper fluttered to the floor. What was wrong with me? I was the calm, logical one! Since when did Moo keep her head in a crisis?

But this wasn't a crisis, was it? It was just a group of words – silly words – sent randomly from an unknown source. A mistake, a prank. Nothing more.

'Is there such a thing,' I asked feebly, 'as sending "funny" faxes? You know, like the jokey phone calls children make.'

'I daresay there is.'

'Though not many households or businesses have fax machines any more,' I said, 'so I doubt it would be kiddies playing games. Maybe a youngster on a training scheme did it as a joke. Or a pharmacist, because they still use fax machines, I think.'

'Perhaps.' Moo sounded thoroughly bored. 'I'd imagine doling out HRT and antidepressants day in, day out might get tedious after a while. Do us both a favour, Ruth, and throw this in the bin. And let's agree to not speak of it again.'

But I did speak of it again – two hours later, when I was out shopping. I had to unburden myself to someone. It is so stressful living with Moo, with all her ups and downs and colourful moods that, at times, I think my head might explode with the upset and anxiety of it all. I briefly considered tele-phoning Stephanie, Moo's ex-daughter-in-law, but I knew if Moo found out about that there'd be absolute hell to pay. She would see it as a betrayal, which I can't really blame her for, because Stephanie isn't a pleasant person at all. She's rough and crude, the sort of woman who'll say: 'I'm like Marmite – people love me or hate me, and I don't give a shit.' But Stephanie is also a no-nonsense soul and I used to find her practical and, well, *basic* presence in our lives a welcome anti-dote to Moo's airs and graces. In fact, I rather miss her. When Stephanie still visited us, she'd always bring her daughter Courtney too, and it was nice to have a part of Barnaby with us for a while. Even if it wasn't quite the finest part.

I told Moo I'd be gone for less than an hour, that I was getting us something nice for lunch – fresh tomatoes, ham, and artisan bread from the organic shop on Lyttleton Road. It's very expensive, and Moo and I can't really afford to buy anything there, but the food tastes so much nicer than the supermarket produce. There were nasty rumours a while ago that the food isn't organic at all – that it's all bought in from a wholesaler in Walthamstow, repackaged in hessian sacks and brown paper bags to 'fool the local lentil-munchers' (according to the man behind the counter at the Jiffy-Kwik Convenience Store). But you can't fake quality, I said to Moo, or the wonderful level of personal service you get at Lyttleton Road.

And it means so much to have regular, friendly faces to engage with. This street, for all its well-heeled residents, is nowhere near as neighbourly as it was twenty years ago. Joanna-Next-Door I have known for two decades; the neighbours on the other side, Lucy and Tony Patterson-Moore, we have known a little longer. But they live in France most of the year, and the house is currently rented out to a smiley young American couple whose names I do not know and whom I rarely see or hear. The other houses have exchanged hands many times since we moved here, and are typically bought by young families desperate to get their children into the good local schools. Once the kiddies grow up, the parents move out and move on – generally somewhere detached, with a much larger garden.

I passed Mrs Number 73 on my way to Lyttleton Road. She was back inside, standing at the ground-floor window, wearing a vest and jogging bottoms (elegantly cut, not slummy), talking animatedly into a mobile phone, while twisting a strand of smooth black hair around her index finger. There was no sign of the little boy, clinging either to her breast or a stylish leg. She was probably negotiating her return to work after a lengthy maternity leave, or plotting to get her son into one of the more selective private schools. She looks the type: slick, ambitious. That poor child. I noticed that several petunia heads (pink and purple striped – ugh!) still littered the front path, and shook my head as I continued on my merry way. Hanging baskets? *Petunias?* Vulgar, vulgar, vulgar. In the good old days, Moo and I would have sent Mrs Number 73 a stern anonymous letter, pointing out her lack of taste and urging her to correct it at her earliest convenience.

The Lyttle Shop on Lyttleton Road – that's what it's called (a weak play on words if you ask me) – wasn't too busy, thank God, and I was pleased to see Joanna-Next-Door was there, paying for several bottles of organic wine at the till. I hadn't forgotten about my 'date' with her father, though she still found it necessary to remind me. She thinks that because I am old I have a colander for a brain.

'Ruthie!' she cried. I shuffled obediently towards her over the stripped-pine floorboards, circumnavigating a wicker-basket display of ethically sourced truffle oils. 'You haven't forgotten about Daddy now, have you? Or,' she pursed her lips, 'had a better offer from somebody else? You'd better not stand him up!'

'Joanna.' I touched her arm and lowered my voice. 'Can I have a word?' Her face dropped. 'Oh, tonight. Yes,' I laughed. 'I'm still game, if your father is?'

'Oh, he can't wait! Of course, you can have a word . . .' She steered me towards the less frequented aisle, between the dried beans and pulses. 'What is it, Ruth? Is something wrong?'

'Well, yes. Something odd has happened and I'd like to know what you think. Two odd things, actually.'

And I told her about Moo predicting her death so precisely, and the threatening fax that followed.

'I know it sounds silly,' I said, 'but I feel uneasy about it all. Moo claims she can't remember saying she was going to die in seventy-two hours, and I'd have forgotten about it myself by now, if it hadn't been for the fax. Common sense tells me the two aren't connected. Moo is no more a fortune teller than I am, and the fax was clearly random, a wrong number. It must be. But still.'

'Mmmm.' Joanna frowned. 'I don't know Muriel very well,' she whispered, 'but she doesn't strike me as an easy person. She's very dramatic and demanding, isn't she? Is there anyone who'd want to upset her, do you think? Someone with an axe to grind?'

I didn't even have to think about it. 'Lots of people,' I said. 'She's annoyed loads of people over the years, including me, but I love her. Nobody else does.'

'Oh!' Joanna looked rather taken aback.

'Of course, she can be charming,' I added hastily. 'Very charming indeed, and was quite the It girl during her modelling days. But she's alienated pretty much everyone over the years. Even Barnaby, her own son! And we all know how that turned out.'

Joanna nodded sadly. 'And because of what happened to Barnaby, she's fallen out with his wife and her only grandchild. Oh, it's all so sad . . .'

'Well,' I said, 'she blames Stephanie for everything. Absolutely everything.'

'So, is Stephanie behind the fax, do you think?'

I considered this for a moment, but it seemed highly unlikely. Stephanie might not be a pleasant woman, but she isn't spiteful, or remotely dramatic, or prone to playing pranks. And, God knows, she has good enough reason to do something awful to Moo, who continues to hold her responsible for Barnaby's death.

\* \* \*

'Her name is Stephanie, and she's a cleaner at his student hall of residence! What in the name of all that's insane does he think he's bloody well playing at?' asked Moo.

That was my introduction to the existence of the unfortunate Stephanie, in a telephone call with a nigh-on hysterical Moo, during the summer of 1994. I was sitting in my Cardiff office at the time, working as the Women's Editor at *South Wales Weekly* and discussing redundancies with the publisher (including my own, as it turned out), when the telephone rang. It was Moo. My PA asked whether she'd care to call back. Moo said she damn well did; that this was a matter of life or death.

'They've been living together for three months,' Moo exploded down the phone at me, 'and she's pregnant! Ten years older than him – ten bloody years – and she has,' she lowered her voice to a whisper, 'even lost some of her teeth. She is common, ugly, thick as a plank, smokes like a steam train, and is every mother's nightmare. He says she's the first truly loving, caring woman he's ever known. I ask you!'

I felt quite hurt at that, I must admit. Had I not always shown Barnaby lots of affection? Had I not been his darling Auntie Roo? I certainly loved him very much – every inch of his pinched, freckled face, his soft auburn hair, the pink pointed tongue that he'd stick out when he was deep in concentration – and he was a walking, talking, carbon copy of Harvey, after all. But I understood what Barnaby meant and remember thinking: well, you've brought this on yourself, Muriel Hinchcliffe. You and Harvey packed that poor child off to boarding school when he was six years old – the baffled look on that little boy's face! – because neither of you had time for him, you only had eyes for each other, and how that has come back to haunt you now that your husband is dead and gone! And, by the way, I still haven't forgiven you for stealing Harvey from me, twenty miserable years ago. I am glad Barnaby is causing you pain. Long may it continue!

'Gosh,' I said, 'how awful! Is there someone at the university you can complain to?'

'Not a soul, you fool! He's a grown man, he can do as he likes. Oh, what on earth would *you* know? You've never had children.'

\* \* \*

'Ruth?' Joanna was staring at me. 'Ruth, you've gone very pale. Are you feeling all right?'

'Yes,' I said. 'I'm fine. I'm just a bit tired, that's all. No, I don't think the fax was from Stephanie. I'm not sure whether she's capable of hating anyone. Unlike . . . well.' I swallowed hard. 'She certainly wouldn't want to hurt or frighten Moo, I can assure you.'

Joanna glanced at her watch. My time was up, it seemed. 'I'm sorry, but I must go,' she said. 'Daddy's a stickler for routine and needs his lunch at noon.'

I nodded. Oh God, he's one of those. 'Set in his ways, is he?' I asked.

'Oh, no, he's great fun and up for anything! But I do have to dash. Give me a knock if things' – she lowered her voice –

'progress. Which I very much doubt, because it'll just be Muriel being a bit silly and attention-seeking, coinciding with a complete stranger sending a nonsensical fax as a joke. You'll see.'

# Three hours after lunch, following
## a lengthy nap

Harvey came to me just now, in a dream. He appeared in the living room, sprawled over the chaise longue in the bay window, rolling himself a cigarette, like he owned the bloody place. He didn't look up, but simply said, 'Why did you leave me, Ruth? Why did you do it?'

He looked just as he had when we first met at Oxford, dressed in a too-tight, too-short-in-the-leg black woollen suit, his copper hair brutally parted and slicked down one side of his face, the sharp edge of his fringe pointing at an angry crop of spots threatening to colonize his right cheekbone. Back then, he was so uncertain, so lacking in finesse, so desperately in need of my guidance and protection.

I sat up in my chair and glared at him. 'Why are you eighteen again?' I said. 'You look as though your mother dressed you and combed your hair.'

'She did,' he said. 'She did it to annoy you.'

This, I told myself, is not how our reunion was meant to be. I have loved you, Harvey Hinchcliffe, for fifty-eight years – or at least, for the last thirty-four of them, the *memory* of you. But now that you are here in front of me, I feel no love at all. Just irritation that you have dared to present yourself to me in this manner – the way you were when we first met, before your transformation.

'Why did you do it?' he said.

'Shhh!' I gestured at Moo, snoozing opposite in her wing-backed chair, crusty feet splayed either side of her pom-pom cushion. 'You'll wake up Moo.'

'I'm a bloody apparition,' he said. 'She can't hear me. I'll ask again, Ruth. Why did you leave me?'

'Excuse me,' I said tartly, 'but I think you'll find that you left me. For her.' I nodded at Moo, who emitted a sharp, somnolent snort. 'Don't you dare rewrite history, don't go reapportioning blame! You said to me, as I recall, "I'm so sorry, Ruth, but Moo and I have fallen in love. There is nothing I can do other than beg for your forgiveness, because we both love you very much and never wanted to hurt you." There, you see? I remember what you said, every brutal word of it. Each patronizing syllable, every treacherous pause for breath, you bastard, is carved into my heart by your cheating, cork-screw tongue. And thanks to the pair of you, I have not trusted a soul since!'

'That's not what I mean,' he said, 'and you know it. Why did you leave me?' He shook his head disapprovingly. 'You're a dangerous woman, Ruth.'

'What? Dangerous – how?'

'You know.'

'I do not!' I struggled – but failed – not to raise my voice, and Moo's eyelids flickered. 'I think you had better go,' I said, reaching to pull the blanket that had slipped down to Moo's ankles back over her knees.

But when I looked up, he'd gone, and I realized that I was awake.

The dream unsettled me very much. It was all so vivid: the afternoon sun shining on the copperish crown of Harvey's head, the creases running down each of his trouser legs, so sharp I could imagine them pressing against my fingertip, the astringent stink of the TCP liquid he used on his spots back then – each detail so real, so graphic, that the reek of him lingered long after I'd woken up. And then there was the hurt I'd felt. The actual physical pain, the gnawing in the pit of my stomach – that remained too, finally easing to a dull ache. A hollow reminder of his rejection and betrayal of me.

I went into the kitchen and drank a large glass of water. The saltiness of the lunchtime ham (which had been disappointing – perhaps the man at the Jiffy-Kwik store has a point after all?) and the late afternoon heat and humidity had made me incredibly thirsty and triggered the mother of all headaches. I looked at my watch – nearly five o'clock. In three hours' time, Lawrence would come to call for our 'date', and I still had Moo to deal with. Allowing her to sleep so long was something of a gamble. If she was too well rested, she might not conk out when required; she might even get wind of my going out for the evening, and I really didn't fancy a visit from the Angel of Death and her icy palm during *EastEnders*. But the over-stimulation of a game of Scrabble generally exhausts Moo, so I let her slumber on while I prepared supper, confident that I could slip out for my date with Lawrence once she was asleep.

I would eat with her, I decided, just after six o'clock. It would be half an hour earlier than usual, but give us time for a lengthy and taxing tournament. Moo would possibly smell a rat, but I'd simply insist I needed an early night because of my headache and the upset of the evening before.

I reached into the cupboard under the sink and took out my medicine chest. It was my mother's originally: a lovely cedarwood thing with a glossy, dark red cross painted boldly on the lid, where I keep my paracetamol, herbal remedies, and an emergency stash of nitrazepam. Such happy, comforting memories I associate with that little wooden box: my mother gently tending to a cut on my knee, a graze on my elbow, or popping a junior aspirin on my tongue in the middle of the night to quell a fever –

*There, there, my darling, Mummy's here. Tell me where it hurts. You'll feel better soon, I promise – you're all safe and sound and loved.*

Did she really say those words to me? I wish I knew for sure.

I know I heard her say such things. But the more I struggle to remember the details, the more everything shifts and blurs. And I can't tell whether the weeping child sitting on my mother's lap, pressing their face into her soft, warm neck, is Muriel or me.

# Suppertime

After preparing Moo's chilli, I was pleased to see Puss again, despite catching him doing his business beneath my prized hydrangea. I needed some form of absolution, I think, even if it meant pretending it came from a cat that lived, ate, and crapped where it liked with impunity.

'Will Puss forgive naughty Ruthie, then, for what she's going to do tonight?' I enquired, placing a saucer of tuna next to the uneaten saucer of salmon on the patio. 'But naughty Ruthie can't forgive naughty Puss for wasting all that expensive food! Muriel's favourite, too.' I tutted half-heartedly. 'Moo adores red salmon.'

I reached out a hand to pet Puss, who'd finally finished kicking mounds of dirt over his deposit, but he hissed and backed slowly away from me, until he was swallowed up by the shrubbery.

I don't know why I bother.

'Supper is served!' I said, nudging the living room door open with the toe of my slippered foot.

Moo has one of those trays on a stand that slides over the arms of her wheelchair. I, however, am still able to eat off my lap without spilling. It is fascinating, I thought, as I tucked

Moo's napkin into the neck of her blouse, how our standards slip as the day progresses: breakfast eaten formally, at opposite ends of the dining table, followed by lunch, eaten less formally, side by side, and finally supper, eaten in the living room on a tray or lap in front of the TV. It is an analogy for our decline as we age, I concluded, watching Muriel smack her lips as she ingested a large chunk of mince.

She narrowed her eyes. 'You've changed your outfit,' she said. 'You're wearing a dress.'

'I stained my top with tomato puree while I was cooking,' I said casually. 'Now, how about playing Scrabble once we've eaten? We're a little earlier than usual because we both need an early night, but we'll have enough time for one or two games, I think.'

She blinked at me. 'I'd have thought you'd had all the rest you needed this afternoon,' she said. 'You were out for the count for most of it, making an absolute racket too. Snoring like a walrus, muttering away to yourself, grinding your teeth . . .'

'Was I?'

'Yes, you were. Anyway, I really don't see why you had to change clothes on my account. I wouldn't have bothered changing for you.'

'Well, it takes a lot more work for you to change.'

We ate in silence for several minutes.

'It's your favourite dress too,' she said suddenly. 'You wore it to Courtney's eighteenth birthday party, as I recall.' She shook her head. 'Ghastly child. Feckless and lazy, just like her mother.'

'It's nothing special, Moo,' I said, a little too sharply. 'Just something from the catalogue, but it happens to be the only clean dress in my wardrobe at the moment. And that's hardly my fault, is it?'

This was partly true. I was very behind with my own laundry, thanks to Moo's worsening incontinence adding to the usual weekly load. It was also true that this dress is my favourite, green gingham with a wrap-around top and gently flaring skirt. The cut is very flattering, giving the illusion of my actually possessing a pair of breasts, while minimizing the size of my over-generous *derrière*. It is difficult for a shorty like me, with my Hobbitesque proportions, to find anything stylish or elegant in the high street stores, but *Little Women* catalogue comes up trumps every time.

By now, I was nearing the end of my meal, though Moo was only halfway through hers. I glanced at my watch. Half past six. One and a half hours to go, and I still had to get (a hopefully dead-to-the-world) Muriel onto the stairlift, upstairs, undressed, and into bed. I felt a twist of anxiety. What if Moo was wide awake when Lawrence came to call? Well, that would be a fine start to the only date I'd had in years: Moo in the background, yammering on about how I was an abusive, sex-starved satanist – whatever it took to put the kibosh on my love life.

'I need the loo,' I said. 'You can set the Scrabble board up while I'm gone.'

Moo sniffed. 'You'd better not disappear again, the way you did last night. And you still haven't given me a manicure, Roo. I've a rough nail that keeps catching on my cardigan.'

*Oh, do it yourself*, I wanted to say. *You can still use your hands, can't you?*

'Manicure coming up after we've played Scrabble,' I said. 'I'll get some varnish while you set up the board. Pale pink, yes? Which shade would you prefer? French Kiss? Mademoiselle?'

'Dear God,' she groaned. 'French Kiss, I suppose. How peculiar it sounds, asking you for that.' She giggled coyly, yawned, and rubbed her eyes with the heel of her hand. 'Oh, Roo . . . I'm very tired, you know.'

Things were looking up. 'I'll be back in a jiffy,' I said.

I have not been in the sole company of a man for many years now. There were lovers after Harvey (well, not so much lovers as sexual facilitators – brief, perfunctory liaisons, not unlike the fleeting connection between my fingernails and back when I scratch it: a physical need pleasantly met, but with no emotional attachment whatsoever). Lately, however, over the last decade or so, my needs have changed. I no longer crave physical stimulation quite as much as I did, though the companionable touch of a hand on my own, the affectionate brushing of lips on my cheek, or even a good old-fashioned shag would be nice once in a while. No, I long for someone to talk to, for conversation, for an intellectual excitement which I no longer get from Moo.

While Moo has never been the most intelligent of women, she was very entertaining in her prime: beautiful, witty, delightfully manipulative, and a highly amusing storyteller. How else would she have penned five bestselling novels? But her ability to scintillate has faded over the years. These days, Moo is a dulled version of her former glittering self, not the sort of woman Harvey would fall for at all, and how I wish I'd made more of the fact when he visited me this afternoon! I should have said: *Just look at her now! Not so fascinating these days, is she? It should have been you, emptying her commode this morning, but you wouldn't have hung around for five seconds, would you? No, when the going got tough, Harvey Hinchcliffe got going, because that's what Harvey Hinchcliffe did to me.*

Oh, I'm probably being unfair. Perhaps Harvey's sudden rejection of me and intense attraction to Moo was down to the seven-year itch after all, just as my mother suggested. I am sure it had nothing at all to do with my multiple miscarriages, with the bonkers, howling mess I'd become after my body expelled one embryo too many, with the fact that for the first time ever I needed Harvey more than he needed me, and Moo had just been photographed by David Bailey for *Vogue* and needed nobody.

'Men do lose interest after a while,' my mother said at the time, 'especially when women get over-demanding. You should smile a little more, darling. Babies aren't everything.'

By the time I returned to the living room, Moo had finished her dinner, stacked our plates and cutlery on the hostess trolley at her side, and set up the Scrabble board on the green-baize card table in front of her. She had even upended the tiles in the upside-down lid of the Scrabble box, in preparation for us making our selection. She smiled brightly up at me.

'I'll let you go first,' she said. 'Just for being so kind. For putting up with me.'

Oh, Moo. Why do you always say such lovely things when I'm about to do my worst to you?

I plonked myself in the armchair opposite, carefully placing the bottle of French Kiss nail polish on the nest of tables at my side. 'For later,' I said. 'Now, let's get playing.' I bent forward to shuffle the tiles in the box around a little more, picked out my letters, and placed them right side up on my grey plastic rack.

ETARTHB

I placed the B tile on the board, following it horizontally with REATHE. 'BREATHE,' I said triumphantly. 'And the B falls on a double-letter score. Seventeen points, Moo, if you please.'

Moo, scribbling down the score, looked up and blinked at me. 'So I see.' She cleared her throat, before swiftly placing a U and a D vertically either side of my R.

'URD,' she said flatly. 'Only four points, but it'll have to do.'

'Urd?'

'Yes. Urd.'

'Is urd a word?'

'Of course it's a word! It is,' she added haughtily, 'an Indian plant. Of the bean family.'

'Golly,' I smirked, 'you learn something new every day in this house. Will the thrills never end?'

'If you don't believe me, you can check the Oxford English Dictionary.'

'No, no, Moo. It's quite all right. I believe you.' I placed my new seven chosen tiles in my rack. I had one blank tile, and the other letters were an uninspiring CNPZAD. Bugger.

Ah! Of course!

'CAN'T,' I said, placing the CAN and a blank tile vertically above the T of BREATHE.

'Can't,' Moo repeated.

'Yes,' I said. 'That's right. With . . .' I swivelled the T away to read the square beneath, 'a triple-word score just *here*. Which means a total of—'

'No, no,' Moo said. 'I meant you *can't do that*.'

'Do what?'

'Use a blank tile for an apostrophe.'

'I most certainly can!'

'No, you can't. You've never done it before.'

'Well, I've never needed to before,' I said. 'But now I do, which means a score of . . .'

'But it's representing an apostrophe. That's punctuation.'

'I know it's punctuation,' I said. 'I was a journalist, Moo, I know what punctuation is. Don't patronize me.'

'Well, I was a novelist,' she replied primly, 'and anyway, punctuation isn't in the rules. Otherwise, we'd all be extending words with blank tiles on to triple-word-score squares with punctuation. You know, full stops, commas, semicolons, colons, exclamation marks, question marks . . .'

'I know what fucking punctuation is!'

Moo lowered her eyes. 'There is no need to swear,' she said.

I took a deep breath. 'In this instance, Moo, the apostrophe represents a missing N and O, which are letters. The apostrophe, therefore, represents two missing letters.'

'Which means,' Moo observed, 'that there should be *two* blank tiles. And you've only used the one.'

'But the omitted N and O are represented by *one piece* of punctuation, to spell out the word CAN'T. If I was using two tiles, I would be spelling out CANNOT. Which I am not.'

'So, you admit it is punctuation!'

'I NEVER SAID IT WASN'T!'

Moo yawned. 'Oh, have it your own way. I'm very tired, you know. Can't be bothered arguing.'

She was beginning to nod off.

I nudged her knee with a corner of the upturned Scrabble lid. 'Moo? You haven't taken your extra letters. Moo?'

'Hmmmm?' She opened one eye. 'Oh, yes. Yes, of course.'

She shuffled the pincered fingers of one hand around the box, sleepily plonking her chosen letters in her rack, while smiling thoughtfully to herself.

'There!' she cried, feebly placing an M above URD, and an E and R beneath. 'MURDER. Double-word score. Eighteen. Do me a favour, dear, and write the score down for me, will you?' She closed her eyes. 'I really don't know what's wrong with me tonight.'

I stared at the board.

CAN T BREATHE MURDER

And then the lid slid off my lap, crashing onto the board, scattering Scrabble tiles all over the carpet.

But Moo, apparently out for the count, didn't flicker an eyelid.

# Just now

My conscience is clear, I keep telling myself, as I fold Moo's bony, slumbering frame into a waterproof-sheet and blanket cocoon. My conscience is clear, completely clear. I've earned this – this precious night out.

I look around Moo's room, the cluttered surfaces and chi-chi decor cloyingly pink and feminine in the westerly evening light. I am going out tonight! The midsummer evening extends far in front of me, dark with uncertainty, fragrant with jasmine, pregnant with possibilities.

Pregnant.

I am weeping on my mother's shoulder, over fifty years ago. *Another one gone*, I'm wailing. *Another bloody miscarriage. Why can't I hold on to my babies? Why can't I be a mother, like you?* And she pulls away from me, sighing, and saying: 'Oh, pull yourself together, Ruth! Harvey won't want you if you're always like this – whining, weeping, you're an absolute sight! Why can't you be more like Muriel? Muriel doesn't have a husband, but is always so funny and pretty and gay! Babies aren't the be-all and end-all, Ruth.' And she chuckles unpleasantly to herself. 'God knows, I should know that better than anyone.'

'There,' I whisper to Moo as I fold the eiderdown over her

legs. 'I've got a great big baby all of my own now, though, haven't I?'

I take a bottle of Chanel N°5 from her dressing table and spritz it onto my wrists, all the while watching her wide-open mouth emit a series of ghastly snores.

*I've something to tell you, Ruth. I went to Harley Street again today. And the neurosurgeon I saw this time . . . well. I have a diagnosis at last. What I've got is rare. And lethal. The prognosis is awful, bloody awful. A slow, painful decline until I can't do anything at all for myself any more. A living death . . . that's what he's sentenced me to. A living death, Ruth. My God. A living death . . .*

I take a Lancôme lipstick from her make-up bag – a violent shade of fuchsia, far too bright for me – and dab it onto my lips.

*No, I don't know how long I've got left. Could be months, could be years. Yes, of course he told me what I've got wrong with me, and yes, yes, he's sure of it . . . it can't be anything else, he says, though God, I wish it was. Oh, Ruth – I'm scared! No, I won't tell you what it's called. Stop nagging me, Ruth – I won't give the bastarding thing a name because that makes it real, do you understand? I don't want its name mentioned under this roof – I'll kill myself if I hear it, Ruth, so please don't ever ask me again. No, I don't want any doctors or nurses, just you. They can't do anything for me anyway, the specialist made that perfectly clear. You will look after me, won't you, Roo? Please don't leave me! Will you live with me, care for me, until the end? I promise I'll leave you everything, the house, my money, everything . . .*

I remove my floral pinafore, its pockets smeared with Sudocrem, and drape it over the back of Moo's wheelchair.

*Oh, Roo . . . thank you. Thank you! I don't deserve a friend like you. I've brought this on myself. Haven't I, Roo?*

I stand at the foot of the bed and watch her chest rising and falling, smoothing my palms down the front of my dress while I wait for the doorbell to ring.

*God's punishing me for falling in love with Harvey, isn't he, Roo?*

It rings.

*Roo?*

I go downstairs and open the door.

# During my date with Lawrence at the Lamb and Flag

I am positively buzzing!

For years, I have been invisible, but tonight I was actually seen. I have been spoken to, listened to, acknowledged, and admired.

But feeling so happy hurts so very much.

Isn't that strange?

Lawrence wasn't what I expected at all. Joanna is petite, blonde, and rather affected, while her father is tall, well built, and bald-headed, with a rather pronounced loping stride that covered our fifty-yard walk to the pub in about two dozen paces. I jogged along beside him, making breathless small talk, while he emitted terse replies with a cockney accent from the side of his mouth, as though he'd spent his formative years with either a dummy or cigarette jammed between his lips. For the first half an hour or so of our 'date', I was not impressed. The pub was too busy for a start – a live band was playing old Kinks' covers, which evidently pleased Lawrence, who kept tapping his hands against his tree-trunk thighs, but I have never been a fan, and my hearing is a bit iffy at the best of times. I also dislike crowded places, and there were far too many customers hogging the bar and standing in large, unwieldy groups, rather than sitting down at the empty tables. I felt small, lost, and rather pathetic as I asked Lawrence to repeat himself.

'I SAID,' he bellowed, 'WHAT DO YOU WANT TO DRINK?'

I stood on tiptoe and shouted up, 'A gin and tonic please.'

'ASSANDASLASS?'

'What?'

'ASSANDASLASS?'

'*What?*'

He stooped and enunciated in my ear. 'Ice and a slice?'

'Yes. Please.'

Lawrence turned back to the bar to order our drinks, giving me the chance to study his blue shirt and black trousers, which were made from excellent-quality linen and quite beautifully cut. He was, in spite of his roughness, a man who scrubbed up very nicely indeed, and that made me think of Harvey and how unfinished he'd been when we first met.

*Harvey Hinchcliffe, from Huddersfield, studying Philosophy, Politics, and Economics. A raging Commie, before you ask, and yes, coming to a privileged shithole like this goes against every one of me principles, but if I'm gonna force change, then I'll have to do it from the inside out. Know thine enemy and all that crap. Now, who the hell are you?*

Lawrence turned to face me and, without making eye contact, inclined his head in the direction of a wicker two-seater table in the courtyard outside, with a red rose and lit candle at its centre. I trotted obediently after him through the chattering throng.

'Now,' he said, 'I can hear myself think.' He smiled at me,

placed our drinks on the table and pulled out a chair so that I could sit down. I thanked him, wincing at the obvious surprise in my voice.

'And thank you for my drink,' I added. 'My round next, I think.'

'Won't hear of it.'

Lawrence, sprawling untidily in the chair opposite, held a spade-like hand aloft to silence my protestations. 'Joanna tells me you don't get out much because you're caring for a sick friend. I'm a selfish git who goes out as and when he pleases, and only cares for himself. That means tonight's on me. Agreed?'

I laughed. 'Agreed.'

'So.' Lawrence took a swig of his pint and grimaced. 'Let's get the clichés out of the way. Tell me about yourself, Ruth.'

'Oh.' I gave a rather ineffectual wave of my hand. Lawrence, I realized, most definitely did have all his own teeth, and they were in remarkably good condition for a man of his age. He also had very nice blue eyes, with just the right number of laughter lines for a man in his late seventies: not so many as to hint at hours spent lying idle in the sun, but not so few as to indicate a soulless existence lived in pursuit of vanity and self-preservation.

'Come on, Ruth,' he said. 'Spit it out. Talk some sanity to me. I've spent the last three days listening to Joanna and that arsehole Elliott trying to convert me to kinesiology and ear-candling, whatever the bloody hell that is.'

I laughed again. He must have thought me such a gurning halfwit. 'Oh, I don't know where to start.'

'You can start by telling me how you ended up being Muriel

Hinchcliffe's carer. My late wife was a fan of her books. Said they were edgier than your average romantic novel. Earthier.' He grinned. 'Sexier.'

My heart sank. Muriel Hinchcliffe. Why did everything always end up having to be about Muriel sodding Hinchcliffe?

'Not read them myself,' he added. 'Not my kind of books at all. And from what Jo tells me, Muriel Hinchcliffe probably isn't my kind of person.'

I perked up at that. 'Actually, I've not read any of her books either,' I declared.

He sat back in his chair and stared at me. 'Really? Why not?'

I shuffled my feet uneasily under the table. The hairs on my shins were poking through my tights and prickling against the skin of the opposing calf. Why the devil hadn't I shaved my legs before coming out?

'Not my sort of book, I suppose,' I said. 'Not intelligent enough, I'm afraid. That probably sounds arrogant of me. But I don't care for romantic literature, not my thing at all.' I took a sip of my drink.

'You've been let down in love,' he said. This was a statement, not a question.

'Yes,' I said. 'I have.' I cleared my throat. 'My ex-husband, Harvey, fell in love with Muriel, who happened to be my best friend at the time. Years ago, now.'

'I'm sorry.' He shook his head. 'I had no idea.'

'Not many people do,' I said. 'Not even Joanna. Most of the neighbours we had back then have since moved on or died, so . . .'

'But you're telling me, a stranger?'

I shrugged. Why shouldn't Lawrence know what had

happened? What did I have to lose? I had nothing to be ashamed of!

'It's something we just don't talk about,' I said. 'Not even with each other. Certainly not since the man in question . . .' My voice must have trailed away, because Lawrence leant forward a little, straining to hear me. 'The man in question died. Over thirty years ago.'

Lawrence sat back in his chair. 'That must make looking after Muriel very hard, I would have thought.'

'Oh, but it doesn't!' I exclaimed. 'It really doesn't.'

'Are you sure? Joanna thinks you're being taken advantage of.'

'*I'm* being taken advantage of?'

'Yes. Joanna says she's worried about you. That you are – how did she put it? – in an isolated and vulnerable position. That you're pretty much Muriel's slave.'

I felt all at once flattered by Joanna's concern, surprised by her insight, and insulted by the assumption that I was a pathetic old biddy, entirely at Moo's mercy. If only people knew the truth of the matter! And I actually had to bite the inside of my cheek to stop myself from laughing and blurting everything out. I wanted so much for him to see *me* – not Ruth the Martyr, the Victim, the Wronged, but Ruth the Avenger, the Brave, the Astute.

I smiled knowingly. 'That's very kind of her,' I said, 'but there's nothing vulnerable about me, I can assure you. I am in excellent health, have all my faculties, and know exactly what I've got myself into with Moo.'

He folded his arms and stared at me. 'Do you, now?'

'Yes,' I said. 'I can assure you that our arrangement is not entirely one-sided.'

'Ah, well.' He shrugged. 'That's a shame. I had a little bet with myself that you'd be the first example of true altruism I'd ever come across. Turns out you're only doing this 'cos there's something in it for you after all.' He took a gulp of his pint and winked at me.

'I'm no fool,' I said.

'I know that. I can tell you're a very intelligent woman.' I could feel my cheeks reddening. 'But,' he went on, 'you're making a hell of a sacrifice, aren't you? Living out your twilight years—'

'My golden years,' I corrected him. 'There's plenty of life in this old girl yet.'

'Well, okay, your golden years. But you're living them out caring for the woman who ran off with your husband!'

'They fell in love with each other,' I said defensively. 'They couldn't help it. Yes, it hurt very much at the time, and I moved away for a while until I'd recovered, but Moo and Harvey were meant to be together in a way that Harvey and I were not.' I smiled. 'I bulldozed him into marrying me. The writing was on the wall when he turned up ten minutes late at the registry office and forgot my name during the vows. But hey-ho, I came to terms with it all, came back to live in London again, and everything was fine. All fine. More than fine, actually, because by that time there was Barnaby, whom I grew to love very much indeed.'

'Barnaby?'

'Harvey and Muriel's son.'

'Ah.'

'He died a few years before Joanna moved next door.'

'I know,' he said. 'Jo told me what happened. I'm sorry.'

'So, yes, I look after Moo because she was – and continues to be – my best friend, and in spite of what she did to me, which was a very long time ago, she has more than paid for it, don't you think, with the dreadful losses she's had to bear? And without me, there's nobody else prepared to look after her. And I'd have nowhere to go, anyway, so . . .'

Lawrence frowned. 'But why wouldn't you have anywhere to go? Jo told me you were a journalist. Women's mags and newspapers, isn't that right? You must have built up a bit of a nest egg.'

So, that was his game, was it? Charming diamond geezer worming his way into wealthy old bat's affections. Well, I was about to disappoint him. 'I worked on a variety of upmarket women's periodicals and the women's pages of the better newspapers,' I said. 'And yes, I was paid very well for it. But then I lost it all.' I fixed him with my most self-assured smile.

'Lost it? How?'

'Dodgy investments and questionable lifestyle choices.' My smile was starting to slip.

'So, you're pretty much dependent on Muriel Hinchcliffe?' Lawrence said.

'I suppose I am,' I replied chirpily. 'And she on me, of course. It's mutually beneficial.'

'Remind me,' Lawrence said slowly, 'what exactly it is that's wrong with her?'

'I don't actually know the name of it. Moo refuses to discuss it. It's a muscle- or nerve-wasting disease of some sort – astonishingly rare, apparently. A highly regarded Harley Street neurosurgeon diagnosed her twenty years ago.'

'Highly regarded neurosurgeon, you say? What was his name?'

I shrugged. 'I can't remember. I'm not sure Moo told me.'

'You can't remember? You don't know the name of her illness or the person who diagnosed her with it? You were a journalist . . .' He laughed, not unpleasantly. 'Curiosity should be your middle name! You're telling me you never wanted to find out?'

'She didn't want to tell me, so I . . .'

'You've never googled the symptoms?'

'We don't have the internet. We don't even have a computer.'

'Or looked at a medical dictionary?'

'I don't believe we have one.'

'Or asked a visiting doctor or nurse?'

'Moo refuses to see anyone medical. She prefers a natural approach. And I'm in perfect health, so . . .'

'So, you're caring full-time for the friend who stole your husband, who suffers from an unnamed disease diagnosed by God-knows-who, with a prognosis of Christ-knows-what, while putting your own life completely on hold. And for what, Ruth? Why?'

I downed the rest of my drink in one, sat back in my chair, and took a deep breath.

'Because Harvey and Moo took my house, and I want it back,' I replied.

\* \* \*

That was the meeting between Harvey and I, post-split, that hurt me most of all: when we came together at my mother's – supposedly 'neutral territory' – to negotiate our divorce, to wrangle and haggle and fight over the splitting of our jointly acquired worldly goods. Eight years of a life bound legally – twelve years together in total – reduced to a piece of A4 paper with two wobbly columns drawn down each side in bright red biro:

| Ruth's share | Harvey's share |
| --- | --- |
| The money | The house |

Looking back, I was a fool, relinquishing my home to him. But how was I supposed to know its value would rocket in the way that it did? It cost five thousand pounds over fifty years ago, two and a half million less than it's worth now. All thanks to gentrification, of course, and for that I have only myself to blame. For it was People Like Us – me, Moo, and Harvey – performing gentle clearances of People Not At All Like Us that led to the stratospheric rise in property prices over the years, although, in our defence, that wasn't our intention at the time. No, we simply saw leafy avenues and spacious unloved houses, where People Like Us could squat, smoke pot, and macramé our way towards world domination.

What was I thinking? But I wasn't thinking at all, was I? I was barely functioning, because Harvey had moved out to move in with Moo, and I was left in the house by myself: just me and my broken heart falling apart over every square inch of the place; my leaking eyes blind to the future potential of this Edwardian villa, oblivious to whatever lay beneath the woodwormed, mouldering interior, smothered in woodchip paper and boarding-house paint. I do, however, remember lying on a bare double mattress late one evening, staring up at the bulb dangling high above my head, noticing – for the very first time – that it was surrounded by a ceiling rose, where gambolling cherubs etched in plaster entwined themselves with ivy leaves, and wondering if this was a suitable spot from which to hang myself.

But I digress. To return to *that* meeting with Harvey (Lawrence has gone to replenish our drinks, thank God), I think I can allow myself a little wallow until his return.

\* \* \*

'Well,' Harvey said, handing me something to sign (I didn't know what, but signed it regardless). 'That was pretty straightforward, I must say. You're being very decent about this, Roo. You look great, by the way. When do you start the New York job?'

'I leave London tomorrow,' I said.

'Features Editor of *Women's Political Digest*, no less!' He whistled long and low. 'Huge congratulations, Roo. You've come a long way from making tea at *The Observer*. It's a dream come true – just what you always wanted!'

'No, it's not,' I said. 'All I want is you, and to have your baby.'

'Oh, Lord . . .' He rubbed his face with his palms. 'We've been over this so many times! Roo, *I* was your baby. I'd become your creation. We weren't lovers any more, hadn't been for a very long time. We were parent and child, and with Muriel – well, I finally feel like a grown-up! What with my bloody mother telling me what to do and think and wear, and I escaped from her only for you to take over where she left off . . .'

'Rubbish,' I said. 'You just don't want me because I can't get pregnant. Because I'm barren. Admit it!'

'I'll admit nothing of the sort,' he growled, 'because it isn't true. Ruth, this is the best thing for all of us. You deserve a proper husband, not a replacement child. You're a strong, intelligent, ambitious woman. Look at where you're going tomorrow! Look at the job you have waiting for you! Your future is amazing, if only you could see it.'

He thrust a tissue into my hand. I blew my nose. 'I've made an idiot of myself again,' I said.

'Not at all,' he murmured, rubbing my shoulder, and my lower belly ached for him.

'I hear you're doing well,' I sniffed.

Mother had let slip that Harvey had been promoted to something important at Labour head office (she was, of course, more excited by that than by my New York posting). She couldn't tell me exactly what it was that Harvey had been promoted to, but knew it had something to do with recruiting young members – with giving the Party a more fashionable (*groovier*, I suppose we said back then) image to attract the hippy-dippy types and Bowie wannabes.

I shot Harvey a sideways glance – one final look for posterity, for at that point I fully intended never setting eyes on him again. He looked delicious, of course: clipped beard, fashionably long but not unkempt hair, tight-around-the-crotch, flared jeans – the epitome of the sexy, acceptable face of socialism, that was Harvey Hinchcliffe now. Exactly how I'd moulded him.

Mother bustled into the room. 'All sorted?' she said brightly. 'Muriel just telephoned. She's coming to visit shortly.' She looked at me entreatingly. 'Why not stay a little longer, Ruth? She'd very much like to be friends.'

I stood up clumsily, slinging my handbag over my shoulder as I swayed on the ludicrous platform soles I'd worn to appear taller, slimmer, stronger. 'I shared my bed, my toys, and you with her, Mother, and now she's got my husband too. I've had quite enough of her so-called friendship, and so, if you'll excuse me, I have a case to pack.'

Mother trotted after me into the hall. I could hear her talking under her breath, something about bitterness, then muttering about God and forgiveness, and my father.

'You leave Father out of this!' I spun around to face her. 'You've no bloody idea what he'd make of what's happened between Harvey and me, but I can pretty much guarantee he'd be on the side of God and his only child, and would do anything to keep my marriage intact and make me happy! *You*, on the other hand, you only give a damn about Harvey and Moo, while *I*, it seems, can go to hell. Because I am in hell.' I turned away, tugging feebly at the front-door handle. 'What about me, Mummy? What about me?'

I took a deep breath, straightened my back, turned on the threshold to face her again – battling to remain certain and firm, desperate to be seen to be standing my ground. But my shoulders, shaking with misery, gave the game away.

She walked slowly towards me. There was something in her eyes – pity? Shame? But it only lasted a second. I held out my arms to meet her.

'Goodbye, Ruth,' she said, taking one of my hands in her own and giving it a perfunctory pump. 'Call me when you get to New York, just to let me know you've arrived safely.'

* * *

'So, the house was *yours* before the divorce?' Lawrence, plonking a fresh gin and tonic in front of me, could barely conceal his amazement.

'Yes. Moo assures me it's bequeathed to me in her will. I'm sure it will be mine again after she dies. She's leaving me all her money too.'

I studied Lawrence's face. Would his eyes light up like cash registers? Would I even care if they did? But he looked down quickly at his mobile phone.

'Excuse me,' he said curtly, 'it's Joanna. I'd better take it.' He turned away.

Ah, the 'escape call'. I'd heard of such things on the rare occasions I'd watched modern situation-comedy programmes. There would be a couple on a blind date, and a friend or family member primed to telephone one of them at a certain time, in case they needed an excuse to release themselves from tedious or physically repulsive company.

'Shit,' Lawrence muttered. 'All right, then.'

My heart sank.

'You need to go,' he said. 'Drink up.'

'*I* need to go?'

'It's Muriel,' he said. 'Jo found her on your front step when she came home from that reading group of hers. Lying flat on her back and screaming blue murder, apparently.'

# A late-night confession

Moo, it turned out, wasn't injured in the slightest, just a little disorientated and very distressed. By the time I arrived at the house, she was safely inside the hallway, propped up in her wheelchair, weeping untidily over the fringed breast of Joanna's poncho, and shooing away a concerned thirty-something man in a pin-striped suit, who I recognized as the male half of the American-Couple-Next-Door. On catching sight of Lawrence, she shrieked, 'No visitors! Send those ghastly men away!'

Joanna winked at Mr American, who turned and gave me a toothy smile. He is a good-looking specimen, albeit in a chiselled, tall, dark and handsome sort of way. He's not my type at all – too Barbie's-Ken-like – though I once enjoyed a fleeting convo with him over the garden fence. It had been nice to have the attention of a young male for a change, even if I was only telling him to deadhead his lupins.

'She's fine, Ruth,' Mr American said.

'Bloody cheek,' Moo muttered.

Joanna mouthed, *I think you'd better go* to him, and Mr American mouthed something back, before squeezing past me with a cheery 'If you need anything, please let me know', and then he was gone.

Joanna touched my arm. 'Go back to Daddy, Ruth,' she said, 'and say a proper goodnight to him. I can hold the fort a little while longer.'

'No!' Moo cried. 'Roo stays here with me! I want Roo here with me NOW!'

'Now, you're not being very fair, are you, Mrs Hinchcliffe?' Joanna murmured. 'Ruth, pop out for a moment, do. Muriel will be fine with me.'

'I won't, you know,' Moo grumbled.

Lawrence was waiting for me on the pavement. I hobbled down the steps to meet him.

'She's okay, then?' he said.

I snorted. 'Of course she's bloody okay.'

'I'm so sorry, Ruth. We were having a really good time, weren't we?'

'Yes,' I said. 'We were. Such a shame it ended early.'

'Let's do it again. Soon.' He took my hand, lifted it to his lips, and gently kissed my knuckles.

I quickly pulled my arm away. 'I must go now,' I said, patting his elbow. And I made my way back up the steps towards the front door as elegantly as possible, acutely aware of his eyes firmly fixed on my backside as I did so.

'Ruth?'

I turned at the top of the steps. 'Yes?'

'Muriel Hinchcliffe, MBE. What's the MBE actually for?'

I chuckled darkly. He did too. 'Services to literature,' I said.

'You're joking!'

'I'm not.' I shook my head. 'Baffling, I know. But Moo still had friends in very high places back then.'

\*

Joanna stayed for as long as it took to get Moo back into bed. After that, she couldn't get out of the place fast enough – a rat deserting a sinking ship if ever there was one, though I really couldn't blame her. Moo's bedroom smelt vaguely of pee, because the commode needed emptying, but nobody mentioned the fact because nobody said a word the whole time, at least nothing meaningful. Just a few *oofs* and *uuughs* and *ouches* as we hauled Moo into a reclining position, and shoved a few pillows under her head.

'There!' Joanna cried, with ill-concealed relief. 'I'll love you and leave you. I can let myself out.'

We waited until we heard the front door slam behind her.

Then, 'You left me!' Moo exploded.

'Well, you were fast asleep!' I hissed. 'When you go sparko like that it's impossible to wake you up. And Joanna said her father needed company, so I—'

'I needed company!'

'You were asleep, you stupid cow!'

But Moo didn't hear me. She was too busy ranting and raving, berating me for neglect, for selfishness, for being a slut, a trollop. Just what had I been doing with that man I'd been out with, hmmm? Screwing him behind the wheelie bins at the Lamb and Flag, that's it! Because we all know that Ruth Donne has a taste for rough sex with rough men in rough places! 'It was one of the things Harvey detested you most for,' Muriel was shrieking. 'For fetishizing his background – his poor, lowly background—'

'You leave Harvey out of this!' I cried.

'Why should I? He was my husband!'

'Well, he was my husband first! And in the eyes of God—'

'Oh, do shut up about God, Ruth. There is no God.' Moo, apparently spent of emotion, was speaking quietly now.

'Yes, there is!' I insisted.

'No, there is not. No decent God would treat his servants the way he's treated you and me.'

I sank down on the bed beside her, and put my head in my hands.

'I am a very sick woman,' Moo said coldly, 'and you left me alone. That was very bad of you, Ruth.'

'Well, how was I to know you'd wake up? You never normally do! You wouldn't have noticed . . . there would have been no harm . . . and what the bloody hell were you doing outside, anyway?'

'I was woken by a noise. I thought someone had broken into the house. So, you see, Ruth, I could have come to harm after all, even if I'd been asleep.'

'But what on earth were you playing at, a woman in your condition, confronting a burglar? Are you mad?'

'Well, what else was I supposed to do? Lie here, waiting for the burglar to find me and bash my useless brains in?'

'So, what was it, then?'

'What was what?'

'The noise.'

'Oh.' Moo lowered her eyes. Her hands, which had been neatly folded over her chest the entire time, now began to tremble and fuss, tying knots in the pink satin bow of her nightgown. 'It was the fax machine again.'

'Oh!'

'Yes, *oh*. It was another malicious fax, I'm afraid. You'll find it in the pocket of my dressing gown. Anyway, I was very frightened when I heard the noises downstairs, and I shouted for you, but you didn't come, so I went looking for you. And I realized the fax machine was whirring away, so I went into the study and picked up the fax and read it. Well, you can imagine how I felt. I just wanted help, so I wheeled myself into the hall, and opened the door, but lost my balance and fell out of my chair, and ended up in a pickle on the front step. All very embarrassing.'

'Oh, Moo!' I flung my arms around her neck. 'I am so sorry!'

Moo, remaining perfectly still, spoke without emotion. 'You should read the fax,' she said. 'I think I know who it's from.'

'Who?'

'Read it first.'

Moo's dressing gown was hanging behind her bedroom door. I fished out the fax from a tissue-rammed pocket, unfurled it, and there it was – the same typeface, but this time there was more:

To: Muriel Hinchcliffe,
I know exactly what you did and now I'm going to make you pay

'So, you see,' Moo said, 'the fax wasn't from a random sender at all. It's from someone who knows me, someone with an axe to grind. And I believe that someone can only be Kate Porter, that journalist from *The Sunday Herald*.'

'Yes, yes, I remember who she is. But why?'

'Because I got her sacked from her job.'

'You did what?'

Moo took a deep breath. 'Well, as you know, she sent a fax

last year requesting to interview me, about my books I believed at the time. Claimed she was a fan. What you don't know is that she wasn't a fan at all, but an old university friend of Barnaby's. I smelt a rat, you see, the moment she turned up on the doorstep, because I was sure that I had seen her before, and I had – at Barnaby's funeral. She was that dreadful, crop-haired girl with the multiple piercings, making a scene at the back of the crematorium – all that weeping and wailing and gnashing of teeth, and haranguing me for letting Barnaby down. The hair and piercings have gone, of course – she's altogether more polished these days, and was wearing a rather fetching pair of red suede heels, as I recall—'

'Yes, yes,' I said, 'I remember what she looked like. But what did she actually do to you?'

Moo swallowed hard. 'Well, once you were out of the room, she told me she had no intention of promoting *The Camelford Chronicles* at all. Instead, she was going to publish an exposé.'

'Of what?'

'Of me. She said I was a phony and a fake, and now she was a big-name writer for a national broadsheet, she had the power to let everyone know the piece of shit I really was – her words, not mine. She had already approached Stephanie, she said, but Stephanie refused to talk to her unless there was proof.'

'Proof of what?'

'Oh. Well, she didn't say. But she did say that when they were students together, Barnaby told her what an appalling, neglectful mother I'd been, and that he'd been brought up in a seriously buggered-up household – again, her words not mine – and that I'd refused to see what was going on under my nose, whatever that means. She claimed he'd been depressed all his life, and that I was responsible. And a lot more besides.'

'Such as?'

'Well, that's enough to go on with, isn't it? I received my bloody MBE for the books I dedicated to his memory, and she—' Moo was starting to cry now. 'That bloody, bastarding bitch was going to spoil the only decent thing I'd ever done in my life; was going to ruin my reputation, the memory people would have of me once I was gone, and she was doing it, she said, because she *loved him*. Because Barnaby was the most decent person she'd ever met. Because he was her best-ever friend. Because people deserved to know the truth, because his wife and daughter deserved—' Moo's upper body collapsed in an avalanche of shuddering sobs. 'Oh God, Ruth. I was so frightened!'

'But how,' I said, 'did you get her sacked?'

Moo closed her eyes. 'She'd put her bag down by my wheel-chair. It was one of those big leather shopper things, completely open, with no zip. Her mobile rang, and she left the room for a few minutes to take the call. So, I took off one of my rings – the diamond solitaire I inherited from Mummy – and pushed it into the bottom of her bag. And then, when she finished the call, I told her to get out of my house and do her worst. Publish and be damned.'

'I see.'

'And the minute she left, I telephoned her office. I spoke to her editor, and said that the features writer they had sent was a most disagreeable woman, who had tried to make me say horrible things about Harvey and Barnaby unless I paid her a five-figure sum not to twist my quotes. I said that I refused, and that I could not believe a reputable newspaper like *The Sunday Herald* would stoop to such gutter-press tactics. I explained that I'd told Kate Porter to go, and after she left I noticed a diamond ring of great sentimental value had vanished from my side table. So would they mind . . .'

'. . . searching her bag on her return to the office.'

'Yes. In exchange for my not telling the police and creating a big stink, which would, of course, damage the *Herald*'s reputation. I was happy, I said, to let the matter rest if they returned my ring and sacked Kate Porter. Which they duly did.'

We sat in silence.

'Roo,' Muriel said at last, 'do you think I'm a terrible person?'

'I'm not sure,' I said.

'I keep thinking Kate Porter is going to come here and kill me. Or frighten me to death. But the funny thing is, I *want* to die. I *long* to die, Ruth. I hate my life. I want it over and done with. I want to be with Harvey and Barnaby again. But I want to die on my own terms, and I'm terrified she'll get to me first—'

'Moo, don't say such things!'

'So, you'll kill me, yes?'

'*What?*'

'You'll do the job before Kate Porter gets to me. Drug me, smother me in my sleep . . . I don't know. Just find a way that's quick and not easily detectable by post-mortem, so you won't get into trouble. Oh, you're so clever, I just know you'll think of something! And do it when I'm not expecting it . . . it'll be our little game!' She reached out and gripped my hand. I stared at our linked fingers, aghast. 'Do it for me,' she said. 'Yes?'

'No!' I cried, snatching my hand away.

'But why not?'

'Because I love you!' I bloody hated her too at times, but the love always won – always had, always would.

'But if you truly loved me, you'd spare me from this awful life. My body is a prison, Ruth. You can release me! Do it, tonight!'

'No, no!' I said. 'Moo, if I killed you – oh God! I couldn't live with myself. I could never live – my life would be hell. It would be a living death for me, knowing what I'd done to you. Please don't ever ask me again!'

She made a strange grunting noise and turned to face the wall.

'Moo?' I said. 'Talk to me! Have I said the wrong thing? Have I let you down?'

'No,' she whispered. 'Your response was exactly what I expected. At least I can always rely on you, Ruth, to be hopelessly predictable.'

Wednesday, 26 June 2019

# Early-morning musings in the shed

I don't know how long I've been sitting here, staring at the sun rising over the row of houses backing onto ours. Long enough, it seems, to have witnessed the fat little spider living in the window frame next to my head trap a wasp in its web, cocooning the poor, convulsing thing in layers of thin white silk.

It should have been Harvey's birthday today. He would have been seventy-six. I suppose I am meant to declare how astonished I am that so many years have gone by. *Where does the time go? Why, it only seems like yesterday we were celebrating his thirty-first birthday in a 'luxury' hotel on the Suffolk coast!* But it actually feels a lifetime ago. Several lifetimes, in fact. Interminable, miserable lifetimes, drowned in loss and regret.

The hotel wasn't even particularly nice, let alone luxurious. It had a television room, with a television that didn't function, shared bathrooms with sticky linoleum flooring, nylon sheets on the beds, and a cracked window that wouldn't open, offering uninspiring views of flat, grey marshland. Harvey and I had sex, of course, but the sex was very poor by then: perfunctory, apologetic, a sorry excuse for a shag. I thought he was being considerate, because I had just had another miscarriage, but it was only days before Harvey confessed his love for Moo, and his guilt and regret post-shag, I suspect, were all for her and not for me.

I arrived back in London from New York exactly two years later: 26 June 1976 – a complete coincidence as it turned out, though I doubt Harvey and Moo saw it that way. I am quite sure they believed I had plotted it all along, that I'd engineered my being sacked from my job for falsifying an 'exclusive interview' with Jacqueline Onassis; that I was willing to endure professional humiliation to find an excuse to see them again – making a 'birthday gift' of my return and desire for reconciliation. *She always was such an attention-seeker*, I can imagine them muttering to each other. *Such a drama queen!*

The truth of the matter was this: I had not been in touch with either of them since relinquishing the house to Harvey, and that had served me very well. I was over it. Over *them*. I barely missed them at all. I was not in denial; I was not being avoidant – I was simply not allowed to be, for my ridiculous mother saw to that with her frequent, gushing letters describing their progress: a marriage at Marylebone Registry Office, followed by a reception at Annabel's nightclub; a baby boy (Barnaby James); a new car (Jaguar E-type); followed by the birth of Harvey's new company – Harvey Hinchcliffe Public Relations (HHPR).

'He manages publicity for politicians and other very important people,' Mother enthused in one particularly epic epistle, before listing various 'luminaries' whose names I did not recognize.

And I read all of her letters, every single word of them, if not with a smile etched on my face, then at least with a stony acceptance. Once or twice, I even found myself wishing Moo and Harvey well. No, the monumental New York cock-up had nothing at all to do with them, and everything to do with me. I was professionally out of my depth, that's all, and the powers that be knew it. They'd been snuffling around for a while, trying to find an excuse to get rid of me, and Jackie O was an absolute gift. Her 'people' withdrew her from our arranged interview at the eleventh hour, leaving me with three thousand words to file and a deadline of twenty-four hours. What else to do, other than cobble together an 'exclusive' from old newspaper cuttings? Every bugger did it!

I landed at Heathrow at seven o'clock in the morning, and was immediately struck by the heat. England was not supposed to be this hot, and most definitely not so early in the day. I telephoned Mother from a box in the arrivals lounge. Following Father's death, she had moved to a modest, purpose-built flat in East Finchley, where she eked out her existence on a church widow's pension.

'Mummy,' I ventured, 'I'm home.'

'That's nice,' she said. 'I suppose it must be the early hours there. Why are you up so late? We're having a heatwave here, you know. I spent the whole night sleeping naked! The whole country is in drought. There'll be riots in the streets when the water runs out. Just as well you're in America, Ruth. You never did like sharing.'

'No, Mummy, you don't understand. I'm home, in London. I'm back here to live.'

'Good God.'

Silence.

'Can I come and stay with you?' I asked tentatively. 'I've nowhere else to go.'

'Certainly,' she said, without hesitation. But she didn't sound certain, or particularly pleased.

'I don't have a lot of luggage,' I said, 'so I won't take up much room. The rest of my stuff is in storage. I'll have it shipped once I'm settled . . .'

'You can have the box room,' she said stoically. 'There isn't much space in the flat, but I'm sure it will be all right.'

'Of course it will,' I said. 'Mummy?'

'Yes?'

'Don't tell Harvey and Moo I'm back. Not yet. I don't want them to know until I'm ready. I've lost my job . . .' I started to cry.

She sighed. 'Ruth, you can't hold a grudge against Muriel forever.'

'I'm not holding a bloody grudge,' I said. 'At least, not any more. I just feel so humiliated. Can't you understand that? I don't want them to know yet . . . to know that I've failed.'

There was a long pause. Then, 'Of course,' she said gently. 'I won't say a thing. I'll see you in a little while.'

I'm not sure why I did it – why I got off the Tube at Highgate rather than riding on to East Finchley, towards my mother's spare room and her uncertain, unwelcoming arms. Clearly, the desire to see Moo and Harvey was too great, after all. But it wasn't just that, because even then I felt an almost preternatural draw towards Barnaby – the little flame-haired boy who should have been mine.

It was mid-morning when I emerged from Highgate Station, blinking, coughing, and dragging my suitcase through an onslaught of traffic fumes and the smell of melting tarmac. While waiting at the bus stop, I briefly questioned the sanity of my diversion, and very nearly scuttled back into the Underground. But, I reasoned, I had to face Harvey and Moo some time, and my appearance today would be unexpected. In that respect, I had the upper hand. Catch them on the back foot – that was it! Before my bloody mother changed her mind and tipped them off.

I remained on the lower deck of the number 134 bus for three stops, getting off just after Queen's Wood. From there, it was only a fifty-yard walk and a sharp right turn to the home I'd owned with Harvey just two years earlier. But now it was Harvey and Muriel's home – a significant difference, except everything around me felt the same, was exactly how I'd left it.

I saw Moo before she saw me. She was standing in a stand-pipe queue, wearing a grubby cream pinafore over a dark brown dress that pinched the sunburnt skin of her upper arms. She was cradling a washing-up bowl under one elbow, a nappy bucket under the other, and nudging an oval baby bath along the pavement with a sandalled toe. I nearly laughed out loud. Muriel Hinchcliffe, socialite and model, had been reduced to this: a dowdy, blowsy milch-cow, awaiting her turn at the watering hole (she'd clearly put on several pounds and they really didn't suit her).

She looked up then, and broke the spell. 'Roo!' she exclaimed, dropping the bowl and bucket, waving her hands above her head. 'Oh, Roo, I'm so happy you're here!'

The queue stared inquisitively as my squeaky suitcase on wheels and I made our inelegant approach. And I realized that

I had not washed for forty-eight hours: my underarms reeked of BO, while my hair – tacky with oil and sweat – was stuck to either side of my face. Moo, however, wasn't even perspiring. Not only that, but she didn't look remotely surprised to see me.

I stopped several feet away, determined not to be the first to step forward and offer my hand. Moo seemed equally reluctant, lest she give up her place in the standpipe queue.

We locked eyes, Moo with a smile on her face. 'Your mother phoned with the good news,' she said. 'Oh, Roo, don't be cross with her, she couldn't help herself! She was so excited, bless her!'

And everything went black, because I think I must have fainted. Either that, or I momentarily lost the will to live.

When I came to, I was indoors and flat on my back, lying on something cool and soft. There was no sign of Moo. It was Harvey leaning over me – clean-shaven, much to my annoyance – and he didn't look happy to see me.

'Where is your beard?' I murmured. 'I distinctly remember telling you to keep your beard, on account of it hiding your weak chin.'

'Shut it, Ruth,' he said. 'You've completely ruined my birthday.'

I lurched upward and forward, holding my hand to my mouth as the dry heaves kicked in. 'I feel sick,' I said.

'You're hungover, I expect. Nothing ever changes, eh?' He slumped on a sofa opposite.

'That's not true!' I cried. 'I have not been drinking! I feel sick because I'm hot, tired and upset, and would it actually kill you, Harvey, to show a little compassion for me, just once in your life?'

'What a mess.' He sighed, rubbing the stubble on his chin. 'What an absolute bloody mess.'

'Can I have a cigarette?' I said. 'I ran out on the Tube. I haven't had one since Hounslow.'

'I've given up,' he muttered.

'What? You?'

'I've got asthma, Ruth. It started just after you left.' And, as if to highlight the fact, he drew a glass inhaler from his jeans pocket, thrust it into his mouth, and started sucking furiously.

'I'm very sorry,' I said, hardly able to hear myself over the racket he was making. 'I had no idea,' I added, raising my voice so he could hear me. 'Mother told me lots of things in her letters, but she didn't tell me *that*.'

He removed the inhaler from his mouth and shrugged. 'Could be worse,' he said, sounding unconvinced. 'So, what are you doing here, Ruth? Why didn't you go straight to your mother's, like you told her you would?'

I rubbed my eyes. My vision was clearing, and I realized I was sitting on a brown leather sofa in the largest ground-floor room at the front of the house. It had been mine and Harvey's bedroom once, because the upstairs was barely habitable when we first moved in. Our mattress had been on the floor, just *there* – where a matching leather sofa now sat, button-backed, respectable.

As did Harvey.

At his feet was a light-brown, shagpile rug, with a cream swirl pattern that matched the wallpaper in the alcoves either side of the mahogany mantelpiece. The original Edwardian stove had been ripped out, replaced with a flame-effect electric fire. I looked up at the ceiling. The decorative rose I'd imagined hanging myself from was still there, but its light bulb was now encased in a brass and stained-glass fitting.

'Tiffany lampshade,' Harvey said, following my gaze. 'Genuine Art Deco. Moo's choice. She has a terrific eye for things like that.'

'A terrific eye,' I echoed. 'It's all very tasteful, I must say. Very nice. Very *beige*.'

'Drop the sarcasm, Ruth.'

'No, really, I mean it. The place really does look lovely.'

Which was more than could be said for Harvey. He'd aged quite a lot, I thought – the result of too many night-feeds, because I was damn sure Moo wouldn't do them. No, she'd have him well trained all right, with nappy changes, midnight burping, cleaning up sick, the works. You could tell: he had bags beneath his eyes, his sideburns needed a bloody good trim, and there was a pale-pink bald patch burgeoning on the top of his head. The stupid sod oozed the sour-smelling, defeated air of a first-time parent entirely at the mercy of its infant tyrant. There was a hole in the seam of his sock too, and his stomach bulged over his waistband, a sure sign of a man driven to comfort eating because he wasn't getting enough sex. None of this, I imagined furiously, none of this would have happened had Harvey remained married to me! I would have held on to a baby, eventually – I would have been an excellent mother. All I'd needed was time!

'I don't know why she didn't just chop off your balls,' I muttered.

'Pardon?'

'Hmmm? Sorry.' I raised my hand to my head, feigning wooziness. 'I'm feeling quite disorientated . . . still not quite right.'

'Yes, yes, of course. You should probably see a doctor.'

'No doctor!' I said. 'I'll be fine, really. I just need a shower, a glass of water, and something to eat. Then I'll be on my way.'

'The shower,' he said, 'will be a problem. Water rationing, Ruth. We're in the middle of a drought and water is scarce. You'll have to make do with a second-hand wash after Moo's given Barnaby his bath. But the sandwich won't be a problem. And I think we have some milk, unless Barnaby's had it all.'

Barnaby!

'Can I see the baby?' I said.

'Not yet,' Harvey growled. 'You've been on a plane and the Tube, and you're not going anywhere near my boy until you've had a damn good wash. He has allergies, Ruth – dust, pollen, nuts . . .'

'Nuts?'

'Yes. He's allergic to nuts.'

'Well, I might be considered eccentric by some, but I'm definitely not nuts.'

Harvey stared at me.

'I suppose you can have the guest room until you feel better,' he muttered at last, rising from the sofa, absent-mindedly scratching his backside as he ambled towards the door. From behind, I thought with a pang, he still didn't look half-bad. 'And then you can see Barnaby,' he added, turning to look sternly at me. 'But you can't stay here, Ruth. You need to go home to your mother. She is your family, this is my family, and you need to accept that. Understood?'

I nodded obediently. 'Absolutely. Message received, over and out.'

# An early-morning phone call

I think Puss is poorly. He hasn't budged from the shrubbery overnight, hasn't touched any of the food I've put down for him. He just lies listlessly on his side, ignoring the capricious comings and goings of bluebottles and bees. I should probably take him to the vet, but I can't afford to pay for treatment, and what if he's on his last legs anyway? It might be the right thing to do, I suppose, have the poor thing put out of his misery. It's what Moo wanted me to do to her yesterday evening, though hell will freeze over before I . . .

'What do you think, Puss?' I ask.

His amber eyes regard me warily through the blackened tangle of undergrowth.

'What,' I repeat, 'do you think I should do?'

I can't do it.

I replace the pillow next to Moo's head and leave the room, softly closing her bedroom door behind me. She is sleeping soundly for now, but my body and mind are too restless for sleep. Lawrence, I want to see Lawrence again! Oh, life could be so perfect if it weren't for Muriel and Kate Porter!

I rest my head against the cool, gloss paintwork of Moo's bedroom door. What to do? Call the police? Tell them about

Kate Porter and her faxed threats? But threats of what? *I will make you pay.* Well, that could mean anything, couldn't it? Pay with Moo's life for wrecking Kate Porter's, or pay for Porter's bloody dry cleaning! And, if I phoned the police, it could all backfire. Moo might end up in terrible trouble for what she did, for the lie she told in getting Porter sacked. There are laws against that sort of thing, aren't there? Wasting police time. Porter could sue Moo for loss of earnings, and where would that leave me? Destitute, for sure.

I could telephone Stephanie. I *should* phone Stephanie. According to Moo, Porter door-stepped her. Stephanie will know what to make of this, what Porter might be up to.

I hobble downstairs to the study. I am not used to seeing the room this early in the morning, the dust-coated surfaces stippled with an unforgiving easterly light. I settle myself in Moo's leather chair and take several deep breaths. Finally, I pick up the phone and dial Stephanie's number.

It's ridiculously early, of course, and I don't know what to expect. No reply? An angry 'what the bloody hell d'you think you're playing at phoning at this time of day' reply? I don't want to frighten Stephanie and Courtney – that's the last thing I want to do, because I know that a telephone call so early in the morning is never good news. It is often bad, tragic, sickening, life-changing news.

'Hullo?'

I am taken so off guard by the swiftness of Stephanie's answer that, for a moment, I can't speak.

'Hullo?' she says again.

'Stephanie? Just to reassure you, Moo is still alive and well. Well, well-ish, because I suppose it's all relative . . .' I'm speaking too fast, tripping over my words – an anxious, rambling delivery. I pretend to cough. 'Sorry,' I say, 'I have a touch of flu. I'm not quite my usual—'

'Hullo, Ruth.' Stephanie's Midlands accent is a dull monotone at the best of times, but sounds especially flat this morning. 'What do you want?'

'I need help, Stephanie.' I'm struggling not to cry. 'We're in a bit of a mess here. Someone's causing trouble – a woman called Kate Porter. You know her, I think?'

'Not really.'

'Well, she came to see you a year or so ago. Is that right?'

'Yes.'

'And she was trying to get you to say bad things about Moo.'

Silence. Then a laugh, a nasty, guttural laugh. I hear Stephanie take a lengthy drag on a cigarette, and automatically fumble about in my skirt pockets for one of my own. But my pockets are empty.

'If I wanted to say bad things about Muriel, I would.' Stephanie exhales forcefully down the receiver at me. 'No one would have to make me. Anyway, yes, that Porter woman came here for about five minutes. Until I sent her packing.'

'Why? What did she say?'

A sigh. 'Look, Ruth, I don't want to be rude, but I'm going to have to be. It's six o'clock in the morning and I've just this minute come in from work . . .'

'Work? You're working nights?'

'Yes, Ruth, night shifts. I'm working in a care home. Some of us need to do shitty jobs, just so that we can eat.'

'Well, I can completely empathize with that.'

'No,' Stephanie says matter-of-factly. 'You really can't. Call me later.'

'There might not be a later!'

Another sigh. 'Ruth, I have tried and tried with Muriel. I have written to her, I've tried calling too, but nobody in that house of yours ever picks up the bloody phone and nobody bothers to reply to my letters, so Courtney and I have come to accept that Muriel can't be bothered with us. A shame, but there you go. I admit I'm surprised that we haven't heard from you either, and you haven't done more to encourage Muriel to stay in touch. But I suppose' – there was that nasty guttural laugh again – 'that's not really in your interests, is it? So, I'd like you to think on this. Is it really fair, after the effort we've made, to phone us out of the blue when I'm just in from a ten-hour shift, to talk about some silly cow Barney went to college with?'

I struggle for an answer.

'Well?' she says. 'Is it?'

'No,' I say quietly. 'No, I suppose it's not. But we're old, and we're scared!'

'We're all scared, Ruth.' She stifles a yawn. 'Life's fucking scary. Look, I don't know what Kate Porter has said to you . . .' I try to interrupt, but Stephanie – getting into her stride – talks over me. 'But she's never struck me as a dangerous person. Messed-up in the head, though. I'll give you that. She held a torch for Barney at uni and never liked me because she was jealous, and so we lost touch after he died. She was an odd one. Very dramatic. Very obsessed with him for a while. And it seems to me that once she got a big job on some bloody newspaper, she got it into her head that Barney had been screwed over by his mum, and the whole world needed to know. That she had to tell his story.'

'Screwed over? How?'

'Look, I lived with Barney for two years, and he was hardly ever out of my sight, so I'd have known if he was up to something. And when he was ill and out of my sight, he was too ill to be up to anything, so . . .'

'Up to what?'

'Writing.'

'Writing? Writing what?'

'Well, he certainly wasn't writing any books, that's for sure. And I told her so. Look, I've got to go. Phone me later.'

'What books?'

'*The Camelford Chronicles*. Porter kept going on about Barney being the real author. And I told her that Barney was as much the author of *The Camelford Chronicles* as I was, because I never saw him write a line of anything other than his essays, and that soft-porn bodice-rippers really weren't his style. Look, I've got to go. Phone me later. Actually, tell Muriel to give us a call. Courtney has some news for her. Not that she's expecting her grandmother to actually give a shit.'

# A terrifying experience

I am huddled, weeping and trembling, on the sofa in the living room, wrapped in Joanna-Next-Door's poncho while she hovers over me, offering tea.

'Ruthie,' she whispers, carefully placing a mug between my shaking hands, folding my fingers around it. 'Drink this, it's hot and sweet. Excellent for shock. Now, listen, there's nothing to be afraid of! Look. Come on, be a big, brave girl and take a good, long look.'

I slowly raise my head, sideways and upwards.

Above me is the ceiling rose and stained-glass Tiffany lamp-shade.

'Nothing there,' Joanna says.

'Nothing there,' I echo.

I brought it on myself, of course, for having a soothing glass or two of Cab Sav after my phone call with Stephanie, then falling asleep in the study chair. The wine and emotional strain of the previous few hours had finally proved too much for me, providing fertile ground for a nightmare or hallucination – call it what you will.

Also, before I fell asleep, I was ruminating wildly – that wouldn't have helped my mind one little bit. I began by mulling over Stephanie's revelation: that Kate Porter believed Barnaby was the true author of Moo's novels. What to make of that? Well, nothing, of course. It just wasn't possible. Where and when would he have written them? How could Moo have known of their existence, never mind get away with passing them off as her own? Barnaby would have shown me his writing before her, surely? I was the one who had encouraged his love of literature. I was the one who first spotted his intelligence. Certainly, neither of his useless parents gave a damn!

I couldn't help thinking, turning things over in my head, remembering long-forgotten events, while staring at the dozens of photographs hanging on the study walls. And then I realized that very few of them featured Barnaby. How, I raged inwardly, just how could the life of that lovely boy slip by so unnoticed?

Then I thought back to the times Barnaby and I had spent together: the glorious years I'd been a part of his life, until he was sent off to school. And I wept when I recalled the bond between us – so evident from our very first meeting, when Harvey and Moo let me hold him at last because I had sufficiently cleaned myself up after my flight from New York, and he smiled at me, and I at him, and Moo cried, 'Oh, everything's going to be all right!'

Barnaby was six when I first felt the full force of Moo's maternal jealousy. Until then, his devotion to me had served her and Harvey rather well. They had to travel a lot, you see, to promote Harvey's business; lots of hobnobbing – 'schmoozing' was the term Moo used – with the great and good, who might become clients of HHPR. And where better for Barney to stay, when Mummy and Daddy were out of town, than around the corner with Auntie Roo – who knew Barney's routine inside out, and was awfully careful about his allergies – and her mother, funny old Mrs Donne?

Mother and I had moved closer to Harvey and Moo shortly after my return from the States, an arrangement that suited everyone – particularly me, as it turned out. I had found a delightful two-bedroom maisonette in a large Victorian villa on the southern side of Muswell Hill. Mother's moving in with me was, at first, a temporary measure, while her flat was being redecorated, but to everyone's surprise we rubbed along rather well. She had mellowed during my time overseas and, if not completely placid in nature, was at least no longer the gorgon she'd been in her heyday. She was also keen to cook and clean (she had always been an impeccable housekeeper, if not a decent wife and mother), and I was glad of the domestic help, given the all-consuming job I'd landed as Features and Entertainment Editor at *A La Mode* magazine, a position that involved plenty of 'schmoozing' of my own, as it turned out.

For a good few years, I was content. The loss of Harvey still rankled, of course, but his rejection of me was partly offset by the adoration of his only son, and my occasional dalliances with unsuitable young men. Life was good. I had money in the bank, an impressive job with important contacts, and an attractive home in an up-and-coming part of north London.

Mother was becoming an issue, though. Her memory was not what it was.

Nor was her personality. She needed me more, which I quite liked at first, but her acid tongue had been replaced with a querulous, peevish one, and our relationship became progressively fraught as time went by. She had to know where I was every hour of the day and night. I would receive frantic telephone calls at work. Where was I? Why had I not said goodbye that morning? And I'd find notes, in her increasingly erratic hand, pushed under my bedroom door:

*Who is sleeping here? Who are you? Why are you living in my house?*

She was dementing, of course. And I was in denial.

Things had to come to a head eventually, which they duly did on 29 July 1981, Royal Wedding day – a bank holiday for the country, though not, alas, for me. I had been briefed by *A La Mode* magazine to write a thousand-word opinion piece on Lady Diana Spencer's wedding dress, a detailed critique of its design, with a feminist slant.

I was cross about this. I did not want to spend the day researching, writing, and editing; I wanted to attend the street party and have a few drinks, like everyone else. And so, I prepared as much as I could in advance without having a clue how the dress would look: if it were tailored and fitted, I could argue it represented the stifling confines of the princess's future role. A long train was a given – all royal brides tried to outdo each other with the length of their trains – and that, I reasoned, would signify the burden of tradition that would follow the poor girl around wherever she went. Finally, a frou-frou, fairy-tale number would be an absolute gift. I could wax lyrical about 'Lady Di' carrying the weight of expectation of a clapped-out nation on the shoulders of her puffed-up sleeves; that this malleable young woman represented the happy ending that everyone wants, but nobody gets.

I had it all planned. A couple of hours writing, then Cinderella could go to the ball! What I did not anticipate, however, was the telephone call that came at eight o'clock that morning.

I was in the bath when the telephone rang, so Mother got there first. By the time I emerged, wrapped in a towel, she was in the hallway wearing nothing but a girdle, gazing down at the receiver in bafflement and wonder.

'Harvey,' she muttered. 'I know the voice, but I can't place the name . . .'

'Give it to me!' I snatched the phone from her hand. 'Go and get dressed!' I barked. 'And get some pants on. Now!'

Mother slowly looked me up and down, at my dripping arms and legs. 'No,' she said, 'I won't. Not until you do.'

I turned my back to her. 'Harvey? What's the matter?'

'Nothing's the matter, Ruth. It's just that Moo and I were wondering whether you could do us a favour.'

'What sort of favour?'

'Well, could you have Barnaby for the day?'

I didn't even have to think about it. 'Yes,' I said. 'Of course!'

'Moo said you had to work.'

'It's an opinion piece, Harvey, and I've practically written the thing. We'll sit and watch the wedding together, then go to the street party. It'll be fun!'

'Well, if you're sure, that would be fantastic. You'll be helping us out of a spot of bother.'

My schadenfreude antennae twitched. 'What sort of bother?' I said.

And I ran through a possible list of delicious botherations in my head: he and Moo had had a furious row and divorce was the only thing left for them now; HHPR had gone into liquidation and they owed thousands and thousands in tax; Moo had crabs; the boiler had broken; his appalling mother had finally died . . .

'Well, it's not really bother, as such,' Harvey said coyly. 'It's actually a very nice problem to have. You see, Moo and I have been invited by a famous rock star – I'm afraid I can't say who – to watch the wedding procession from his penthouse suite, then join him for luncheon, so we can't really take Barnaby with us. You do understand, don't you, Ruth? Ruth?'

'Hmmm? Oh, yes. Of course.'

'I'll drop him round in an hour, so Moo has plenty of time to get ready. Thanks so much for this, Ruth – we owe you one. Right, must go. Oh, and is your mum okay? She sounded a bit strange just now.'

Mother pulled herself together just in time, and appeared as sane as bootlaces for the duration of Harvey's brief visit.

'You caught me off guard, Harvey Hinchcliffe,' she said, admonishing him with a flirtatious wink. 'Telephoning so early in the morning. Gracious, I was barely dressed! Ruth tells me you'll be celebrating the wedding with a famous singer. How exciting!'

'Yes, indeed!' Harvey beamed. 'So you'll understand if I can't stop. Ruth . . .' He beckoned me to the front door. 'Can I have a quick word before I go?'

Mother was coaxing Barnaby into the kitchen with the promise of a glass of lemonade. I watched him trot eagerly after her, his adorable, spindly legs sprouting from a pair of denim shorts with Mister Men patches sewn onto the back pockets. Mister Happy and Mister Bump. I hugged myself inwardly. Today was going to be a good day.

'He's grown again.' I sighed. 'Oh, a quick word. Yes, of course.'

'So,' Harvey said, 'if you're taking Barney to the street party, keep an eye on what he eats. Remember his allergies. No nuts.'

'Of course!'

Harvey lowered his voice: 'And booze, Ruth. Stay off the booze.'

I raised an eyebrow in mock surprise. 'Are we still discussing Barnaby?'

'Don't try to be funny, Ruth. Barnaby stays away from the nuts, you stay off the booze. You're in loco parentis, and I don't want you pissed.'

I was deeply hurt and offended by this. Enthusiastic tippler I may be at times, but raging dipsomaniac I am not, and I did not care for his accusatory tone. 'That is most unfair!' I cried. 'I don't drink. Much. In fact, I hardly drink at all these days!'

He opened his mouth in reply, but was silenced by the approach of my mother, clutching a packet of biscuits to her breast.

'Jammie Dodger?' she enquired.

'No. Thank you, Vi.'

'Custard cream? Garibaldi?'

'No, really, I'm fine.'

She scuttled back into the kitchen.

I touched the lapel of Harvey's jacket. Linen. Straining a little around the buttons, from where he'd put on a few more pounds, but the beige really suited him and his softer colouring. His hair was no longer as red as it used to be – its vibrancy blunted with flecks of white – while his once-startling blue eyes had mellowed to a muted grey.

'You look tired,' I said, tenderly patting his chest. He leapt as though I'd scalded him. My hand fell to my side.

'I'm fine,' he said, 'completely fine.' And he turned on his heel, striding down the garden path without a backwards glance.

Then, at the gate, he paused.

'I'm sorry, Ruth,' he said, head bowed.

'Not as sorry as I am,' I replied.

Just as I was closing the door, Barnaby appeared at my side.

'You're crying,' he said.

'No, I'm not. I've just got something in my eye.'

'Mrs Donne is being odd.'

'Odd?' I said. 'In what way, odd?'

'She put a whole packet of Jammie Dodgers on a plate, then said if I didn't eat every single one of them, I couldn't have my dinner.'

I tried to hide my expression. Too late.

'You don't know whether to laugh or cry, do you, Auntie Roo?' he said.

'No,' I chuckled, and I drew him towards me, holding him close, inhaling the warm, oily scent of his scalp and the sweet aroma of biscuits and jam around his lovely, chubby chops. And I kissed his freckled forehead, gently squeezing the exquisite flesh of his cheeks between my fingers and thumbs. 'No,' I whispered, 'I don't. I really don't, you clever, clever boy.'

'Auntie Roo?'

'Yes?'

'Do you mind not holding me quite so tightly? Or pinching my cheeks like that? It hurts.'

The three of us – a cosy, companionable trio – watched the royal procession and ceremony on the TV in the kitchen-diner, but the whole thing went on for far too long, and by the time the 'happy' couple had exited St Paul's Cathedral, I was finishing my gin and tonic, while Mother and Barnaby had started their third (or was it fourth?) game of snakes and ladders. Even so, I considered the morning a success. I had only to type up the notes I'd made, and then I could relax. The article had practically written itself. I had been most fortunate that the dress in question was the full-on fairy-tale type after all, and with an extraordinarily long train.

'I have a bad feeling about this marriage,' I said to no one in particular.

'Well, you would, wouldn't you,' Mother sniffed from the dining chair next to mine, 'given *your* history.'

I was disinhibited owing to the gin, I admit, and more than a little narked at having to work while Moo and Harvey lunched on lobster with their mystery rock god. I was also caught off guard. Mother had not been so sharp, so unpleasant, for quite some time. What had provoked such a shitty remark? What on earth had I done to deserve it?

'That,' I said, 'was most uncalled for!'

'What does she mean?' Barnaby asked.

'It doesn't matter,' I muttered.

'Oh, but it does,' Mother said archly. 'She's never got over it, that one.'

'Mummy!' I cried. 'Can you please not speak to me like that in front of Barnaby? He's a child!'

Barnaby shook the dice in his hand and let it roll onto the dining table. 'Auntie Roo never got over what?' he asked.

'Your daddy,' Mother said. 'Marrying your mummy.'

'But who else,' Barnaby enquired, looking puzzled, 'would Daddy have married?'

Before I could interject or protest, or do anything to distract their attention, Mother replied, pointing at me, 'Why, *her*, of course. He was married to her before he married your mother. Don't you know anything?'

I don't remember exactly what I said to the pair of them next, but I think I berated Barnaby for asking too many damn-fool questions, and I seem to recall slapping Mother, and I *might* have called her a four-letter word, much to my eternal shame and regret. And then I walked out on the pair of them, slamming the front door behind me with such force that the stained-glass panels rattled in their frames. And I stumbled into the street, where the Union Jack bunting I'd strung so happily from lamp post to lamp post the day before rippled like applause in the breeze, twinkling wickedly in the sunshine.

I sat on the kerb and wept.

Then a woman's plummy voice yelled, 'Hey, Ruth, fancy a drink?'

It was Bunty Wright from the Street Party Committee, cutting a stately figure in a plus-size, turquoise two-piece and wide-brimmed straw hat. She had commandeered a wallpaper-pasting table on the opposite pavement, from where she was buttering mountains of bread, and barking commands at troops of coiffured, aproned women.

'Ruth, if you help me with these sandwiches,' Bunty boomed, 'there's a gin and tonic going spare. It's either that or helping Rufus with the barbecue, and he's never lit one before in his life. So, come to me, my darling, if you value your eyebrows.'

The coiffured women tittered. I laughed too, and wiped my eyes with the hem of my skirt.

'I'll be there in a minute,' I said.

'Good-oh. Will your mad mater be joining us?'

'Not if I can help it,' I said, and Bunty let out a raucous roar.

I lose all concept of time when I've had a drink or two. One minute, it was noon, and I was scraping potted meat onto sliced white bread, the next I was helping to judge the kiddies' fancy-dress competition and three-legged race. Unfortunately, a little alcohol mixed with spite made me louder than usual – I know I raised my voice and laughed too much, in the hope that Mother and Barnaby would hear me, and beg to come out and join in the fun. But when neither appeared, I became ashamed and morose, because I noticed that people were staring at me and whispering behind their hands. And so, as dusk descended, I found myself sulking in a deckchair in Bunty's front garden, and I must have fallen asleep, because the next thing I knew it was dark, and I could hear music and singing and laughter ebbing and flowing through the night air from the far end of the street:

*You put your left foot in . . .*

And somewhere, Harvey's voice yelling, 'Ruth! Where the bloody hell are you? Ruth!'

*Your left foot out . . .*

And Moo, a very angry Moo, her high-pitched calls edging closer: 'Ruth! We need to talk to you – now!'

Then Bunty's deep, placatory tones. 'She's over there. But I really don't see why you have to make such a . . .'

*In out, in out, shake it all about . . .*

'RUTH!'

Someone shone a torch in my face. I couldn't see exactly who, but recognized Harvey's bulky outline behind the shaft of light. I blinked.

And then, his voice: 'You BITCH!'

He dragged me upwards from the chair by my throat, his fingers crushing my larynx. I spluttered and choked and, in a blind panic, bit down hard on his arm. He yelped and pulled it away, gripping my wrist, raising his other hand to hit me, but I plunged my nails into his face to claw myself free. He shook me off, shaking me over and over, until my head hurt.

'We nearly lost him, you stupid cow!' he was screaming. 'We nearly lost him!'

Then Moo's voice. 'Harvey, stop it! You'll kill her!'

'Good! Good riddance!'

Moo again: 'Harvey, for God's sake, please . . .'

I was released and fell to the ground, wheezing and panting, clutching my throat.

'Harvey,' I gasped, 'for the love of God. I don't under-stand . . .'

Moo sank down on the ground beside me. 'Are you okay?'

'Yes,' I whimpered. 'I think so.'

'Ruth,' she said, 'Barnaby nearly died tonight. We came to

pick him up and found your mother trying to feed him a packet of peanuts. She said he couldn't go out to join the party unless he ate them all.' She stifled a sob. 'He hadn't eaten any, thank God, but your mother wafting an open packet around was enough to affect his breathing, and he was extremely distressed. We called an ambulance—'

'My God!' I cried. 'Is he all right?'

'He is now.' Harvey, who had collapsed in Bunty's deckchair, was sucking on an inhaler as though his life depended on it. He glowered at me. 'The paramedics stabilized him. He's going to be okay. Ruth, how could you?'

'Me? But it wasn't me who gave him the nuts! It was my bloody mother!'

'Who is clearly,' Harvey hissed, leaning forward, jabbing his inhaler at me, 'as mad as a March hare.'

'She is not!' I cried. 'Yes, she gets forgetful sometimes—'

'Ruth,' Moo said gently, 'your mother is senile, isn't she?'

'No!' I shook my head. 'No, she isn't. She's getting old, that's all.'

'Ruth,' Moo said again, 'Harvey and I have suspected for quite some time, though you're both skilled at hiding it. But she's clearly a very unwell woman and you left her by herself, in charge of Barnaby.'

'You left him,' Harvey added, 'in the sole care of a senile old woman who tried to feed him a foodstuff that could, quite frankly, have killed him, just so you could get drunk at a party. I will never forgive you for this.'

'I am not drunk!' I cried. 'I never get drunk!'

Moo and Harvey exchanged an odd look. They stood up.

'Where are you going?' I said.

'To spend the night with Barnaby in the hospital,' Moo replied. 'He's being taken in for observation.'

'Take me with you! Please! I want to see for myself that he's all right . . .'

Harvey shook his head. 'After this latest episode, Ruth, we will be limiting contact between you and Barnaby for quite some time. As it is, he needs a break from you. He's been complaining for a while now that you make him feel uncomfortable. That you hold him for too long and too close—'

'LIAR!'

Harvey peered down his nose at me, as though I was something he'd scraped off the sole of his shoe. 'Are you calling my son a liar?' he said.

'No, no! YOU! I'm calling *you* a liar. Barnaby would never say something like that!'

'That's exactly what he's told us,' Moo said. 'Just now. He said that you ask him too many questions about us, that you kiss him too often, and hug him too much—'

'But I love him!' I cried. 'I'm just showing him how much I care and how much I love him! It's impossible to love a child too much!'

But Harvey was already walking towards the blue ambulance light pulsing away at the end of the street, his furious stride parting the crowd of gape-mouthed onlookers.

Moo lingered at my side for a moment.

'Actually, Ruth,' she said sadly, 'I do think it's possible to love a child too much. Or rather to love a child too much in the wrong way for the wrong reasons.'

I stood up to follow her, but my legs buckled beneath me.

Everything started to spin. 'Ho hum,' I heard Bunty boom, 'nothing to see here, folks. I'll just help Ruthie home.'

And I felt Bunty's firm hands under my arms, lifting me onto my feet, then guiding me down her paved path until I felt smooth tarmac beneath me. 'Let's get those legs of yours moving,' she was saying. 'Come on. Quick march. One-two. One-two.'

I did as I was told.

'I've done something awful,' I sobbed, burying my face in Bunty's fleshy upper arm, shielding my eyes from the neighbours' judgemental stares. 'I've done something awful,' I repeated. 'I've ruined everything, for everyone.'

'Nonsense,' Bunty scoffed. 'Harvey and Muriel were upset and frightened, that's all, but they'll come round. You'll see. That's what happens when kiddies get into scrapes. Parents have to find someone to blame.'

'Yes, I suppose you're right.' I sniffed. 'And it is partly their fault! They were the ones who left him for the day, because they wanted to go to a party!'

'That's the spirit!' Bunty cried. 'They needed someone to blame, Ruth, because they felt guilty, you see.'

I nodded, butting Bunty's shoulder with my tear-stained face. 'And none of what they said makes any sense,' I wailed. 'None of it at all! If Barnaby dislikes me or finds me frightening, why would they leave him with me? WHY?'

'Bastards!' Bunty boomed in my ear.

'Bastards, yes!' I cried, triumphant.

And then I opened my eyes.

The street around me, while it was my street, was now very different indeed. It was dark, because none of the street lamps were lit, the Union Jack bunting had vanished, and the houses looked taller and thinner, distorted and insubstantial. All was silent, the pavements deserted, with no sign of the party from seconds before. There were twists and turns in the road ahead, too, that I did not recognize, and it seemed very much longer than usual, stretching far into the distance.

'I don't like it here,' I said, closing my eyes. 'I don't like it here one bit. I don't know where we're going!'

'Why, you're going home, Ruth!' Bunty said. 'Here you are now! Look!'

I opened my eyes again, this time to daylight.

And I wasn't standing on the street, or in my little maison-ette. Nor was Bunty at my side.

I was quite alone.

And it wasn't 1981 any more. It was today, this morning, just minutes ago, and I was in Moo's front room, gazing up at her Tiffany lampshade, from where a plaited length of rope swayed gently to and fro above my head. Someone had done an expert job, tying one end tightly to the light-bulb flex and fashioning the other end into a noose, which – I knew with absolute certainty – was the perfect circumference to slip over my head.

They had even taken the trouble to move Moo's wheelchair directly beneath it. Just to give me a leg-up, so to speak.

'There now,' Joanna's saying. 'There's nothing to see, is there? No rope hanging from the ceiling. And Muriel's wheelchair is where we left it last night, in the hallway.'

'Nothing here,' I echo.

Joanna rubs my shoulder. 'Dear me, what a to-do!' she sighs.

'Having you hammering on my door just now, after that rumpus with Muriel last night . . . I don't know. What *am* I going to do with the pair of you? It's just one thing after another at the moment, isn't it?'

# Alone again

Joanna stayed for almost half an hour, which was really very decent of her, given how busy she always is.

'As soon as Daddy's back from his morning walk, I'll be driving him home to Colchester,' she explained, as we said our goodbyes on the doorstep just now.

'Oh!' I said. 'I was under the impression he was staying a little longer. I think he was keen for the two of us to meet up again.'

'Well,' Joanna replied quickly, 'that absolutely goes without saying, and I'd simply love for you two kids to get together for another date, of course. But I'm afraid there's been a change of plan. Rupert wants me to drop off a few bits and bobs for his end of exams party – he's just finished his finals, Ruth! Isn't that incredible? – and it seemed silly not to take Daddy home at the same time, as he's pretty much en route.'

'Well, a one-hundred-mile round trip to Cambridge with a detour to Colchester is hardly dropping off a few bits and bobs, Joanna,' I laughed. 'It'll be an exhausting day for you. Surely Rupert can sort out his own bits and bobs, and your father can stay a little while longer?'

'No can do, I'm afraid.' Joanna smiled sadly. 'And of course I won't do the trip in one day – I'll stay with Daddy for a night or two. Elliott's been nagging me to get out of the house for a few days, anyway. He wants to renovate the orangery.'

'The orangery?'

'Yes, you know. At the back of the house.'

She meant the conservatory, of course. 'Lucky you,' I said. 'Getting away for a couple of nights with your father. How I wish I could join you!'

'Now, do take advantage of Elliott while I'm gone,' she said, clearly not taking me on. 'He'll be happy to tackle any odd job, or just use him to have a good old moan about Muriel if you need to. He's an extraordinary listener.'

'It'll be all the ear-candling,' I said. 'Look, Joanna' – I lowered my voice – 'I'd be very grateful if you could . . . well, you know, what happened just now with my funny turn . . . If you could just keep it between the two of us, and not tell your father.'

Joanna smiled and patted my hand. 'Don't you worry. You can trust me to do the right thing.'

'Because we did get on very well,' I said, 'and I'd hate for a silly misunderstanding to spoil things between us. Will he visit again soon? Perhaps he'd like to stay in touch in the meantime?'

'Oh, yes! Super idea. I'll ask him.' Joanna glanced at her watch. 'Sorry, need to crack on. And you, Ruth, need to rest. I'm sure that's what all this is about, sheer exhaustion. Make the most of Muriel being asleep and get some shut-eye yourself.'

I saluted her. 'Message received,' I said.

'That's my girl. And Ruth,' she added quietly, 'just keep an eye on the drink, darling. You're, you know . . .' she wafted her hand around her nose. 'You're a bit, you know, fumy.'

Before I could protest, she was already skittering down the steps, poncho flapping behind her, waving enthusiastically at Mr American, whose chiselled, quizzical head had popped up over our privet hedge.

'Everything okay?' he enquired. 'I was halfway to work, but the cleaner called my mobile. Said someone was screaming your house down, but she was too scared to check it out for herself.'

'All fine and dandy!' Joanna called. 'Just a misunderstanding, that's all. But how sweet of you, Adam, coming all the way back to make sure Ruth was all right!

'How sweet of you, Adam,' I echoed.

And then I noticed Mrs Number 73 standing at her front window, staring across the road at me. She tentatively raised a hand in salutation, but I was too tired and confused to engage, and so I shut the door.

When I went to check on Moo, she was lying in bed with her curtains drawn. I could just about make out through the gloom that she was flat on her back, staring up at the ceiling, and for a moment I thought she might be dead. But a fluttering of fingers on her left hand, followed by a ladylike cough, indicated that Muriel Hinchcliffe was still very much with us, and preparing herself, no doubt, to demand the commode, a mani-cure, poached eggs on toast, or all three at once. I hovered on the threshold, awaiting orders.

'I heard voices just now,' she said at last. 'Downstairs and outside.'

'Joanna-Next-Door,' I replied. 'She came to see how you were after last night.'

'Ah.'

'Shall I open the curtains?' I said. 'But just to let you know, Moo, I'm not feeling at all well.'

'No, no. It's all right. Keep them shut.'

Her voice sounded bunged-up, adenoidal. 'Have you got a cold?' I asked.

A heavy sigh erupted from the bed. 'It would have been Harvey's birthday today,' she said.

'Yes,' I replied. 'I remembered.'

'I'd like to be alone for an hour or two, if that's all right with you. Oh, you said you weren't feeling well?'

'I have a headache, I'm afraid,' I said. 'I could do with shutting my eyes for a bit. But what about your breakfast?'

Moo lifted her fist, and feebly rubbed her eyes with the heel of her hand. 'It's all right,' she said. 'I'm not hungry. I think a morning in bed would suit us both, after the drama of last night.'

I nodded and took a step back.

'Goodbye, Moo.'

'Goodbye, Roo.'

I have been lying here for thirty-eight minutes, unable to drop off. I am not afraid of sleep, nor am I trying to avoid another nightmare, because surely that was all this morning's rope-and-wheelchair business was. The mind plays tricks when it is stressed – I know that better than anyone. No, I think I am simply no good at going to bed during the day. Mother didn't approve of daytime nappers, you see, labelling them lazy degenerates. I was once severely beaten for lying on my bed in my daytime clothes. That kind of indoctrination stays with a child for life.

Mother didn't approve of many things, actually, not just daytime sleeping, but visitors (even overnight ones) defecating in her lavatory, people eating in the street, and any post-pubertal female wearing red shoes. She did, however, appear to approve of extramarital sex, even if it destroyed her own child's marriage. I have often wondered how Moo and Harvey viewed her for that; how they judged her betrayal of me (though they clearly had no issue excusing their own). Sometimes, I'd catch Harvey regarding Mother in a rather odd way – a look of frightened disgust would flit over his face when he thought no one was watching – and then, in the immediate aftermath, he'd be especially loving towards Barnaby, scooping him up, holding him close, as though he'd never let him go.

Which is why what happened next completely knocked me for six.

Following the Royal Wedding peanut debacle, I was in the doghouse with Moo and Harvey for the rest of the summer. It was early September when Moo finally phoned. Her voice sounded hoarse and wobbly, as though she'd been crying for quite some time.

'I'm so sorry, Ruth,' she said. 'I think our reaction was quite excessive, looking back. I'd like very much to be friends again, if that's all right with you.'

'Moo!' I cried. 'Of course it is! I've missed you all so much, you know!'

'Yes,' she said. 'I think I do. Look, Roo . . .'

'Yes?'

'We'd like to come around and see you. This afternoon, if that's convenient.'

'It's always convenient, Moo,' I said.

'It'll be all three of us.'

'But of course!'

'Will your mother be there?'

I looked across at Mother, who was sitting at the dining table, staring out of the window at the garden we shared with Henry Bossington, the owner of the maisonette upstairs – a middle-aged gent with a taste for loud opera, cravats, and elaborately embroidered smoking jackets; a cat-fancier, too, who had recently acquired a large ginger tom with a spectacularly bushy tail. He was exercising the creature the whole time I was speaking to Moo, leading the cat around the lawn with the aid of a scarlet harness and leash, encouraging it to scratch and sniff around the herbaceous borders.

'Lord Cedric Bristlerump!' Mother exclaimed delightedly. Her thick grey hair, unwashed for days, stood up in tangled clumps at either side of her head.

'Yes,' I hissed down the receiver at Roo, 'of course Mother will be here. This is her home!'

'I suppose' – Moo's voice faltered a little – 'what I'm really asking is, how is she? We don't want Barnaby to feel uncomfortable or frightened, you see.'

Mother, leaning forward in her chair, had planted her splayed palms against the window pane. 'Fred!' she cried plaintively. 'My darling cat! Oh, Fred!'

'She's senile, Moo,' I said. 'The doctor confirmed it a couple of weeks after . . . well, what happened with Barnaby and the nuts. And then she had a funny turn a week or so later, a fall of some sort, though the doctor said it was a stroke. She's gone downhill quite a lot, I'm afraid. I suppose I'm in for a long and bumpy time of it. But she really is quite harmless.' I took a deep breath. 'I've handed in my notice at *A La Mode*,' I added. 'I had no choice. I can't leave Mother alone any more. She's deteriorated so much in the last month, as it is.'

'Oh, Roo – I'm so sorry! I feel terrible we left it so long to get in touch, that we blamed you for what happened with Barnaby. Of course, we'll bring him with us, although I have to tell you . . .'

But Mother was pounding her fists on the window, shrieking at a visibly shaken Henry Bossington. 'Leave my cat alone, you pervert! Remove your shackles of bondage from his body forthwith!'

'I've got to go,' I said. 'I'll see you later.'

They arrived just after Mother had retired for her afternoon nap.

I opened the door to a photogenic – if unsettling – tableau: the three of them standing in a row on my doorstep, in descending order of height. There was something of the religious sect about them, because they were all wearing their best clothes and peculiarly fixed smiles, and I half expected Harvey, who was dressed to the nines in a pin-striped suit and natty red tie, to ask whether I'd ever considered letting the Lord Jesus Christ into my life. Moo, red-eyed and puffy-faced, and wearing a cream silk day dress, stood nervously beside him – quite the little woman. Only Barnaby seemed his usual self, wearing grey flannel shorts and a smart navy blazer, beaming angelically up at me, his little feet skipping from side to side in a pair of black patent lace-ups.

Harvey made the first move, reaching forward and shaking my hand.

'I am sorry, Ruth,' he said, 'for being so aggressive. It was really quite uncalled for.'

'You tried to choke me,' I said. 'You could have killed me.'

'Could you really, Daddy?' Barnaby exclaimed. 'That would make you a murderer! Would you go to jail for that? Would you, Daddy? Would you?'

'Be quiet, Barney,' Moo murmured.

'Yes, I would.' Harvey spoke sternly. 'I would go to jail, Barnaby, and quite right too. What I did was very bad and most unfair on Auntie Roo.' He smiled sheepishly. 'Forgive me?' he said.

'Of course!' I cried. And Moo and Barney lurched forward to hug me, while Harvey stood aside, looking on approvingly.

'Come in, come in!' I said. 'Mother's asleep, so you need to be quiet, but I'll make some tea, and I'll get you some biscuits, Barney. You'd like that, wouldn't you?'

'Not if they're Jammie Dodgers, I wouldn't,' he said, and everyone laughed.

They'd been with me for well over an hour when they finally dropped their bombshell. Or rather, Barnaby did.

We were playing Ludo, he and I, while Moo and Harvey looked on, offering murmurs of encouragement to Barnaby, while updating me on the progress of HHPR. From what I could gather, the company was doing extremely well – too well for them to manage, in fact. They simply didn't have enough staff, and the staff they did have weren't up to the standards of copywriting HHPR required.

'I don't know. Nobody these days can actually write; everyone has such dreadful grammar!' Moo exclaimed. 'I don't know what the state schools are teaching our children, but the young people nowadays haven't a clue.'

'How to write, or spell!' Harvey added.

My heart started beating a little faster. Were they about to offer me work? Freelance copywriting from home, perhaps, work I could fit in around the capricious nature of Mother's sleeping habits? Because she'd barely slept through the night over the past month, preferring to take her naps in unpredictable chunks here and there – wherever the fancy took her.

'I could help!' I blurted, unable to contain myself. 'Oh, let me, please!'

Something passed between Moo and Harvey. A shifty, anxious exchange.

'Oh, Roo.' Moo shook her head. 'It's not that we don't think you'd be brilliant at it – you're the best writer I know! But you're clearly exhausted looking after your mother, and working for us as well might be the final straw, don't you think? No, I'll be helping Harvey with the copywriting.'

'*You?*' I said, immediately regretting the obvious surprise in my voice.

'Well, yes!' She laughed mirthlessly. 'Little old me! You weren't the only one to get an A in your O-level English, you know. Besides, my modelling days are well and truly over, and I'm very keen to get back to work, so . . .'

'Will I get an A in my O-level English?' Barnaby enquired.

'Of course, darling!' Harvey patted his back. 'You're a very clever boy. A very clever boy indeed.'

'So, is that,' Barney mused, 'why you're sending me away to boarding school?'

I dropped the dice. It fell to the board with a heavy *clop*, revealing six gold dots. Everyone stared down at them.

'You're doing what?' I said.

Moo cleared her throat. 'The boy needs an education.'

'He needs a loving family!' I cried. 'Good God, Moo, you've been to boarding school, you know the hell you went through! And you want to inflict the same on your son?'

'It was different then!' Moo insisted. 'This is a wonderful school. It's very progressive. He can come home at weekends, if he likes – it's only thirty miles away! And they do the most wonderful things there. Not just the three Rs: there's den-building, music-making, dancing, Greek theatre . . .'

'He needs his mother and father!' I was shouting now. 'He needs his Auntie Roo!'

'He needs a stable environment that will stimulate his intelligence,' Harvey said, still staring at the dice.

'I don't mind,' Barnaby piped up. 'I'm looking forward to it! Boarding school's supposed to be fun. I'll meet lots of boys just like me, and we'll have midnight feasts and adventures. And best of all, Mummy and Daddy won't have to worry about what to do with me when they have to work, and they can't leave me with you and Mrs Donne any more, because Mrs Donne is totally batty, and Auntie Roo is always . . . Mummy? What does three sheets to the wind mean?'

Moo's eye twitched. 'Shhhhh!' she hissed. 'I'm so sorry, Roo. I simply don't know where he gets these phrases from . . .

the playground, I suppose. Just as well we're sending him to boarding—'

I glared at her. 'Don't,' I said. 'Just don't. And don't try to justify what you're doing, because you and I both know that sending him away at six is wrong – plain wrong! I still have your letters from boarding school. Would you like me to get them out for you? Read them to you? Remind you of the misery you endured? And you were more than twice his age!'

'Yes,' Moo replied coldly. 'I know what boarding school did to me. I also know that, at the time, my distress barely registered with you, because you rarely replied to my letters. It is 1981, Ruth, and there are some very nurturing schools out there. What we're doing is right, for all of us. It's absolutely the only—'

'As for you,' I interrupted her, swivelling in my chair to redirect my wrath at Harvey, 'you damned hypocrite! You call yourself a socialist, yet rather than continue to send your son to the perfectly adequate state school at the end of the road, where he will be educated as an equal to his peers, you . . . you *buy* him privilege!'

'I am not a hypocrite,' Harvey replied, looking me straight in the eye. 'I pay my taxes – a considerable amount, actually. Can't you be flexible in your thinking for once, Ruth? By doing what we're doing, we're actually freeing up Harvey's state-school place to a child who can't afford private education. Everyone's a winner. I am not compromising my values in any shape or form.'

'You're deluded!'

'You're entitled to your opinion, Ruth.'

'Don't be such a sanctimonious prick.' I rose unsteadily to

my feet. 'You'd better get out. All three of you. Get out of my house, now!'

Barnaby started to cry.

Moo tried to take my hand, but I shook her away. 'Darling Roo,' she was saying, 'please don't be cross with us. It really is all for the best—'

'Go,' I sobbed. 'Go, now. I can't bear it, I just can't bear it. You'll lose him. *I'll* lose him. He'll never be the same . . . Please leave me alone. Just go.'

I heard Harvey mutter, 'As you wish,' and seconds later, the front door slammed.

All was silent for a moment.

Then, a sudden shriek – Mother, roused from her daytime nap:

'RUTH! Come quickly! I need the loo. I'm desperate. RUTH!'

# Just now, in the box room

I am so restless this morning. I do not want to wake Moo, but at the same time I do not want to be by myself, or un-occupied for long. I do not want to be left alone with my thoughts, which have developed a life of their own these last few days. I do not trust my brain.

I rarely venture into the box room. This is partly because it is next to Moo's room, and whenever she hears me in here – God, the questioning I have to put up with! What was I doing? What did I want? What on earth did I hope to find? Nothing and nothing and nothing, I always reply. Is it not enough that, occasionally, I'd just like a change of scenery, that I want to stand in a different room with a fresh perspective, once in a while?

Not that this room has much to commend it. It measures eight foot by nine foot: too small for a decent-sized bedroom, although it was Barnaby's until he left home. I have never understood why this was so, why he wasn't offered the room I occupy – the second-best bedroom in the house, with a delightful view of the garden. I suppose it made sense in his infant years, sleeping in the room next to his parents. But later, as he grew – when he became all arms and legs and clumsiness, a cauldron of hormonal rage – the box room barely contained him! Why restrain him and crush him like that? It seems cruel somehow.

There are still traces of Barney in this room, though they bring me no comfort at all. His bed has gone, but the wardrobe remains, where his blazer still hangs in its plastic dry cleaning bag. The navy-blue curtains have never been changed, nor the striped turquoise and white wallpaper, even though it is peeling in places and stained brown with blooming patches of damp.

On top of the G-plan wardrobe are three brown leather suitcases, stacked on top of each other. These contain Barnaby's clothes, some schoolbooks, old photographs, and a few stuffed toys, including a one-eyed teddy bear that Moo owned before him. His other possessions remain with Stephanie, which is how it should be, I suppose.

The rest of the room contains Moo's 'gym' – a selection of fitness contraptions she acquired during the late 1980s, a few years after Harvey's death. This was when she'd given up drinking and was ready to meet someone new, was keen to put right the havoc she'd wreaked on her body after boozing her way through the inaugural months of widowhood. The equipment sounds impressive, but really isn't up to much. Each item – a rowing machine, stationary bike, and treadmill – was purchased from the free catalogues abundant in TV listings magazines back then, aimed at Persons of a Certain Age, rather than fitness enthusiasts.

The rowing machine and bike have been redundant for years, remaining folded against the wardrobe, perfectly positioned for clouting me on the ankle or elbow on the rare occasions that I squeeze past. Only the treadmill is in working order, set up in front of the sash window, from where Number 73's petunias hang a perpetual forty feet away, however briskly one walks. There is a decent enough view of the street in both directions – I can see pretty much everyone's comings and goings, without being observed myself. I'm overlooked only by Number 73's upstairs windows, which are shielded by what Joanna-Next-Door calls 'plantation shutters', a ghastly trend that screams *nouveau riche* to me.

Just after I moved back in with Moo, I used the treadmill every week. But I haven't done so in years. I'm busy enough as it is, with all the cooking and cleaning and shopping for Moo, and it's always struck me as silly anyway, walking on the spot, going nowhere. Still, the treadmill has its uses – I can stand on it just now, for example, all the better to peer down at Lawrence. And I thank my lucky stars that the treadmill elevates me an extra few inches, enough to see the curve of his buttocks as he bends forward, folding his strapping body into the passenger seat of Joanna's red Mini. She's already inside the car, flapping her arms impatiently, and she toots her horn with her elbow – unintentionally, I suspect.

'Get a bloody move on, and stop making such heavy weather of it!' I can hear her saying. 'I haven't got all day!'

And Lawrence, uttering something inaudible, slams the door, and off they zoom.

I stand for a while, gripping the treadmill bars for support, gazing up the hill long after they've gone. And then I start moving my legs. The rubber belt glides smoothly beneath my feet, the motion oddly soothing. Maybe I should do this more often. Exercise is good for the body and soul, and no, cooking and cleaning and shopping for Moo doesn't count, because exercise should be for me.

*Me time*. I used to write articles extolling the virtues of me time, for some of the fluffier women's magazines back in the 1990s. The importance of me time – of taking a luxurious bath, surrounded by exotically scented candles; of buying oneself a pair of impractical knickers in silk and French lace. Husband screwing your oldest friend? Book a massage, get some me time! Can't get pregnant? Multiple miscarriages? Paint your nails, have some me time! Wondering why the hell you should bother getting out of bed ever again? No matter – just stay there, apply a face mask, and enjoy a lifetime of me time!

I walk a little faster. Me time. Me time. Faster and faster. Me, me time. I remove my grip from the bars, preparing to pump my arms at my sides. *Me time, me time, lovely, lovely me time*. I glance at my palms, which should be covered in dust. The supporting bars of the treadmill, like everything else in this room, should be plastered in the stuff, because no one has cleaned in here for years. *Me time. Me time, lovely, lovely me time . . .*

But my palms, inexplicably, are completely dust-free.


'I'm telling you, Stephanie, we're in trouble!' I wail. 'That bloody Porter woman's been in this house – she's been in the box room, I'm sure of it! The treadmill's been used recently. It's the only thing in that room not covered in dust. The supporting bars have been touched in the last few days, I'm sure of it!'

Stephanie exhales noisily down the phone at me. My own cigarette is already lit, jammed between my lips.

'Two phone calls in one morning,' she says with a sneer. 'My word, you're spoiling us, Ruth.'

'I'm frightened, Stephanie!'

She takes another drag of her cigarette. 'Let's go over this again. You're telling me that Kate Porter has been sneaking into Muriel's house to use the treadmill.'

'Yes!'

Stephanie wheezes gleefully. 'You should charge her a membership fee, Ruth. Or tell her to piss off and use Virgin Active, like everyone else.'

'It's not funny! Please don't make fun of me, Stephanie. I don't think she's jogging on it – I don't think that at all. But I do think she's breaking into the house when I'm out and Moo's asleep, and she uses the treadmill to look down the street to check my comings and goings . . .'

'No.' Stephanie's tone is serious now. 'No, Ruth, you're right. It isn't funny. Have you checked the house? Are there any signs of a break-in?'

'Well, of course I have! And there's nothing – I've looked absolutely everywhere.'

And I had: in wardrobes, in cupboards, the attic. Explaining my actions to Moo had required quick thinking – I'd made the excuse of a misplaced slipper, pointing shakily at my stock-inged feet, before launching myself under her bed. *But I don't understand the urgency*, she'd cried. *I just want to be left alone!*

'And Stephanie,' I continue, 'all the windows are locked, and both front and back doors have mortice locks. I use them whenever I leave the house, and at night. I can only imagine that when Porter was here a year ago, she took a set of keys with her and . . .'

'Ruth . . .'

'But,' I can hear myself musing, 'no keys are missing! And

there are only two sets anyway – mine and Moo's, not that Moo uses her keys any more because . . .'

'Ruth!'

'. . . she doesn't go out and hasn't for years, but they're still in the kitchen drawer – I'm sure of it, because I only saw them yesterday morning. Oh God, what if Moo finds out that Porter's got into the house? What will it do to her?'

'RUTH!'

I pause for breath. 'Yes?'

'Ruth, to be honest, I'm more concerned about your state of mind than I am about Muriel. You're telling me that Kate Porter wants Muriel dead, keeps sending her faxes to tip her off to the fact, then breaks into your house to stand on your treadmill, even though there's no evidence that anyone has been in the house at all and no keys are missing. Listen to yourself – none of what you're saying makes any sense.' She clears her throat. 'Ruth,' she says, 'do you need to see a doctor?'

My mother's vacant, dribbling face flashes into my mind for a moment. I swipe it away, appalled.

'That's ridiculous!' I say. 'There's nothing wrong with *me*. This is all about Moo! Please could you have a word with Kate Porter? Sound her out, ask her in a friendly way if she's up to something? Make it sound as though you're on her side! And then tell her Moo's a very sick woman who's coming to the end of her life . . .'

'What? Me?'

'Well, did Porter give you her telephone number?'

'Yes.'

'And do you still have it?'

Stephanie takes a lengthy drag of her cigarette. I do too. 'I believe so,' she says.

'Then please call her!'

'I can't just call her out of the blue with loony accusations . . . Oh shit. Hang on a sec. There's someone at the door.'

There's a clunk as Stephanie places her phone on a hard surface, then atmospheric crackling broken intermittently by her background nasal drone. Then the sound of laughter – lots of laughter.

'Hullo?' Stephanie's back again. 'Look, I can't stay, Ruth. I've got neighbours and friends coming round. We're having a party here today, so no, I won't call Kate Porter, because I'm up to my eyes and ears in it. Call me tomorrow, if you're still worried, and I'll see what I can do.'

'Party?' I say, inexplicably irked at not being invited. 'What sort of party?'

'Courtney wanted to tell Muriel first.'

'Muriel's not well enough to come to the phone.'

A sigh. 'All right, I'll tell *you* then, and trust you'll pass on the news. Courtney's been offered a scholarship to train as a barrister.'

'What?'

And I picture Courtney, surly, slug-browed Courtney, with the fake-tanned face and trout-pout lips, addressing a bewildered High Court judge. 'Courtney?' I say. 'A barrister? Are you sure?'

'When did you last see her?' Stephanie snaps.

'Well, six years ago, I suppose. At her eighteenth—'

'She's grown up,' Stephanie interrupts me. 'And achieved a lot, which you'd know if either you or Muriel ever bothered to read the letters we send you. Courtney got a first in law from Birmingham uni last year. Took her ages to get it, because she had to resit her GCSEs and do A levels at night school – it's not easy, you see, growing up with a widowed mum who has to work all the hours God sends, just so there's food on the table. She went off the rails quite a few times, as I know you noticed and judged her for, but she got there in the end.'

'Oh, Stephanie!' I exclaim. 'Moo will be so proud!'

That nasty, guttural laugh again. 'Well, Muriel-arsing-Hinchcliffe has no right to be proud of Courtney. This is *my daughter's* achievement, helped by the support of our neighbours and friends – our *real* family – who'll be drinking Prosecco with us all afternoon. And we'll raise our glasses to love, loyalty, and friendship, something you and Muriel will never understand or experience, because all you care about is yourselves and looking down your noses at people like us, and grinding decent, hard-working folk into the ground to make yourselves feel better. Jesus. You people – you London snobs – you're all the same. Bastards!'

'I am not a snob!' I cry. 'I've voted Labour all my life!'

'I'd piss myself laughing at that, Ruth, if it wasn't so tragically lacking in self-awareness. Know what? I'm not going to phone Porter on your behalf. Not today, not tomorrow, not ever. You've insulted us once too often, I'm afraid.'

'What?'

'Asking me just now, *Are you sure*? Am I sure that Courtney is going to be a barrister! My daughter has a brain, Ruth. Her father was a very bright man, and I'm a very clever woman. I just never had opportunities, unlike you, because I was poor.

But Barnaby saw that – he actually saw that – he believed in me. He *knew*.'

She chokes back a sob.

'And now you've made me cry,' she wails, 'on what should be one of the happiest days of my life! You just don't get it, do you? People like you – you're just so THICK!'

'That's not true!'

'You live there, the pair of you, in that bubble of smuggery, judging people like us on how we live, telling us where we're going wrong in our lives and thinking you're so virtuous. I nearly wrote to Muriel, you know, to ask if she'd help with Courtney's tuition fees. But I tore up the letter, because I knew what the answer would be – a big fat no, because we're the undeserving poor, and we should know our place, because we're no better than we ought to be, because Muriel still blames me, she blames me and Courtney for Barnaby, blames us when it was all her fault, all her fault and all *your* fault . . .'

She's struggling for breath now. 'Don't you dare telephone me,' she whispers hoarsely. 'Me, or Courtney. Ever. Again.'

# I remain in the study with unhappy recollections for company

I replace the telephone receiver with a shaking, chastened hand.

Stephanie is right. I *am* thick.

Why did I say that? Why on earth did I say, 'A barrister – are you sure?'

I replay my words – rewinding, fast-forwarding them over and over again in my head, but whatever I do, my utterance can only be heard as an insult. I can't blame Stephanie for reacting the way that she did, because I would have done exactly the same.

If only I'd said, 'A barrister – oh, Stephanie, aren't you proud!'

If only I'd said, 'I'm so sorry, Stephanie. I've been a total fool.'

If only I'd said nothing at all.

If only I hadn't left Barnaby alone with my mother and a packet of peanuts that day, then Moo and Harvey might not have sent him away. He might have been schooled just down the road, spending all his free time with me. Then he would have known constant affection – not the intermittent love doled out by his parents outside of term-time, subject to the demands of the glitzy clients of HHPR. He might even have gone to university in London, lodging with his darling Auntie Roo, and never have met Stephanie at all. He would still be here, living beside me, helping me to care for his mother: easing the burden, making decisions, holding my hand when it all got too much.

If only. If only.

\* \* \*

I decided to forgive Harvey and Moo, or at least give the impression of doing so. I telephoned Moo the day after she dropped the boarding-school bombshell, apologizing profusely for my overreaction to their news. I said I'd thought long and hard about their decision and understood their reasoning. But please, I begged, would they let me see Barnaby one last time before he left?

'Of course,' Moo said. 'And we *do* understand, Roo – if it's any consolation, we're very upset about Barnaby going away. But it's all for the best, and he assures us it's what he wants.'

But the boy's shaking hands and tear-stained face on his day of departure told a very different story.

'You look so smart,' I said to him, popping his one-eyed teddy bear under his arm.

'Say cheese!' Harvey boomed. 'And please smile, the pair of you. Come on, let's try one more time.'

I turned away from the camera and squeezed Barney's hand. 'I'll miss you so much,' I whispered.

'They grow up so fast, don't they?' Moo trilled from the sidelines, unable to look me in the eye.

*They grow up so fast.*

That's what parents always say about their children. What they really mean, of course, is that they've ignored the inconvenient, unpalatable changes that have been brewing under their noses for quite some time. But the same goes for the children of parents growing older, I think. It had suited me to ignore so much for so long that once Mother's dementia was finally diagnosed, she seemed to decline at breakneck speed. *They grow old and mad so very fast*, I'd say to anyone who'd listen: the district nurse, the postman, but most often of all to myself.

Mother lingered for four more years. In retrospect, those years sped past, though each day felt interminable at the time. Moo and Harvey rarely visited, choosing instead to throw their not-inconsiderable wealth at easing their conscience by treating me to 'respite breaks': a night-nurse took over nocturnal duties on alternate weekends, so that I could sleep, and every six months or so I was given a week's holiday, while a carer moved in.

'It's the least we can do,' Moo said at the time, 'after everything your mother did for me.'

Barnaby, however, was not permitted to visit during his school vacations. Mother's condition was too upsetting, Moo said. Instead, I was encouraged to visit them on the rare occasions Barnaby's holidays and my respite breaks collided.

And on each visit, it seemed to me, he'd grown a few inches upwards and away from me, eventually barely acknowledging my presence. By the time he was ten years old, we had become so distant from each other that I might just as well have been living in a different country. He became paler, skinnier, fussier in nature – not the Barnaby I knew at all – and had also developed the annoying habit of addressing me via his mother and father:

'Did Auntie Roo study Latin?'

'I *am* here,' I said, laughing, 'sitting on the sofa next to you, Barney. You can ask me, you know!'

'Auntie Roo was marvellous at Latin!' Moo, a vision of elegance in a green silk shirt-dress, was wafting around the living room in a cloud of Chanel Nº5, all the while balancing a platter of canapés on an upturned palm. 'Roo was the cleverest person I knew! Nibbles, anyone?'

Barnaby turned to his mother, completely ignoring me. 'Was she as clever as I am, Mummy?' he asked, sliding a vol-au-vent onto his plate with a delicate forefinger.

Moo winked at me theatrically. I pretended not to notice. 'Oh, no,' she cried, 'no one's as clever as you, Barney! Especially when it comes to maths. He's marvellous at maths, isn't he, Harvey?'

Harvey, hiding behind a copy of *The Times* on the sofa opposite, grunted approvingly.

'I thought,' I said, 'that this school of his was meant to be progressive? You know, Greek theatre and den-making, rather than Latin and quadratic equations.'

Barnaby scowled. 'Greek theatre is for girls.'

'Now listen, old man' – Harvey chuckled, folding his newspaper with a flourish – 'that's not factually correct, is it? Everyone knows that in Ancient Greece the men played all the parts.'

'And den-making,' Barnaby added derisively, 'is for babies. Girls and babies.'

I already knew from bitter experience that it was entirely possible to love and thoroughly dislike a person at the same time, so my ambivalence towards the pre-pubescent Barnaby Hinchcliffe did not come as a shock to me. But it did come as a disappointment, and with a great deal of heartbreak. I had lost him for the moment, I knew.

But I was too exhausted by the constant threat of losing Mother to dwell on Barnaby for long, though in truth I had already lost a significant part of her as well. First to vanish was her short-term memory, then her capacity for self-care. I fed, changed, and bathed her, only for her to immediately forget I had done so. I read, talked, and sang to her, massaged her feet, styled her hair, being all at once nurse and entertainer, only for her to repeatedly demand: *Where is Muriel? When is Muriel coming? Will Muriel come and see me today?*

I drank too much and slept too little, sometimes screaming and punching the walls in frustration. A couple of times, my upstairs neighbour, Henry Bossington, appeared at my door in his smoking jacket, tentatively enquiring if something was wrong and whether he could be of any assistance. I tried to kiss him once. He never called again.

My relationship with Mother grew ever more mercurial. We would switch – within seconds – from screaming in one another's faces to sobbing in each other's arms. I cradled Mother, I smacked her legs. I brushed her hair, I slapped her face. For years, for every second of every day, I walked the line between angel and abuser. And whatever I did, however well I did it, however much I abased myself, turned myself inside out to please and care for her every need and whim, it was never, ever enough. Because it was *me*, you see – *me* at her side, not Moo. And all Mother wanted was Moo.

*Screw Moo!* I'd yell in her face. *It's me – Ruth – wiping your backside, sponging spittle from your chin. It's me, your only daughter, Ruth. Can't you see me, Mummy? Can't you see me AT ALL?*

It came as a relief, actually, the day – two years or so post-diagnosis – when she finally stared at me blankly and muttered: 'Who the hell are you?'

She could not hurt me any more, because she did not know me.

Mother's body, however, in contrast to her brain, remained stubbornly strong until the end. Only in the final months did she completely lose the use of her legs, followed by her arms, and then her mouth – that pursed, bullet-hard orifice that had once instilled in me such fear and self-loathing.

Her eyes still spoke, though – God, they spoke. Of fear and confusion mainly, but sometimes of joy and gratitude. Or did I dream that? In those interminable, sleep-deprived days and nights of her final weeks, I suspect I imagined so very much. Was that really a thankful squeeze I felt from her fingers when I took her hand? Did I honestly see a brief acknowledging nod of the head as I sponged her down? I am sure that I hallucin-ated. I saw my father once, or at least the impression of him, the back of his cassocked figure standing, poker-straight, by the fireplace, oh so sure of its Christian conviction.

*Daddy*, I whispered, *oh Daddy, thank God! You've come for her at last. You've come to take her home!*

But he faded clean away.

Father's fleeting apparition, however, gave me a morsel of comfort. I reasoned his appearance was a message: that he wasn't ready to take Mother away because I wasn't ready to let her go. Something had to happen first – she had to acknow-ledge she loved me, of course! She had to admit that she loved me more than Moo. I could not allow Mother to leave me forever without that reassurance.

'Blink if you love me more than Muriel, Mummy.'

Was it a blink I saw, or an automatic fluttering of her lashes?

One day, I showed her the little cedarwood medicine chest, with the bright red cross painted on its lid.

'Remember this, Mummy? Your lovely old medicine chest?'

Did her eyes flicker? I am sure that they did.

'Do you remember me sitting on your lap when I hurt myself, and you brought out this box and said to me, "Now then, Ruth, where does it hurt? There, there, Ruth, there, there." Please blink, Mummy, if you can remember.'

Nothing.

'I know someone was sitting on your lap, Mummy, but was it Muriel or me? Please, Mummy, it's important. Blink if it was me.'

Still nothing.

Then her mouth began to move – uncontrollably – and she exhaled a feeble but unmistakeable 'ooooooooooooo'.

'Oooooo, Mummy? Are you trying to say "you" or "Moo?" Which is it, Mummy? Who was sitting on your lap? Are you trying to say "Moo"?'

No answer.

'Or are you trying to say "you"?'

Nothing.

I never tried again after that.

The morning Mother lost consciousness, I telephoned Moo. It was a humid, overcast Saturday in mid-July, with a peculiar sense of static in the air. There was no breeze at all; everything seemed stuck and slow. Even the birds were silent.

Moo took ages to answer the phone. I was about to replace the receiver, when I heard a faint, distracted 'Yes?'

'You need to come and see Mother,' I said. 'She's dying. Speak to her, please, just one last time. She needs you, Moo.'

'Oh, Ruth, I can't!'

'*I* need you, Moo!'

'Ruth, I really can't. It's work. I have to work today, because of this blasted concert.'

'Concert?'

'Live Aid, Roo – remember? Some of our biggest clients are involved, and there are VIPs flying in from all over the place! Harvey says it's a project of gargantuan proportions that could go tits up any second, and some of these people have the strangest requests I think I've ever—'

'But she's dying!'

'Roo, I have to do this, I can't let Harvey down. And it's not just about him, it's the starving millions.'

'Oh, spare me your self-righteous nonsense!' I cried. 'You don't give a shit about the starving millions. You only care for yourself!'

'Ruth, how could you?'

'Oh, send them a platter of your vol-au-vents, why don't you, and one of your old silk dresses!'

'You're being ridiculous, Ruth, and actually very offensive. I will let this go, because I know you're upset, but I have to warn you that Harvey and I—'

'Just five minutes,' I wailed, 'five lousy minutes of your precious time!'

'Ruth,' she sighed. 'I'm sorry. It's impossible. I'll call round later tonight.'

'So, it's possible for you and Harvey to fly a VIP into the country from a different continent,' I mused, 'but impossible for you to walk half a mile to spend a few minutes at the deathbed of the woman who effectively raised you.'

'I'll see you later, Ruth.'

'Don't bother, Muriel. It'll be too little and far too late.'

# I venture back into the box room

I am giving myself a good talking-to. There is no one in the house but me and Moo; there was no noose hanging in the living room earlier – it was just a bad dream brought on by being sleep-deprived, that's all. As for the dust, or lack of it, on the treadmill . . . well. A further close, cool-headed examination of the support bars confirms that any absence of dust was simply down to me. I'd have been rubbing my hands up and down the bars while gawping at Lawrence's backside, before wiping my palms absent-mindedly on my skirt. I didn't register it at the time, because I was far too busy staring. No one is out to get me. I have done nothing wrong!

I deserve happiness. I deserve Lawrence. I deserve a second chance at love. Everyone deserves a second chance – even the Muriels of this world, guilty as hell of stealing love from those far less beautiful than themselves. Though many times, over the years, I have wondered whether Moo truly understood the power she had over men. The charitable part of me believes she did not, that she did not mean to fall in love with Harvey, or encourage him to fall for her. She had no history of husband-stealing – was remarkably chaste, in fact, was still a virgin, as far as I knew. No, Moo was always so sickeningly nice about everything, facing the world with a wide-eyed incredulity that anything could possibly be her fault. She never set out to hurt me, so why should this be any different?

Though I did suspect, in the days and weeks following Mother's death, that Moo experienced guilt of some sort, after all. Even if it was too little, and far too late.

\* \* \*

Minutes after Mother passed away, Muriel appeared on my doorstep, resplendent in her Live Aid gear: a pair of drainpipe snow-washed jeans, tie-dyed T-shirt, and a blouson leather jacket with bejewelled lapels and yoke. I'd have laughed in her mutton-dressed-as-lamb face, had I not been bawling my eyes out at the time.

'Well, I'm here,' she panted, patting down her bird's-nest hairdo. 'I got away from the after-party as soon as—'

'She's dead,' I said.

Moo clamped the palm of her hand over her mouth, suppressing a mounting wail or gasp. I couldn't be bothered to find out which. I started to close the door, but she jammed it open with a pink stilettoed heel.

'I am not leaving you on your own,' she said. 'Not tonight. However much you hate me just now, Ruth, you can't be alone tonight.'

'Moo,' I said wearily, 'I've been on my own for years. It's just that nobody's noticed.'

'I'm coming inside, Ruth, whether you like it or not. I'd like to see Auntie Vi just one last time. And then I'll sit with you. I'll hold your hand. Or sit in a different room, if you'd rather, even outside in the garden – whatever you want – but I'm not leaving you on your own tonight.'

I shrugged. 'Do what you like,' I said.

I let Moo handle everything after that: the undertakers, the wake, the administration of Mother's paltry will. Everything seemed such an effort at first, even breathing, eating, and dressing myself. I just wanted to sleep. My mouth was dry; I kept swallowing. I couldn't stop shaking with cold, even though it was high summer and terribly hot.

My grief was not without its benefits, though. Harvey was very much nicer than usual. He even kissed my cheek.

The funeral, everyone insisted, would be a major turning point. 'You'll feel better after that,' Moo said. 'Closure,' she added. 'Funerals help draw a line under things.'

'Did a funeral draw a line under the suicide of your mother, Moo?' I enquired. 'Or under your father's sudden, sordid demise?'

Her eager-to-comfort face fell.

'No,' I said. 'I thought not. I do wish people wouldn't talk such bollocks.'

The funeral was scheduled for the final Friday in July – a wait of two weeks for my 'closure', though the funeral director assured Moo and me that it really couldn't be helped. A backlog of bodies, apparently, owing to considerably more deaths than usual; these anomalies sometimes happened for no reason, he added, nervously nudging his spectacles up his nose, though it did make you wonder what the good Lord was up to, did it not? I assured him that no, it really didn't, and any more nonsensical talk like that and I'd be looking elsewhere for an undertaker to undertake my mother's exequies.

Barnaby, Moo informed me, would not be attending, even

though he would be home for the school summer holidays (too upsetting, she said). There was, thankfully, a respectable enough turn out anyway: the few surviving members of Father's old congregation, a second cousin twice removed, the district nurse, the postman, and some representatives from East Finchley Women's Institute. Bunty Wright and Henry Bossington also made an appearance, sharing a pew at the back of the crematorium, giving some much-needed welly to 'The Lord Is My Shepherd' and 'Love Divine'. They even returned to my maisonette for the wake, though I couldn't be bothered to speak to either of them. Moo was the perfect hostess, of course, passing around drinks and canapés while I sat outside on the garden bench, using a slug-eaten potted hosta as a makeshift ashtray. From there, I could safely observe the shadowy figures milling around my living room, while wishing with all my heart that they'd just fuck off.

But grief passes with time – at least, the rawness of it does. By Christmas, I was back at work. I had to be, because my savings had dwindled to practically nothing, and the meagre amount Mother had left in her will covered her funeral costs, but no more.

I had Harvey, of all people, to thank for my new job.

'Remember Frank Keen from university?' he asked me, fourteen weeks and two days after Mother's death (I had popped round to visit Barnaby during his October half-term – a pointless exercise, as it turned out, since the boy remained in his room throughout).

'How could I not?' I replied. 'Keen was that slimy little mathematician who sold pornographic images to pay off his gambling debts. What's he up to these days?'

'He's a multi-millionaire,' Harvey said, 'with a magazine empire and portfolio of titles as long as my arm. He's also one of the Labour Party's biggest donors.'

'But why on earth,' I mused, 'have I not heard of him? I thought I knew everyone in the publishing industry.'

Harvey cleared his throat. 'Not everyone, Ruth. Put it this way, the magazines he publishes are not the sort of publications *you'd* write for.'

'Oh?'

'No. They're not the kind of magazines people buy for the standard of writing, if you see what I mean. They buy them for the *photographs*.'

'Ah.'

'Ah, indeed. Anyway, he was asking me if I knew anyone interested in a sub-editing position on a new title of his. Someone mature, with experience, a decent grasp of grammar, a broad mind . . .'

'Oh, Harvey! You surely didn't think for one second that I would be prepared to work for that creep on . . . on . . .' I could barely begin to utter the words, 'a girlie magazine?'

'But that's the thing, Ruth. He wants to branch out, equalize things between the sexes, so he claims. He has this idea of launching an erotic magazine for women. Lots of rippling torsos, well-oiled buttocks in studded leather G-strings, the odd well-written saucy short story. That sort of thing.'

My interest was piqued, I must admit. While I did not approve of the exploitation of my own sex, the exploitation of men was a different matter. But exploitation was exploitation, was it not? And porn was porn. And yet, Frank Keen – odious arsehole that he'd been in our twenties (and arseholes, in my experience, rarely become less troublesome with age) – could be onto something here. Why shouldn't women look at photographs of naked men? Where was the harm? It was 1985, not 1885, after all.

'It's pioneering stuff, Ruth,' Harvey said.

'Don't be absurd,' I replied. 'It's selling mucky photographs to line Frank Keen's pockets, and you know it. Don't try to dress it up as a giant stride for equality, because I can assure you it's not.'

Harvey laughed. 'Come off it. You're interested, admit it – I can see it written all over your face. Look, Keen's assured me there's no, ahem, *tumescence*, and the stories are suggestive rather than graphic. The salary's good, the work undemanding. Just the sort of thing,' he added gently, 'for someone who's been out of the game for a while, has had a rough time, and needs something fun to ease them back into the wonderful world of magazine journalism. You'll be writing captions, heads and sells, and topping and tailing some naughty stories. Easy! Three days a week. What do you say?'

I thought for a moment. 'Do you see much of Keen?' I asked.

'Yes,' Harvey replied. 'I'm afraid I do. His offices are in the same building as mine. Two floors up from HHPR.'

'I see.'

'Even worse for me,' Harvey growled, 'the offices for *Venus Blue* – the mag in question – will be on the same floor as mine, because Keen's run out of office space and has to share with us. The daft bastard.'

'Which means,' I added mischievously, 'if I take the job, you run the risk of coming face to face with lil' ol' me three days a week. Are you sure you can cope with the temptation, Harvey?'

He stared at me. 'It's a big floor, Ruth. You're on the south side, I'm on the north. We'll bump into each now and again, I'm sure, but I'm a very busy man and you, hopefully, will be a busy woman.'

When I think about Harvey these days, it's generally his face that October afternoon that I picture: a little grey around the temples, a tad flabby around the jowls, increasingly likely to be sucking on an asthma inhaler, but attractive nevertheless – a far cry from the scabby, scrawny, copper-haired youth in the ill-fitting suit I'd first clapped eyes on at Oxford. Now, here, I remember thinking, is a man at the top of his game: a man exuding urbane *bonhomie*, a man generally at peace with himself and the world around him. I would even go as far as believing he was finally at peace with me.

Smug? I suppose he probably was, but then he had every right to be.

Complacent? Oh, yes. He was most definitely that.

\* \* \*

Over there, on top of the box-room wardrobe, are three cases, one of which contains Barnaby's childhood toys. These include a cat glove puppet, a Kermit the Frog, a shoddy replica of Rod Hull's Emu, and Moo's one-eyed teddy bear. This bear accompanied Moo on every one of her overnight stays at my childhood home, tucked always beneath her arm, its soft, rounded, golden belly pressed against her own.

Until the day Bear disappeared, because I'd hidden him.

We were ten years old at the time, and I had decided that Muriel was too old for bears – too old, in fact, for a lot of things, including sitting on my mother's lap and having her hair brushed when she was perfectly capable of doing the job herself. Yes, the day had finally come for change, and since my mother could not be trusted to do the sensible thing and enforce change herself, I – Ruth Donne – had to be the grown-up by taking matters into my own hands. And so, I took Bear, who had tumbled onto the floor at the side of my mattress during the night while Moo was asleep in my bed, and stuffed him up the unused fireplace in my room.

Oh, the rumpus the following morning! The tears, the wailing, the flailing, fumbling panic. Where was Bear? How could Bear just vanish? What on earth would Moo do without him? She felt sick – she was actually going to be sick!

'Ruth.' My mother eyed me suspiciously. 'What have you done with Bear?'

'I can assure you,' I said, 'that I have not touched Bear.'

For, strictly speaking, I had not. I had been careful, you see, to put on my woollen mittens before taking Bear and shoving him up the chimney. I had pre-empted my mother asking this question, and my response to it. I could not tell the truth, because that would incur a heavy thrashing, but nor did I want to lie, because that would incur the good Lord's wrath, and I didn't fancy being struck by lightning or turned into a pillar of salt.

'You'd better not be lying, Ruth. Muriel is very distressed!'

'So I hear,' I replied, listening to Muriel's retching from the lavatory further along the landing.

My mother eyed me menacingly. 'You have one last chance to put this right!'

'But I've done nothing wrong!'

The day wore on. I was denied breakfast and lunch, because Moo was not feeling well enough to eat either, and it would be immoral, I was told, for me to enjoy any form of refreshment while she suffered so much. Moo, meanwhile, shivering uncontrollably with the shock of it all, had been given prime position in the armchair next to the kitchen stove: bundled up in waffle blankets, offered mug after mug of delicious hot coffee, while Mother busied herself at her side with the Saturday afternoon ironing.

I was jealous, I admit. I was also lonely and completely lost. Banished from the company of the two people I loved most in the world to search for a one-eyed teddy bear. Had the human race – apart from me – completely lost its marbles?

'Why me?' I cried. 'Why can't Moo search for him? He's *her* bear!'

'You know why,' Mother snarled. 'And you'd better do the right thing before your father returns from the football. He has a way,' she added unpleasantly, 'of flushing lies out of children. You need to remember that, Ruth. God speaks through your father. They have an understanding.'

'I wish I could go to the football,' I said, keen to change the subject.

'Well, you're not a boy, more's the pity, and so you can't.'

I appeared at Muriel's side just after six o'clock – minutes before my father's return.

'I've found Bear,' I said. 'He was inside your pillowcase. He must have got tangled up in there while you were asleep.'

An overjoyed Moo sprang from her chair, grabbing Bear and flinging her arms around my neck. 'Oh, Roo!' she cried.

'Thank you so, so much! Look, Auntie Vi, Roo's found Bear!'

Mother didn't look up from the ironing. 'Has she indeed?' she said quietly.

Nothing more was said on the subject.

Later that evening, Mother disappeared upstairs for quite some time. On her return, she told me to go to my room and put away my ironed laundry.

Laid out on my bed was my one and only party dress: blue organza, with a white lace collar; a beautiful, much-loved little thing.

It had been burned beyond repair. Great black iron-shaped scorch marks, deliberately placed, at equal distances, all the way around the perimeter of the skirt.

I hung the dress up at the back of my wardrobe, went back downstairs to join Mother and Moo, and did not utter another word for the rest of the evening.

# Preparing lunch in the kitchen

Moo has announced that she is ready to start the day and, having skipped breakfast, is demanding her lunch. So, I'm fishing out Mother's medicine chest, and crushing two nitrazepam into Moo's soup. I shouldn't be doing this, I know that I shouldn't, but I am so tired and anxious today, and desperately need a break from her capriciousness and irrational demands. Once I've knocked her out, I'll go and find Puss, and smuggle him into my room. No matter if he has fleas. More than anything else right now, I want to fall asleep with a warm body and beating heart next to my own.

Moo loves Heinz tomato soup, as do I. It is comforting and familiar, even if it does feel a little silly sipping it on a warm, midsummer afternoon. Nevertheless, we'll sit together, as we often do: me perched on the end of Moo's bed, Moo propped up on her pillows, and drink our soup from matching mugs, just like we did when we were girls. I will open the windows to free the odour that has settled around Moo's commode these last few days, allowing the scent of Joanna-Next-Door's *Trachelospermum jasminoides* to drift around the room. Moo will probably joke – she often does at this time of year – that we're stealing the fragrance from Joanna-Next-Door; that the pleasure the jasmine gives us is not ours to take. And I'll go along with it, as I always do, all the while battling the urge to upend my mug over her silly blonde head and call her out as the filthy, thieving hypocrite she truly is.

Some people steal because they are hungry, others because they are greedy. Some steal because they are angry. My antics with Bear, I believe, put me in the third category – but at least I was able to put things right. The loss of Bear was not permanent for Moo; the damage I inflicted was nothing compared to the loss I endured when she took Mother and Harvey from me.

So many wrongs that were never put right.

Oh God. What have I done?

\* \* \*

I started work at *Venus Blue* in mid-December. The delay was mainly due to the personnel department at Keen Erotica losing all my paperwork, but also down to me dragging my heels on finally accepting the job. And I had to be interviewed, of course. Frank Keen wanted to be seen as fair and impartial, even though those close to him knew he was anything but. At first, I really wasn't sure about the team I would be working with. My fellow sub-editors were incredibly young and took themselves too seriously, especially the chief sub-editor – a bright young thing fresh from Oxbridge, untouched by failure, humiliation, and the general shit of life. The poor child simply oozed untried self-assurance.

'Fiona Hart,' she trilled, shaking my hand so enthusiastically that the pussycat bow on her blouse nodded in unison. She had evidently ingested *Cosmopolitan* magazine's career pages in a bid to create the classic corporate woman image – with some success, I had to admit: trouser-suited, shoulder-padded, a black leather Filofax welded to her palm, Fiona Hart looked the part, walked the walk, and talked the talk, albeit with a Sloane Ranger yowl.

'Now,' she said, smoothing her blonde bob, 'Frank tells me you come highly qualified, and from what I can see from your CV, you've had some very prestigious positions – *Women's Political Digest*, yah? So, Ruth, I have to ask you – why us? Why *this* job?'

'Well,' I lied, 'I think that what you're doing is very forward-looking.'

Her face lit up. 'Oh, yes. It is, isn't it? Pioneering, wouldn't you say?'

*Pioneering*. Harvey had uttered that very word two months earlier, while trying to whet my appetite for the job at *Venus Blue*. Clearly it was the word *du jour*, and I knew I'd gain brownie points for parroting it back.

'Pioneering. Absolutely,' I said. 'Very brave. Very empowering for women. I've never worked on anything like this before, so it'll be a refreshing change. Very, er . . . *pioneering*.'

'You don't see the position of sub-editor as something of a demotion?'

'Most definitely not.'

'And you won't have a problem answering to me? I am considerably younger than you, Ruth, and less experienced, though what I lack in experience I make up for in talent, yah?'

And ego, it would seem. 'Absolutely,' I beamed.

'You will be dealing with some rather unusual copy, Ruth, and some fairly graphic pictures. How do you feel, for example, about coming face to face with a penis?'

'I'm forty-two years old,' I said. 'I've come face to face with a few in my time.'

'They will, of course, be flaccid.'

'Oh,' I smirked. 'I'm afraid I've not come face to face with too many of *those*.'

Fiona stared at me. 'This is a serious job, Ruth. We have a responsibility, you know, and Frank has made it clear to me that I have the final say in whether we recruit you or not. Now, I have a test piece for you to edit. Captions for our Christmas issue centrefold, and a heading too, if you wouldn't mind.'

I blinked at the layout in front of me. A young, spectacularly well-endowed man, with chiselled jaw and laughing eyes – naked as the day he was born, save for a pair of antlers perched atop his crew-cut head – was frolicking and flexing his muscles in a polystyrene snowstorm.

I cleared my throat.

'The heading,' I said. 'I would suggest . . . Ding Dong Merrily, Oh My!'

The job was mine.


On my fourth day at *Venus Blue*, Harvey paid me a visit. It was the morning of the magazine's Christmas party: lunch at Kettner's in Soho, followed by drinks and a makeshift disco back at the office. I was extremely fortunate to be invited, Fiona Hart was keen to stress, because all the places had been paid for and reserved back in September. But Frank *simply insisted* I be added to the guest list.

Harvey, it transpired, had also been invited as a thank you for helping with the magazine launch publicity three weeks earlier. Clearly, he was not best pleased at my inclusion. He appeared at my desk first thing, just as I was removing my overcoat, having donned his steel-rimmed spectacles for the occasion – a sign, if ever there was one, that Harvey Hinchcliffe meant business.

'Nice to see you,' I said. 'I was wondering when you'd come to check on how I was settling in.'

Harvey folded his arms and stared at me. 'I've heard you're coming to the party,' he said. 'I want some assurances, Ruth.'

'Oh?' I carefully draped my coat over the back of my chair. 'What sort of assurances?'

'That you won't get drunk, for a start.'

I blinked at him. 'I haven't got drunk in years,' I said. 'Not since . . . well. The Royal Wedding debacle. And I hardly touched a drop the whole time Mother was ill, because one of us had to be compos mentis, as you very well know. I took my duty of care to Mother very seriously indeed . . .'

'Oh, Ruth,' Harvey spread his palms apologetically. 'I'm sorry if I've caused offence. It's just that I really want this job to work out for you. You've been off the sauce for so long that I'm worried you might drink too much today and make a fool of yourself. I've got a point, Ruth, haven't I? Haven't I, Ruth? Ruth?'

I shrugged.

'Look,' he went on, 'I accept that what I said just now was out of order. I just want you to be careful. All right?'

'All right.'

'So you'll take it easy?'

I shrugged again.

'And you'll leave early?'

'Early? What do you mean?'

'Well,' he blustered, 'perhaps the most sensible thing would be for you to leave after lunch.' He chuckled. 'I mean, the evening do is when the booze will really start flowing. And, let's face it, discos have never been your thing.'

'My *thing*?'

'Well, you don't enjoy dancing.'

'I enjoy watching other people dance!'

His face, I realized, had turned rather red. Not with anger or irritation – most definitely not that – but with something else. Embarrassment – that was it! Harvey was flustered, but why?

'Don't worry, Harvey,' I smirked mischievously. 'I won't take advantage of your drunkenness and seduce you under the mistletoe.'

'Don't be ridiculous,' he muttered.

'But just in case, you'd best not forget your inhaler.' I leant forward and patted the breast pocket of his jacket. 'In case you get *overexcited*.'

Fiona Hart, meanwhile, had appeared at the other side of the desk, from where she was slowly unbuttoning her overcoat to reveal a low-cut, black lace dress. Her breasts were squashed together with the aid of a push-up bra, I suspected, because Mother Nature didn't make breasts as fulsome and buoyant as that. At least, she had no business to.

'Morning, Harvey,' Fiona breathed, casually smoothing a stray strand of hair behind a delicate ear. Her lobe, I noticed, was sporting a dangling earring of pearl and silver mistletoe.

'Gosh!' I exclaimed. 'Don't you look lovely, Fiona! Harvey, doesn't Fiona look lovely?'

I glanced at Harvey, who was busy studying something invisible on the sole of his shoe. The redness of his face had intensified to a rather unflattering shade of puce.

'Hmmm? Oh, Fi,' he murmured, rising quickly, turning on his heel, making a great show of taking his leave from us as casually as possible. 'Good morning. Well, I'll see you ladies later.'

Fiona became increasingly jittery as the morning wore on. By midday, she looked fit to burst with something. I wasn't sure what.

'There'll be a champagne reception first,' she muttered impatiently, handing me a final layout to read. 'Frank's threatening to play the piano for us all, so brace yourself for a chorus or two of "Frosty the Snowman". He *insists* on harmonies at his pissed-up singalongs. All very tiresome. You'll need to get a move on with that layout, Ruth. We'll be leaving soon. The reception's booked for 1 p.m.'

'Champagne reception?' I said. 'Frank's really pushing the boat out!'

'Yes.' Fiona appeared to relax for a moment, actually cracking a smile, which lit up her face and eyes, making her appear quite childlike – a most unsettling effect, given the practically pornographic proportions of her neckline. 'He is. We'll have a three-course lunch – well, prawn cocktail, pizza and a mince pie, so pretty basic really, then we'll do Secret Santa, have a few more drinks, a couple of party games, and back to the office for 8 p.m. Frank' – she rolled her eyes dramatically – 'is insisting on being DJ for the evening. I mean, can you imagine? A DJ? At *his* age?'

'My age too,' I reminded her. 'And Harvey's, of course. I suppose we must seem positively prehistoric to you, Fiona.'

I scanned her face for a reaction, but none was forthcoming. She was too busy plucking pieces of stationery from her desk, while humming Wham!'s 'Last Christmas' under her breath.

'So,' she said, 'I'll be in the darkroom for the next half-hour or so, if you need me.' She had selected a neon-pink clipboard and pom-pom-fringed pencil case, and was hugging the clipboard to her décolletage as though it were plated armour. 'Frank,' she added, 'wants me to help him interview the new picture editor.' She rolled her eyes again. 'He said to me, "Fi, come and meet Jon Moore and his camera with me in the darkroom, and we'll see what develops."'

I groaned. 'Dark room?' I said.

'Over there.' Fiona nudged her head towards what I'd dismissed as a fire door at the far end of the office. 'Awful place,' she shuddered. 'You have to walk through a tunnel to get there. Only a short tunnel, but nevertheless . . .' She shuddered again. 'It's creepy, Ruth. So stuffy. And *dark*. I can't bear to go in there.'

'Well,' I laughed, '*dark room*, Fiona. The clue is in the name.'

'Oh!' she cried. 'I nearly forgot.'

She opened the topmost drawer in her filing cabinet and drew out a key. 'Of course, we won't actually be able to get into the darkroom without *this*,' she said. 'Another reason why I can't wait for Frank to employ a picture editor. I'm sick and tired of being responsible for that bloody room and all its comings and goings. It'll be a pleasure to hand this key over to somebody else, for a change.'

'You can hand it over to me, if you like,' I said.

She shook her head. 'No can do, I'm afraid. Frank's thoroughly anal when it comes to security. Only gives keys to senior members of staff – you'd have been welcome to it otherwise.' She wrinkled her nose. 'God I hate that room. It absolutely reeks of chemicals. I can barely breathe in there.'

'Spent a lot of time in the darkroom, have you?' I said.

But she was already halfway across the office, out of earshot.

I settled down to study the final layout in some detail.

'So Fiona Hart hates spending time in the darkroom, does she?' I whispered to the grinning male model in the studded leather G-string. 'Well, methinks the lady doth protest a little bit too much.'

I disregarded Harvey's 'advice', of course. There was no way on earth I was going to make my excuses and leave before 8 p.m., like a naughty schoolgirl obeying her father's curfew. Not when I was certain there'd be so much scandal to observe and enjoy, which seemed increasingly probable as the afternoon at Kettner's wore on. Yes, it was absolutely worth my while to remain as sober as possible, while everyone else drank themselves senseless. The atmosphere in that upstairs party room was, as I recall, both convivial and threatening: thirty bloated egos rammed around a twenty-person table, jockeying for elbow space, buoyed with free booze, armed with silly string, party poppers, and the firm belief that this would be THE night they'd get a shag/promotion/pay rise – possibly all three.

I felt quite at sea, I must admit. I was not used to so many people – the noise, the chatter, the screeching – and the room felt claustrophobic: thick with cigarette smoke; the two sash windows behind me opaque with breath vapour and condensation, shielding the view of the last-minute Christmas shoppers milling about in the drizzle outside. In desperation, I attempted small talk with the fellow fish out of water at my side – the freshly hired picture editor, Jon Moore, whom Fiona had managed to 'squeeze in' at the eleventh hour. But this earnest young man, wearing a Yasser Arafat-style scarf knotted loosely around his neck, and bearing equally loose opinions on absolutely everything, proved a dull companion. I emitted the occasional 'hmmm' and 'oh?', while he lectured me on the plight of the Chinese pangolin, all the while scanning the room for an alternative source of amusement.

My eyes settled quickly on the surreptitious glances being exchanged between Harvey and Fiona, when they thought no one was looking. Much blushing and batting of eyelashes on Fiona's part, I thought, and a tongue that spent a little too much time darting around her lips. I was right to have been suspicious. Dear God – poor Moo!

I had to speak to Harvey before it was too late, assuming his relationship with Fiona had not already been consummated. And so, on my way to the ladies' loos, I crouched down beside him, having battled my way through the classified department's contest to see who could cram the most paper napkins into the cups of their bras.

'Harvey,' I whispered, 'I need to talk to you.'

He swivelled around in his chair, red crêpe-paper crown slipping over one eye. There was bright yellow silly string clinging to his hair. 'What?' he asked irritably.

But we were interrupted by Frank, a diminutive gargoyle of a man with extraordinarily large hands that might be considered comical, were they not usually engaged in some form of sexual harassment. He leant across Harvey and lunged at my breasts.

'Ruthie!' he cried. 'Come here, you luscious munchkin, and sit on my knee! Let me tell you what I want for Christmas – you owe me one, you know!'

'Not now, Frank.' I batted him off playfully. 'Later, perhaps.'

'I'll hold you to that, munchkin,' he said, turning his attention and welding his palm to the miniskirted backside of a passing young waitress.

'Harvey,' I hissed, 'you need to be careful.'

His one visible eye regarded me warily. 'Careful of what?'

'Of whatever' – I looked back over my shoulder at Fiona, who was deep in conversation with Jon Moore – 'extra-curricular activities you've got planned for tonight.'

'Ruth, you're talking nonsense. You're pissed. Go away. Oh, and merry Christmas.'

I stood up and spoke loudly. 'Is Muriel coming later?' I said.

He stared up at me. 'Muriel? No.' He shook his head. 'No. Of course she's not. Look, you're making a scene. Sit down. And for fuck's sake, stop shouting.'

'Why? Why isn't Muriel coming?'

He tugged at my sleeve, drawing me down to his level.

'What the hell are you playing at?' he growled. 'Of course Muriel isn't coming tonight! She'll be at home, taking care of Barnaby. Which is exactly where she ought to be.'

'Just be careful,' I murmured. 'Of Miss Glitter Tits over there.' I nudged my head at Fiona. 'Don't think I haven't twigged, Harvey. Remember, you cheated on me. I know all the signs. I can read you like a book. And you're so predictable, aren't you? She's a bargain-basement version of a much younger Moo.'

He pulled my face towards his, and kissed me firmly, urgently, momentarily darting the firm, moist tip of his tongue into my mouth. My knees buckled beneath me as he drew his lips away from mine.

'One word,' he murmured in my ear, 'just one word from you, Ruth Donne, and you're dead meat.'

For the rest of the evening, Harvey took great pains to avoid me, while I took great pains to monitor Fiona Hart's every move. She became exceedingly drunk and silly, and took to calling me Donne-Donne, much to my annoyance. I did my best to conceal this by making a great show of taking her under my wing and fretting over her welfare, and we left Kettner's arm in arm, while Harvey and Frank tottered behind us, boorishly singing Christmas carols with very rude lyrics.

'There now,' I said, as we swayed along the Soho pavements together. 'We're nearly back at the office. Plain water for you from now on, my friend!'

'Ooooh noooo,' Fiona trilled. 'The night is still young!'

'Yes,' I smiled, 'and so are you. I suppose there's always the promise of romance at this time of year for someone your age, isn't there, Fiona?'

She threw back her head and guffawed, going over on one ankle as she did so. I tugged her upright by the scruff of her faux-fur coat. 'Thank you, Donne-Donne,' she slurred. 'Don't want to end up in the gutter.'

'Do you have a boyfriend?' I enquired.

'Shhhh! she giggled. 'Might do. Might have a *lover*, Donne-Donne. Meeting him later,' she slurred. 'Midnight assssignation.'

'Oh!' I said. 'At your place?'

She shook her head. 'Mummy and Daddy!' she squawked. 'Ooooh noooo, I live with my mummy and daddy in lovely, leafy Issssslington, Donne-Donne. No naughties if Mummy and Daddy in residence.' She held a waving finger to her lips. 'Ooooh, nooo nooo noooo. Somewhere else.'

'Ah! I see,' I said. 'Oh, let me guess . . .' I squeezed her arm. 'The darkroom!'

She nodded enthusiastically. 'Midnight assignation. Shhhh! You're very good at this. Bet it's because you've been a naughty girl in your time, haven't you, Donne-Donne? Bet you've met some naughty boys in a few darkrooms!'

I laughed. 'I may have,' I said.

She stopped abruptly and thrust out her lower lip. 'Why aren't you married?' she asked petulantly. 'You should be married, Donne-Donne. You're funny. And you've got lovely big boobies.' She sniggered. 'Thing is,' she confided from behind a cupped hand, 'men don't see you how I see you. Harvey says you've got a face like a bag of spanners.'

I smiled stiffly. 'Does he now?'

'Yes, he does!'

'Well,' I said, 'he's a very naughty man who needs to be taught a lesson, isn't he?'

Fiona gave me a knowing look and shrieked with laughter.

I left the party shortly after that, when the dancing started. I made a point of shaking Harvey's hand, just so he knew I'd left. He was sitting on the edge of Frank Keen's desk, pretending not to notice Fiona next to the photocopier, shaking her hips and tits to Abba's 'Dancing Queen'.

'Be good,' I said.

He stared at me.
'Merry Christmas,' I added.
'Fuck off, Ruth.'

I spent the next few hours biding my time in the Dog and
Whistle, directly across the road from the office – a popular
drinking hole with workers during the day and early evening,
but nigh-on deserted after 9 p.m. My table was the perfect
vantage point: out of the way, behind a pillar, and next to an
artificial Christmas tree bedecked with a mismatched selection
of baubles and a lone, shedding snake of dark red tinsel. It
was also next to a large window, through which I could observe
the partygoers leaving the building opposite. First to emerge
was Frank Keen's secretary – the flame-haired, fifty-something,
four-feet-tall Marianne – arm in arm with the man himself.
Fifteen minutes later, Jon Moore appeared – alone and very
drunk. He staggered along the pavement, unwound scarf
trailing behind him, before pausing to vomit enthusiastically
into a litter bin. I ordered a double gin and tonic, and lit a
cigarette. It was going to be a long night.

No one else appeared for at least another hour, but then
there was a flurry of activity as the entire classified department
burst forth from the building. Half a dozen women in vertigin-
ous heels stood squawking and cackling on the kerb, before
piling into a passing black cab. The cab screamed to a halt a
few seconds later; three of the party fell out, and the cab
zoomed off, leaving one of the women in the middle of the
road screaming obscenities and shaking her fist. I noticed she
was only wearing one shoe.

The women dispersed after several minutes. By then, it was

approaching midnight, and time to make my move. I left the pub, crossed the road to the office, and peered through the window into reception. The security guard – a large man with spade-like hands, sparse grey comb-over and gruff voice, known only as 'Bill' – had vacated his seat for one of his rounds, which I knew (from his introductory monologue on my first day at *Venus Blue*) he carried out religiously on the hour, every two hours. I keyed in the passcode, opened the door, and entered the lobby, swiftly concealing myself amid an arrangement of plastic tropical plants.

I could hear the *thud thud thud* of party music vibrating through the ceiling from two floors above – clearly there were still merrymakers in the office other than Harvey and Fiona, who, I imagined, must have been gnawing their knuckles down to the bone in anticipation of their midnight sexy session. It was very hard not to feel bitter, and I started to weep tears of self-pity, grasping the glossy, fingered leaf of a Swiss cheese plant in a pathetic bid for comfort. A sharp *ping* from the lift quickly brought me to my senses. I hurried into the fire escape. I knew it was best to remain undetected, though I could easily excuse my reappearance in the building as a search for mislaid house keys. Nevertheless, I took the back stairs, emerging minutes later – breathless and dizzy – on the second-floor landing, from where I darted into the ladies' loos. Here, I made for the disabled cubicle, which contained not just a lavatory, but two coat hooks, a sizeable sink, soap dispenser, and plenty of paper towels, which I knew would be necessary for Fiona Hart's copulatory preparations.

I understood Harvey's preferences all too well, you see. He'd been brought up by a strict Methodist mother, for whom cleanliness was next to Godliness, and in that regard Harvey was absolutely his mother's son. Because, for him, cleanliness was next to sexiness – he simply could not contemplate inter-course with anything other than a freshly washed vagina, and would have had no shame in making his expectations clear to the eager-to-please, relatively inexperienced Fiona Hart. Certainly, nothing had changed during his relationship with Moo, for periodic examination of their bathroom cabinet during my visits always revealed a sizeable stash of 'feminine' wash, powder, and wipes.

Thus concealed, I waited. First to enter the ladies was the features editor, Sheila Grant, and her deputy, Sue Gately. I perched on the closed lavatory seat and lifted my feet off the floor, lest Sheila and Sue recognize my lace-up brogues and catch me out. I needn't have worried: both were too keen to unburden themselves of urine and gossip to sense my silent, seething presence in the cubicle opposite.

'Jesus,' Sheila was saying, 'you'd think they'd be a bit less obvious about it, wouldn't you?'

'The way they were looking at each other . . .'

'Sue, there's no bog roll in here. Have you got some?'

'Think so.'

'Pass it under, will you? God, they must think we're stupid.'

'That's the worst thing, isn't it? Thinking we don't notice.'

'The way she was throwing herself at him!'

'He's twice her age, as well.'

'And married.'

'With a kid too.'

'Where are they now, Sue? Did you see where they went?'

'Oh, he'll be hiding in the darkroom. She snuck off to

unlock the door while we were doing the conga. She's pissed as a fart, but wily with it. Her coat's gone, but she's in the building somewhere. Haven't a clue where, but she'll be there all right, hiding and waiting for us to leave, because we're the last to go.'

'As always! Christ, we're a pair of pissheads.'

They laughed.

'Bill's finishing his rounds soon. So they've got two hours all to themselves.'

'What a bastard.'

'What a bitch.'

They flushed their lavatories in unison, and I couldn't make out the next few words.

Then, 'She's such a nice lady too, his wife. Really pretty. Used to be a model.'

'Well, he's got a new model now.'

They left, their clacking heels on the tiled floor silenced by the carpeted landing outside. I heard the *ping* of the lift arrive, the doors softly open and close, and then they were gone.

I pulled a scarf from my handbag, unlocked the cubicle door, positioned myself behind it, and waited.

Fiona arrived approximately fifteen minutes later, humming softly to herself ('Last Christmas', naturally). I heard her pause for a moment – probably in front of a mirror – before making her way to my cubicle. My heart was so full of fear and elation that I thought it might actually flip from my chest, limbo dance under the cubicle door, and give the game away – because I felt so happy to be right, you see. So satisfied that I had read the situation so accurately, and yet I felt disappointment too.

I was disappointed in the pair of them, for not knowing better than to cheat on Moo, and for insulting my intelligence. Did Harvey really believe that I would let him get away with it? Did this silly cow – this idiotic child – truly think for a single second that she was any match for Moo, or me?

I was so cross! And my fury erupted the second she entered the cubicle, and I leapt on her back like an alley cat, wrapping my scarf over her head so she could not see my face. She gave a shocked little yelp, but I remained silent the whole time – in spite of wanting to give her a piece of my mind – and I bashed the front of Fiona Hart's head against the edge of the sink over and over, as hard as I could, bashed her stupid brains out, stupid cow, Moo cow, Moo cow, bash her stupid blonde head bash bash bash –

She fell to the floor, unconscious. I placed her in the recovery position, before rootling around in her jacket pocket for the key to the darkroom, which I was sure she'd hung on to – either that, or it would be back in her filing cabinet. My first hunch was correct, though, and I drew out the key, triumphant. I moved swiftly after that. I had very little time before Harvey would get impatient and decide to investigate why his mistress's preparations were taking longer than expected.

The *Venus Blue* office was a very different, almost sinister place without its staff. True, it was dark, and it did not usually smell so strongly of stale alcohol and cigarettes, nor was it normally strewn in tinsel, party poppers, and silly string. But the empty bottles and wine glasses abandoned on the desks gave it an air of the *Mary Celeste*, as though phantom party-goers might, any second, rematerialize in the positions they'd assumed an hour before, and ask me what the bloody hell was

I playing at, creeping across the office like this, holding that key in my trembling hand . . .

Harvey's jacket, I noticed, was draped over the back of Fiona's chair – a protective, proprietorial gesture that only served to enrage me further. Had I considered abandoning my plan, and I believe I was starting to have second thoughts, this sight only made me resolve to see it through. I hurried across the office, crept into the tunnel, saw the darkroom door was ajar, and quietly closed it. I heard Harvey utter a quizzical 'Fi?' from beyond the door, and I turned the key in the lock.

I returned to Fiona immediately. Her nose was bleeding, she was unconscious, and – I admit to being relieved at this, because I had got a little carried away – still breathing. I placed the key on her upturned palm. The explanation they'd give Bill when he found them, I reasoned, was obvious (neither would dare admit the truth!). They'd claim that Fiona had inadvertently locked Harvey inside the darkroom, before drunkenly passing out in the toilet and knocking herself out on the sink. Harvey would look an absolute idiot trying to excuse his presence there, while Fiona would suffer the disfigurement of a broken, bloody nose.

I briefly returned to the office. I wanted to hear Harvey's anger and frustration for myself. Interestingly, he sounded more frightened than anything, and was pounding on the door for help. He must have heard my approach, because he whimpered, 'Help me! For God's sake, help me! Don't leave me – please don't leave me!' And I thought, *Oh, Harvey Hinchcliffe. How many times all those years ago did I utter those very words to you?* And I turned on my heel and left.

\*

The telephone call came about five hours later. It was from a curiously flat-sounding Moo.

She simply said, 'He's dead.'

I thought, at first, that she meant Barnaby. 'What?' I cried. 'But how?'

And then, while my legs lost all sensation, and my body crumpled to the floor, Moo calmly explained the horror of it all. Harvey had not come home last night, which was not unusual after a party. But a security guard had found his body, after noticing his abandoned jacket and keys, and the police had just left after telling her the terrible news. It appeared that Harvey had been locked in the darkroom by the chief sub-editor, who had been far too drunk to know what she was doing. The poor girl had fallen in the lavatory, hitting her head on the sink and floor, was suffering from concussion, and had absolutely no recollection of the evening before.

'Harvey's dead?' I whimpered. 'But I don't understand!'

'We suspect he had an asthma attack,' Moo said quietly. 'His inhaler was in his jacket pocket in the office outside.' She started to cry. 'I suppose he must have panicked when he realized he was locked in, and that set him off. And it wasn't a healthy atmosphere in that darkroom, from what he told me . . . all those chemicals . . . not good at all for his lungs. Oh, Roo. I'm so sorry. For all of us. For me, Barney, but also for you, because you loved him too – *you loved him first* . . .'

I vomited then, into the palm of my hand. And I think I must have blacked out for a minute, because when I came round the phone was silent, and all I could hear was my own voice, screaming.

Thursday, 27 June 2019

# I have been absent for eighteen hours

I wake with a start.

I am flat on my back, fully dressed, sprawled on top of Moo's eiderdown. She is sitting beside me in her wheelchair. The contours of her white-blonde curls are tipped with silvery morning light, her appearance almost seraphic, were it not for the heavily pencilled brows and brightly rouged cheeks.

'Welcome back to the land of the living!' she trills. 'You've been asleep since yesterday lunchtime. Who was a sleepy sausage, hmmm? It'll be all that gallivanting around with strange men.'

'Lawrence isn't a strange man,' I garble. My tongue is stuck to my lips, my mouth bone dry. 'He's Joanna-Next-Door's father.' I sit up too fast and my head starts to spin. I lie back down. 'I don't feel well.'

'Hungover, I expect.'

I attempt to rise again, lifting my upper body, gingerly resting my weight on my elbows. 'No,' I say, 'low blood pressure. I got up too quickly, that's all.' I stare at her. 'You've done your hair and make-up. And you've changed your clothes too!'

'Oh, it's all superficial and top-half only.' Moo wafts the hem of her kaftan at me. 'I'm still in my nightie under all this. I decided to leave you to it, because you went completely sparko yesterday lunchtime – just like that! One minute we were chatting away, the next you were . . .' She makes a fluttering motion with her hand. 'I managed without you, though.' She smiles coyly. 'No accidents, either. I made it to the commode each time – all by myself! I couldn't get into the kitchen to make something to eat, of course, but you'd left a tube of Pringles in the study, so I had those for my dinner instead, along with a glass of that Cab Sav you hadn't quite finished. I felt quite the reprobate, I can tell you! Who'd have thought it, Pringles and red wine going so well together? *And* I managed to catch up with *The Archers* after sleeping through it the night before. All in all, quite a successful evening, I'd say.'

'Moo,' I ask feebly, 'what's happened to me? I don't feel at all right.'

'Well, after our lunch, you fancied a nap, and you climbed into bed next to me, and started talking gibberish about that bloody woman who locked Harvey in the darkroom at *Venus Blue*, and the next thing I knew you were snoring away like a walrus.'

'Fiona Hart? What did I say about her?'

'Oh.' Moo shrugs. 'A load of old nonsense, really. You kept referring to her as "Glitter Tits" and said she was your Kate Porter. You kept saying over and over: *Moo, you have Kate Porter on your conscience, I have Fiona Hart*. What did you mean by that?'

'I don't know, I really don't know!' I'm feeling frightened now. Very frightened indeed. I remember none of this!

'I mean,' Moo continues pensively, 'it wasn't as though you got her sacked or anything like that – you'd worked with each other for all of three days! Of course, she left *Venus Blue*, but that was completely of her own accord because she felt so guilty after what happened to Harvey. Had a breakdown, poor thing.'

I shake my head. 'I can't remember.'

'Really? Gosh, I do. All very sad. Killed herself a year or so later. Threw herself under a Tube train.' She shudders. 'Surely you haven't forgotten that?'

I have a splitting headache. 'Moo, please stop,' I say. 'I really don't remember!'

'But how on earth' – she frowns – 'can you not? There was a child involved too – Fiona Hart ended up having a baby, the August after Harvey . . . well, you know. God, the whole thing was so awful in so many ways. And not just for me, Barnaby, or even for you, I suppose, but also for that poor woman, her parents, her baby. I wonder what happened to the baby? Never found out if it was a boy or a girl. Whatever it was, it would be in its thirties by now.' She shakes her head. 'Poor Fiona felt so guilty, and I couldn't understand it, because I made it perfectly clear at the inquest that I bore her no ill will or blame at all . . .'

shutupshutupshutupshutupshutupshutup

'. . . Don't you remember, Roo? You were there at the hearing! I distinctly remember saying to the coroner, "I accept it was an accident, and bear Fiona Hart no ill will. Is it not enough of a punishment that she'll live with the knowledge of what she did for the rest of her life?" Those were my very words, Roo. Don't you remember?'

shutupshutupshutupshutupshutupshutupshutupshutup

'Don't you remember, Roo? I mean, terrible things happen for no good reason all the time, and we simply have to accept that they do, and pull up our big girl pants and get on with it. Don't you agree?'

I nod.

'Well, I knew you'd feel the same,' Moo says. 'And anyway' – her face falls a little – 'God knows what Harvey was doing in the darkroom in the first place. Meeting someone, I suspect.' She nods sagely to herself. 'He shouldn't have been in there. Up to no good. As always. He never changed, did he, Roo? Roo?'

My mind is working furiously. What happened? What the bloody hell has happened to me since yesterday lunchtime? Why have I lost entire swathes of my short- and long-term memory?

'No,' I say. 'No, I suppose he didn't.'

'Do you think we were fools to love him, Ruth?'

'What?'

She stares at me intently. 'Do you still love Harvey,' she asks slowly, 'even now?'

'No!' I lie. 'Of course not!'

'I do,' she says sadly. 'I suppose I always will. And the funny thing is, I wouldn't have minded too much if he had been having affairs. In fact, I'm pretty sure that he was seeing someone else, but it was fine because he always came home to me. Apart from the time that he didn't, of course, because he was dead. Do you know, I even wondered whether he'd rekindled things with you. In one of my madder moments, I thought it might be you he was planning to meet in that darkroom.'

'Don't be ridiculous,' I mutter. 'I repulsed him. Which you know perfectly well.'

Fragments are finally starting to fuse in my head.

I remember climbing the stairs yesterday lunchtime, carrying a mug of tomato soup in each hand, and remarking on the strong smell of jasmine from Joanna-Next-Door's. Then Moo spilt some of her soup on her nightie, and I went to the bathroom to get a towel. I didn't think she'd spilt that much, though perhaps it was rather more than I realized, because the nitrazepam clearly didn't touch her at all. But then, if the tablets are old and losing their potency . . . oh, shut up, Ruth, and concentrate! What else do I recall? *What else?* I remember sitting back down on the bed, and both of us drinking our soup in silence. Then, when we'd nearly finished, Moo asking, out of the blue, whether I ever thought of Frank Keen, and how he was getting on in prison after that sexual harassment scandal with those young girls he'd worked with years ago. And I said no, that the filthy bastard deserved everything he got, especially after he'd tried to worm his way into Moo's life after Harvey died. And Moo said – rather sadly – do you remember the staff at *Venus Blue*, and do you think Harvey was in love with anyone who worked there? Because she'd had her suspicions . . . Gosh, was it possible that Harvey was every bit as bad as Frank Keen, trying it on with lots of young women? Abusing his position? Would there be women crawling out of the woodwork now, even though Harvey was dead . . . And by that time, I'd finished my soup – I think – I can't remember. I can't bloody remember!

I start to cry.

'Roo? Are you all right?'

'No,' I say. 'I'm not. Moo, is my face lopsided? Is my speech all funny?'

'No!' She laughs. 'Of course not! Why do you ask?'

'Have I had a stroke?' I whimper. 'Or some sort of fit? I can't remember things, Moo. But then, at the same time, I remember things that can't possibly have happened . . . see things that aren't there. Oh God! I'm dementing, aren't I? I'm becoming my mother. I'm turning into my mother!'

'Don't be ridiculous!'

'I'm not being ridiculous! And it's all your fault! I haven't been right since Monday night, when you said you only had seventy-two hours to live. And then those faxes arriving, and all that talk about Kate Porter coming to get you and wanting you dead . . . and then you asked *me* to murder you! And I can't sleep, and I keep seeing things and imagining things, and remembering things I don't want to remember, and I even ended up searching the house for something or someone – I don't know what – and I didn't tell you, because I didn't want you frightened, but I ended up twice as frightened because I'm frightened for both of us . . . so I ended up phoning Stephanie, and now I've upset her.'

'You did *what*?'

'Well, you left me no choice!' I bluster. 'I had to talk to someone, had to get some sort of perspective.'

'You spoke to Stephanie,' Moo says slowly, 'without telling me?'

'I know,' I say. 'I'm sorry. I didn't mean to interfere.'

'And you've upset her.'

'Yes.'

'And how on earth,' Moo asks coldly, 'did you manage that?'

I gulp. 'I insulted Courtney. I expressed surprise that Courtney was becoming a barrister. Courtney wanted to tell you herself, but I've messed that up, and now neither of them will ever speak to us again.'

'Oh, pull yourself together, Ruth. Of course I haven't predicted my own death! And I wasn't serious about wanting you to kill me. I thought you knew me better than that. I was just feeling a little "off" because of Harvey's birthday, that's all. As for those silly faxes and Kate Porter . . .' She waves her hand dismissively. 'Well, what on earth can she actually *do* to me? And, of course, Stephanie and Courtney will speak to us again! You'll see. I'll send a congratulations card and generous cheque. They'll soon come crawling back.'

'I need help, Moo,' I wail. 'I really have felt like I'm losing my mind. I keep remembering my mother's face, the way her face was when she was ill, and I know that will be me very soon. I'm dementing, Moo, aren't I?'

'I can assure you,' Moo says firmly, 'that you are not turning into your mother at all. I see no signs of dementia in you, Ruth, and in all the years I have known you, I have never, ever thought you were anything like your mother. Well,' she falters, 'apart from . . .'

'Apart from when?'

'Well, the one and only time you ever reminded me of her was just after Harvey died. When you came to live with Barnaby and me, and I had that panic attack, and you wrapped me up in some blankets, and popped me into an armchair in the kitchen next to the range, and made me coffee laced with whisky while you did my ironing.' She smiles fondly at the memory. 'Just like your mother did when I lost Bear, but that was without the whisky, of course. Oh, how lucky I was,' she says, 'to have had you after Harvey died. I'd have been lost without you. Though I daresay I wasn't easy company for quite a long time, was I?'

* * *

No, she wasn't.

After Harvey died, the blows kept rolling for poor old Moo. HHPR was, it transpired, in serious financial trouble: a classic case of its deceased owner's overspending, fudging his taxes, lying his arse off about his clients (of whom, it turned out, there were now very few), and crossing his fingers and hoping all would come good in the end. The only option for Moo was to sell the company – either that, or lose her home – and Frank Keen, predictably, stepped up to the plate, seizing the chance to screw a grieving widow in more ways than one. His bid for HHPR – while short-changing Moo – nevertheless bought her precious time, keeping the wolf from her door while she figured out what to do with the rest of her life.

For Barnaby, the change in lifestyle was immediate and seismic. He had to leave his boarding school, because Moo could no longer afford the astronomical fees, and re-enrol at the state primary from where Harvey had thoughtlessly plucked him years before. For the sins of his father, Barnaby Hinchcliffe suffered very much indeed. He was bullied mercilessly, branded a 'snob' and 'gay' by his former classmates, who resented his apparent betrayal of them. Children can be cruel and unforgiving, yet the dear little lamb never once complained. In fact, I only became aware of the bullying after dog excrement was smeared on Moo's front door, and I witnessed the perpetrator – a deeply unpleasant young man called Jonathan Hayes – running away down the garden path. A visit to the class teacher and a 'grassing-up' of the bully boys by a group of eager-to-please young girls brought things to a swift and painful conclusion for Master Hayes and his chums. Yet Barnaby never acknowledged my intervention, nor spoke of any consequent improvements in his school life. He simply retreated to his room each evening to read in solitude. It was like living with a ghostly version of his father's younger self – a situation, I'm ashamed to admit, that I found strangely comforting.

Yes, the year or so following Harvey's death was a tricky time for all concerned. Moo chose to drink her way through it, while I ate my way through it instead. I also had trouble sleeping, and became rather over-reliant on nitrazepam for several months.

I did not go back to *Venus Blue*. I handed in my notice at once, unable to return to the scene of what, in my head, I knew amounted to no more than a terrible accident (my part in the tragedy, I reasoned, was incidental. *I* was not the adulterous husband or lover, *I* had committed no crime!). Yet my heart . . . oh God, my heart, which was aching and breaking constantly, although I dared not show it. I did express it, though – in a series of truly terrible poems, penned in one of my long-lost journals – but catharsis proved elusive, and the horror remained, the black and airless horror of it all, the dreams I still have – his terrified voice calling out in the darkness: 'Don't leave me, Ruth! Please don't leave me! Don't leave me, Ruth . . . RUTH!'

By early February, I'd moved in full-time with Moo. She was incapable of looking after herself, let alone taking care of Barnaby, and my plan made sense for us all. I'd rent out my maisonette and contribute to Moo's household budget, while cooking and cleaning for the three of us – generally playing mother, father, housekeeper, and nursemaid. I admit my actions were not altogether altruistic. On the occasions I'd stayed over at Moo's during the preceding weeks, I had slept very much better than usual and was untroubled by nightmares. The close proximity of two other wounded souls diminished the wounds of my own, I suppose.

'You feed from us,' Barnaby muttered under his breath one morning, as we ate our Weetabix side by side at the dining room table.

'I beg your pardon?'

'You feed on us,' he said.

'Well,' I blustered, 'not exactly, Barney. I always pay my way . . .'

'That's not what I meant,' he said quietly.

'Then what do you mean, dear?' I said, placing my hand over his.

'Nothing,' he said, gently sliding his hand away from mine. 'I don't know why I said that. I just say dumb things some-times. Forget it, Auntie Roo. It was nothing. I just say dumb things.'

* * *

'What are you thinking about now?' Moo says. 'You keep muttering to yourself.'

'Do I?'

'Yes, you do.' She frowns. 'Perhaps you should see a doctor after all. They do say that talking to yourself is the first sign of—'

'I'm getting up,' I say abruptly.

There is only one way to find out how well – or otherwise – I am functioning this morning, and that is to get on with the day ahead. Festering in bed will only make me feel worse, and achieve nothing positive. I need to be busy, busy, busy.

'I'll make some tea,' I say, carefully easing my legs over the edge of the mattress and sitting up slowly. The fog in my head is beginning to lift. 'There we are!' I exclaim. 'I'm feeling better already. I think I was just groggy after sleeping for so long.'

'That's the spirit!' Moo cries. 'I'm feeling better today too. Very much better than yesterday. Today is going to be a *good* day! Let's have a celebration breakfast of poached eggs on toast, and then a game of Scrabble!'

# A brief return to normality

No sign of Puss this morning. I searched the garden, but aborted my mission when Moo caught me crouched in the shrubbery, whistling and making kissing noises. She had evidently extricated herself from her bed to wheel herself into my bedroom, from where I suspect she'd been observing me for quite some time. I only realized she was there when she rapped on the pane and mouthed, 'Get a bloody move on!'

I shuffled backwards on my knees, carefully avoiding my prized lupins as I did so. Moo thrust the window open and glared down at me.

'I said get a bloody move on, I'm starving!' she cried. 'And what on earth are all those saucers doing on the patio? Good God alive, Ruth, is that red salmon I see?'

I am a firm believer in routine, as was my mother. Routine is the punctuation of life; without it our days would be full of senseless ramblings with no pause for thought at all. Right now, for example, I am washing the breakfast dishes, and when I have dried them with my favourite tea towel (featuring a map of the London Underground), I will water the potted African violet on the kitchen sill. This is what I do on Thursday mornings – what I have done for years and years: wash up, water the African violet, then launder Moo's smalls in the cloakroom sink. After that, I will have my bath. This is slightly out of routine for me, because I usually bathe before breakfast. But Moo was so keen for her poached eggs on toast – in fact, we were both exceedingly hungry this morning – that it seemed silly to delay our meal further for the sake of my ablutions. I am not so set in my ways that I am completely closed off to new ideas.

Yes, returning to my usual routine has helped my mood enormously. I have not been this relaxed for days, and this is simply because I am punctuating my time once more; I am finally pausing for breath. My head has cleared completely, all my faculties and limbs are functioning normally – no sign of a fit or stroke, thank God. I slept so long because I was exhausted, mentally and physically wrung-out. And all because of Moo playing silly buggers with her death announcement, and those silly joke faxes we've received. Throw into the mix a little booze, the excitement of a night out with an attractive man, and too little sleep, and . . . well. Overstimulation for anyone, I'd expect, but especially for me. I forget that I have the body of a seventy-six-year-old woman, with all its flaws and foibles, because in my head I am still sixteen and not an old woman at all. I also forget how hard I work; how stressful it is caring for Moo and the toll it takes on my health. I know I should take better care of myself – *who's caring for the carer?* as Joanna-Next-Door would say. But there is no one to care for me.

I'm indulging myself again, wallowing in self-pity. Self-indulgence, my mother said, was the worst sin of all. She had no time for whiners – worse than self-abusers, she said – barking at me to BUCK UP whenever I hurt myself.

Which, in the months following the episode with Bear, happened really rather a lot.

\* \* \*

'You're careless, Ruth. Careless and clumsy! For goodness' sake, buck up! All those scratches on your forearms – whatever are you doing to yourself? Silly girl!'

'I don't know, Mummy. I keep bumping into things.'

'Well, don't.'

I dared not tell her the truth: that I deliberately hurt myself. Broken glass, darning needles, safety pins, knives – it's funny, when I think about it now, that the pain from sharp, steely objects provided such exquisite comfort, while the sharpest, steeliest object of all ignored my silent pleas for help. Time and again, I'd glance up at the kitchen cupboard that housed Mother's medicine chest, hoping – heart in mouth – that her gaze would follow mine; that she would finally take the hint, would understand what had to be done, that her maternal instincts would kick in at last and she'd retrieve the box with its blood-red cross painted boldly on the lid, and pop me on her lap to give me succour, give me love . . .

'Staring into space again? For goodness' sake, BUCK UP, pull down your sleeves, and cover those scratches on your arms. Nobody wants to see them!'

She did soften eventually, several months after the incident with Bear, when Moo's mother was still alive and enjoying a fleeting month or so of sobriety. In a bid, I suppose, to reclaim her daughter, Moo's mother whisked her off to Switzerland for the summer holidays, much to my own mother's chagrin.

'Why?' Mother railed. 'Why must she take Muriel away for so long?'

'Because,' my father ventured, 'Muriel is her daughter and she wishes to spend some time with her?'

'Oh, shut up, Gerald! What do you know about raising girls? The child needs stability and good home cooking!'

'The child needs her mother,' my father pointedly replied. 'As all children do.'

Mother did not reply to this, but instead spent the next week and a half sleeping in the spare room.

'Your father's snoring,' she icily explained, 'is driving me up the wall, Ruth.'

And then – out of nowhere – she returned to the marital bed, as though nothing had happened, surprising me the following morning with the most delightful suggestion:

'Shall we go shopping today, Ruth?'

'Well, yes, Mummy. If you like.'

'I thought we could buy you some clothes. A new party dress, I think. You've outgrown your blue organza one. It's time for something more grown-up. It was quite a babyish thing. Never suited you.'

'Oh!' I cried. 'Thank you! Thank you!'

And I leapt from my chair to wrap my arms around her stout, unyielding waist, while she remained as stiff as a board. Though I like to think she did briefly ruffle my hair.

* * *

The brand-new party dress – black velvet with a cream lace collar – was wasted on me, of course, as all beautiful clothes are. I was built for usefulness rather than ornamentation, and have no problem with that. Here, in my wardrobe, is a selection of skirts and slacks with elasticated waistbands, several long-sleeved blouses in neutral colours, a couple of modest summer dresses, and a few short-sleeved tops – all plain, good-quality garments that allow me to go about my duties without hindrance, or attracting unwanted attention. I am glad to have led a life untroubled by vanity. It must be quite depressing to be like Moo: to live your life with the expectation that you must be as beautiful today as you were the day before, and everyone watching and waiting for the day that you are no longer beautiful at all.

I have selected a pair of cotton slacks and a loose white blouse for today's venture: a trip to the shops to restock our kitchen cupboards, which are looking rather bare. We do have a stash of tins and toilet paper in the cellar, but Moo will not permit any plundering of that. We must always have a stockpile in case of emergencies. 'Because one never knows when something might happen,' Moo explains, whenever I protest at the clutter her stockpile creates. She is coy, however, when pressed on what that something might be. Zombie apocalypse? Ebola pandemic? An alien invasion?

'You may well laugh,' she'll reply haughtily, 'but one never knows what crisis may come. Remember, Ruth – the Blitz. The Cold War. The Three-Day Week. We've lived through them all.'

'And survived,' I always add, 'without eating our way through fifty tins of pilchards.'

So, off to the shops I must go. I have left Moo at the dining table, happily gluing some of her old modelling photographs into a scrapbook. She does this now and again – sorting through the life she's led: cataloguing, captioning, controlling it all, I suppose. I, meanwhile, am heading for the Jiffy-Kwik Convenience Store. It is very much cheaper than the Lyttle Shop on Lyttleton Road, and just before I left the house, Moo made no bones about how tight things are at the moment. She said I wasn't to spend too much, especially now she has to woo Stephanie back with a hefty cheque, thanks to Yours Truly buggering everything up.

Anyway, I am pleased to return to the Jiffy-Kwik Convenience Store. I have not seen the owner, Ray, for several weeks now, and I feel very guilty about that. Ray will suspect that I have joined the ranks of 'lentil-munchers' lured by the artisanal delights at Lyttleton Road, and I do not want him to think less of me.

'Miss Donne!' he booms as I make my entrance, his ursine, black-overalled frame bearing down on me over his counter. 'It's been a long time!'

'Has it?' I enquire, wrestling a wire basket free from a tangled stack.

'Three weeks.' He cocks his balding, bearded head to one side, grinning at me like a razor. 'I have three weeks' reserved copies of *The Observer* in your name under my counter. Would you like them?'

'Oh! Yes, please,' I say, finally liberating the basket. 'I can catch up with them tonight.'

Ray waggles a finger playfully. 'Not until you tell me where you've been.'

'Well, I've been here, Ray. At home. I haven't needed to do as much in the way of shopping, you see. Moo doesn't have much of an appetite these days, and I'm on a diet, so . . .'

He nods sympathetically. 'I understand. I'm just having a joke with you, Miss Donne. I also have some lovely organic ham that you might like.'

'Oh! Yes, please.'

'And some artisan bread.'

'Super.' My cheeks are starting to redden.

'And organic tomatoes.' He grins again. 'I know what my customers like.' He taps his nose and I can't help staring – as I often do – at the dark mass of curled hairs carpeting his knuckles. 'I have my informers.'

I'm thinking of a reply, when a soft, male American voice suddenly speaks behind me: 'I can fully recommend the bread. Just as good as the stuff at Lyttleton Road, I'd say.'

Ray moves his finger from his nose to his lips. 'Shhhh!' he says with a wink. 'Not the L-word! Mind your language, sir!'

I turn to see Adam – Mr American – standing in the doorway, pushing his sunglasses off his face, and flashing me a genial smile. He is dressed for the beach (as most young people are these days, whenever the temperature rises above fifteen degrees) in baggy shorts, a Hawaiian shirt, and leather thong flip-flops. I can't help noticing his incredibly long toes.

'And the tomatoes are to *die* for,' says the woman at his side. Mr American's wife, I presume, who surprises me by speaking with a cut-glass British accent. An English rose, if ever there was one: blonde, fine-boned, freckled, a vision of urban chic in a khaki maxi sundress. Why had I assumed that she'd be American too?

'Ruth, how are you?' Mr American steps forward and pats my shoulder. 'Rebecca,' he says as he ushers his wife towards me, 'this is Ruth. We've spoken over the fence, haven't we, Ruth?'

I nod obediently.

'Ruth lives next door to us,' Mr American explains. 'She's given me a few gardening tips and I'm seriously envious of her summer house.'

'Shed,' I correct him. 'I've seen you in the distance,' I say to the woman, 'but I've not had the pleasure . . .'

She cuts in with a hasty 'I'm away on business a lot', tempering her abruptness with an awkward smile, before looking away and smoothing a blonde tendril of hair behind a delicate earlobe. 'I have to leave poor Adam by himself for days at a time,' she adds, with a shy little laugh. 'He'll be throwing lots of wild parties, I imagine.'

'Yeah, I'm an absolute animal.' Mr American grins.

'I never hear a peep out of him,' I say. 'Your husband is a model neighbour, Rebecca.'

'Well, to be honest, I'm not really there that much either,' Mr American explains sheepishly, 'so I'm not much of a neighbour, period. I stay with my sister a lot. She lives in Clerkenwell, which suits me better for work, and so . . .'

'What Adam means is he's too chicken to stay in the house all by himself while I'm away.' Mrs American pokes her husband playfully in the ribs.

'Well, it's a big house for one person. And I've never understood why we had to move here anyway . . .'

'Green space, Adam,' the woman replies crisply. 'We wanted green space.'

'And the schools are excellent,' Ray adds.

'We don't have kids,' Mr American says.

'Yet,' his wife adds pointedly.

'The houses are Edwardian and beautifully crafted,' I add, not wanting to be left out.

Mrs American nods eagerly. 'I fell in love with the house the moment I saw it.'

'Which is ironic,' Mr American says, 'since you're never there.'

His wife's colour rises swiftly, the way it does on the delicately skinned. 'Look,' she says hotly, 'if you don't like it here, you can always . . .'

Ray clears his throat. 'If I may interject for a moment,' he says. 'I was just telling Miss Donne here that I have some lovely organic ham and tomatoes and artisan bread, and for your good selves I have those beautiful Kalamata olives you requested.'

'Oh, Ray, thank you!' Mrs American claps her hands gleefully. 'They'll be perfect for our picnic! And if I could have some of that lovely artisan bread as well . . . Oh, have I jumped the queue, Ruth? You were here before me.'

'Don't worry.' I smile. 'You go ahead.'

Mr American touches my arm. 'Ruth,' he says quietly, 'can I have a quiet word?'

'Yes,' I say, 'what is it?'

He steers me to one side. 'We've got a bit of a problem.' He grimaces. 'An embarrassing problem, actually.'

'Oh?'

'Yes. Rats.'

'Rats?'

Ray, evidently eavesdropping while wrapping Rebecca's

artisan bread in a brown paper bag, chips in with an enthusiastic 'They say in London you're never further than three feet away from a rat!'

'It's true,' Mrs American says. 'They're all over the Underground! Scuttling over the platforms, running around your feet. Disgusting creatures. Oh, and can I have some ham, please?'

Ray frowns. 'But you are vegetarian!'

'Vegan,' she corrects him.

'My father's coming to stay,' Mr American explains. 'All the way from Oklahoma. You might like to meet him, Ruth? He's been pretty lonely since my mother died, and he's great company – a Vietnam vet, full of amazing stories!'

Oh God. Why is it that younger people assume that a single woman in her seventies must be in want of a widower, even a gun-toting, Trump-worshipping one?

Ray, placing the meat slicer onto the counter, grimaces as he positions a pink clod of ham beneath the blade. 'And what,' he says carefully, 'makes you think that the lovely Miss Donne is not already spoken for? Or has any interest in men?'

Sometimes I could kiss Ray.

'Ray, you're right,' Mr American blusters. 'Apologies, Ruth. None of my business, of course. I didn't mean to offend.'

'Not at all.' I smile. 'No offence taken and no apology needed.' I pat Mr American's elbow, preparing to make my way towards the chilled foodstuffs aisle, where I can lurk by the yogurts until the Americans-Next-Door have left. I wave over my shoulder. 'Lovely to meet you at last, Rebecca.'

'But the rats!' Mr American protests. 'We haven't discussed the rats.'

'I have some poison you can use,' I say. 'And I seem to have acquired a cat, which might be of some use to you, but it doesn't seem very well at the moment. Actually, I think I have some traps somewhere, but most people don't consider them humane, though I can't see how poison, or slow, torturous death by cat, is any less . . .'

'Yes, yes,' he says, 'I have poison too, but I needed to let you know that the rats are coming up from my cellar, which makes it your problem as well as mine. Well, it makes it a street problem, actually, because all our cellars are connected.'

My stomach drops. 'All our cellars are connected,' I hear myself repeating.

'Yes!' he exclaims. 'There's an arch in the wall between my cellar and yours! Not huge, about two feet wide and two feet high, but large enough. All the cellars, up and down the street, are joined like that, apparently. That's what the rental agent told me.'

'Enough gaps for an invasion by a whole army of bastarding rats!' Ray cries.

'Of course,' I say quietly. 'All our cellars are connected. I'd forgotten.'

'Weird as hell,' Mr American adds.

'Not really,' I reply. 'It's just how houses were built years ago. It's perfectly normal around here.'

'Miss Donne?' Ray's voice sounds very far away. 'Miss Donne? Would you still like me to cut you some ham?'

I walk up to the counter and hand him my empty basket. 'I need to go home,' I say. 'I'll come back later.'

Ray accepts the basket with a puzzled frown. 'Miss Donne,' he says, 'are you feeling all right?'

'No. Well, yes – I'm all right,' I reply, 'but Moo might not be. She's terrified of rats, you see. Absolutely petrified. I must get home and warn her. Excuse me. Please excuse me.'

# I hurry home

Well, what on earth do I expect to find down in the cellar? Kate Porter sitting in wait, with a crowbar, perched on Barnaby's old BMX bike? A resurrected Fiona Hart, tampering with the boiler? All I can think as I hurry home is that the cellar was the one and only part of the house I forgot to check for intruders – a foolish, reckless oversight that may have placed Moo in terrible danger! Anyone could get to her, from any house on our side of the road. And yet . . . and yet. The cellar is *always* locked, bolted, kitchen-side, for security. When Harvey and I first moved into the house, fixing a bolt to the cellar door was the first (and last) DIY task he undertook, and all to protect us from the harmless, perma-stoned squatters living five doors down.

'We were squatters once,' I said with a smirk, watching him drill the first of several aborted holes into the door. 'Whatever happened to your belief in share and share alike?'

'I grew up and got a mortgage,' he growled. 'And this house is mine.'

Back home, I unlock the front door as quietly as possible, and tiptoe across the hall. With any luck, I might get away with a quick in-and-out, without Moo even knowing I was there. But I am not exactly light on my feet these days, and her voice chirps from the dining room as I scuttle over the parquet flooring.

'Home already, Ruth dear? What's for lunch?'

I grunt in reply and hurry into the kitchen. The cellar door is, as I expected, bolted. True, it is not the sturdiest bolt in the world, and could be easily sprung with an energetic shove from the opposite side, but there would be evidence of that, surely? Chipped paint, dents in the door frame, loose screws, perhaps. But everything seems completely intact. No, no one could possibly get out of the cellar and into the house unless permitted by me.

'What are you doing? Whatever's the matter?' Moo's voice is edging closer. She must be wheeling herself towards the kitchen at speed. 'Why aren't you saying anything?'

We meet in the hallway, outside the study. 'I forgot this,' I say, hoping my hand doesn't tremble as I waft my purse in front of her face. 'I left it on the kitchen counter. Silly old fool that I am.'

I am still shaking as I close the front door. Across the road, Mrs Number 73 is standing at her front window, holding her wriggling toddler. She is pointing at something in their front garden – a flower or bird, I expect – and is entreating the child to smile at it, even though she is not smiling herself. Like mother, like son, I sniff, although it occurs to me briefly that the boy – blonde-haired and pasty-faced – looks nothing at all like his mother.

Back at the Jiffy-Kwik Convenience Store, Ray is busy restocking the cigarette shelves behind his counter. The rolled-back, grey plastic shutter exposes a plethora of toxic goodies, and I bide my time in the tinned fruit section, summoning up the courage to make my usual request of twenty Silk Cut, while bracing myself for the gentle chiding from Ray that invariably follows. Mr and Mrs American have left the building, it seems. As I did not meet them on my way back to the store, I conclude they must be on their way to their *romantique pique-nique à deux.*

I wonder where? Perhaps they are celebrating Mrs American's return with an afternoon in the grounds of Alexandra Palace. I imagine them sprawled, side by side, on the steep, grassy slopes; fingers touching, faces tilted towards each other, oblivious to the city glittering below. Or maybe they have chosen to take a stroll, hand in hand, through Highgate Woods, pausing to gaze at the kiddies' playground, smiling and sharing the same silent hope that they might one day have a family too.

It has been a long time since I walked for pleasure. Many years ago, I did so daily, in the first few years after Harvey's death, when I was still living with Moo and Barney and freelancing from their home. It was how I began each day: a gentle stroll around Queen's Woods, or a longer amble through Alexandra Park towards the terrace surrounding the Palace. I liked to look down on central London from there, relieved that I was – temporarily at least – spared from taking my place among the scuttling millions earning a crust.

Speaking of crusts, Ray has very kindly saved me the last loaf of artisan bread. He has also been much gentler with me since my return to his shop, just now – resisting the urge to tease me for my defection to Lyttleton Road. He's even reserved some ham for me.

'Thank you, Ray,' I say, placing two plump, fragrant tomatoes on the counter between us. 'You're always so kind to me.'

'Not at all, Miss Donne. You seemed rather disturbed half an hour ago, if you don't mind me saying. Is everything all right?'

I fish around in my bag for my purse, avoiding eye contact. He has a rather penetrating stare, does Ray. 'Oh, yes,' I say. 'I'm fine. But I am quite worried about Moo. She's not been so good these last few days, although she does seem brighter this morning. I left her sticking old photographs into a scrapbook. She likes to relive her past triumphs, which is understandable, I suppose.'

'She wasn't upset by the rats?'

'Hmmm?'

'You said she was frightened of rats. Did you see any rats, Miss Donne?'

'No, no,' I say, 'but I only took a quick look, and I didn't tell Moo because I didn't want to upset her.'

'Such a shame.' Ray hands me my bagged-up ham, bread and tomatoes with a shake of his head. 'She was quite a remarkable woman in her day, was she not?'

'Yes, she was.'

'A model and a famous writer! I've heard the stories, you know. She is quite the legend in these parts!'

'Indeed.'

I'm starting to feel a little cross with Ray and his banging on about Moo. I'm also getting increasingly flustered trying to shove my groceries into my bag, which is proving extremely awkward as my hands are still shaking, and my stupid fat fingers keep getting caught up in the string holes, but Ray does not offer to help me at all! He just stands there, wittering away. Oh, please, please shut up, and just give me my bloody fags!

'What did the queen give Mrs Hinchcliffe again,' Ray muses, finally sliding a packet of Silk Cut over the counter towards me, 'an OBE?'

'MBE,' I correct him sharply, snatching the packet and stuffing it into my bag with a sniff. 'OBE and CBE are *very much better.*'

I feel such a worm. It was churlish of me to correct Ray like that. His manner towards me was decidedly chilly as we concluded our business together, and all the way home I've done nothing but worry about what he must think of me now. And my blasted front-door keys are at the bottom of my stupid string bag, and that awful Mrs Number 73 is watching me from her window. I will not, will not look at her, though I sense she wants me to do so. Yes, I can feel her sly stare crawling over my back as I mount the steps to the door. Well, judge away, you nosy cow! Tell yourself I'm a fat-arsed, stuck-up, hatchet-faced old boot, because that's how Ray sees me now, how Barnaby saw me, how Harvey saw me, how everyone sees me!

There is something going on at Joanna-Next-Door's, some sort of commotion. The door is half-open and, craning my head, I can see that a couple of men with very long beards and low-slung jeans are attempting to manoeuvre a claw-footed bath down the stairs. One of them, I'm guessing, is Elliott – I have never actually met the man, so would not know him if he fell on me, but the other, I am sure, is that odious not-so-little-shit any more, Jonathan Hayes, Barney's old bully. All grown up and in his mid-forties, but Jonathan Hayes I am sure he is, because I recognize his shifty eyes and distinctive over-bite. I'm sure he recognizes me too, as he's just turned away and bent over to pick something off the floor, thus exposing the crevice between his upper buttocks.

I've barely put my key in the lock, when I hear Muriel shriek from the dining room.

'Roo!' she cries. 'Come and look!'

'In a minute.'

'You sound out of breath.'

I lumber through the hallway, dumping the string bag on the kitchen floor with an oof. 'That's because I've been carrying a bag of bloody shopping,' I shout.

'You should lose some weight, dear.'

When I do eventually join Moo, she is exactly how I left her, sitting at the dining room table poring over her leather-bound scrapbook. The table is strewn with old photographs in varying sizes and hues – some black and white images, some in colour, most of them faded. She gives an excited yelp at my entrance, and waves a stubby glue-stick in my general direction.

'Look at this!' she cries. 'Look at the hat I was wearing! Whatever was I thinking?'

I peer over her shoulder. It is a picture of Moo on the day she received her MBE, circa 1999, when Frank Keen was still able to pull strings within the government, and doing all he could to worm his way back into Moo's good books. Yes, it was a most peculiar year, looking back, packed with ups and downs and disruption: the high of Moo getting her MBE, the upheaval of the house renovation, the heartbreak of losing my journals and photos, the worry of Moo's symptoms, her devastating prognosis . . .

And it makes me sad for the Moo in the picture, who is so smiley, hopeful, and glamorous. She is wearing a fuchsia suit with a straight skirt and nipped-in waist, and a matching hat the size and shape of a satellite dish perched on her head. At her side is four-year-old Courtney, stuffed into a salmon-pink dress with puffed sleeves and a lace-up bodice. Such an unhappy-looking child, with a thin-lipped, angular face, still bearing the pitted scars of a recent dose of chicken pox, and swamped by a mop of auburn ringlets bound in oversized bows. I feel a stab of something. Pity, I suppose.

'What a sight,' Moo sighs. 'What an absolute sight.'

'Well, she was a rather graceless child, I agree,' I say, 'but that's rather harsh, Moo. Besides, if what Stephanie claims is true, it seems she turned out all right after all.'

'I wasn't talking about Courtney. I was talking about me!'

'Oh! Well, I don't see why,' I say. 'The hat's a bit much, but you looked all right otherwise.'

'But it doesn't matter any more, does it?' Moo sighs. 'However I looked, whatever I wore, it didn't actually change a thing, because Barney was dead. He should have been there,' she says sadly. 'Barnaby Hinchcliffe should have been there. And he wasn't there, because he'd gone and killed himself. And . . .' She grips the edge of the table with surprising ferocity, '. . . because, oh God!'

We have these episodes from time to time. Barnaby's name is barely mentioned for months, then suddenly – out of the blue – there is a violent outburst of grief and rage, and I must forget my own agonies, while I cuddle and cajole Moo back into a state of equilibrium.

I rub her back. 'Moo, please don't torture yourself!'

She flinches from my touch, yanks a tissue from her sleeve, and blows her nose. 'I am not torturing myself,' she snaps, shooting me an odd look. 'What a bloody farce all this has been. Since Harvey died, then Barnaby . . . everything. Everything! Such a performance. An exhausting performance.'

She turns to the table, tucks her tissue back up her sleeve, and continues daubing glue onto the photograph as though the previous few minutes had never happened. I watch her position the photo in its allotted space in the scrapbook and thump it into place with the heel of one hand.

I prepare to leave, shaken somewhat by the more intense than usual outburst I have just witnessed.

Then, 'Barney left a letter, Ruth. For me,' Moo says quietly, without looking up.

'Yes,' I reply, pausing in the doorway. 'I know. We both know I know.'

'You never read it.'

This is a statement, not a question. Moo knows damn well that I never read the stupid thing.

'Of course I didn't read it,' I say. 'I never saw it, it wasn't mine to read.'

She wipes her eyes with the back of her hand, and takes a deep breath. 'He was frightened,' she says. 'A very frightened and confused young man.'

'What's all this about, Moo?'

She shakes her head. 'Ignore me. I'm being overemotional,' she murmurs. 'I don't know what's wrong with me at the moment. Up one minute, down the next. I should be more careful,' she nods to herself, 'in what I say and do.'

I stare at her, unsure how to react, lest it spark another outburst.

'I'll go and put the kettle on and put the shopping away,' I say tentatively, 'if that's all right with you?'

But she doesn't seem to hear me. 'We should all be careful in what we say and do,' she says, selecting another photograph, appearing to address it. 'Words can cause such damage. So much damage.'

# Putting the shopping away

And now I feel even worse about Ray, because while I was unpacking my shopping, I found a Post-it note stuck on the wrapping of the artisan bread. Ray had written in capital letters: 'TAKE CARE OF THE CARER MISS DONNE.'

No mention of Moo, only me.

I do not deserve such kindness.

I do, however, deserve a glass of wine and a cigarette. But I must not – will not – ruin my good intentions for the day: a return to routine, to decent sleep, and wholesome, healthy food. What was it Moo said this morning? *Today will be a good day*. No, it will be better than that – it will be a great day! I will do some baking. I will make some flapjacks, then take them next door to the American couple, to thank them for telling me about the rats. Then I'll give a batch to Ray to apologize for my earlier rudeness, and I might give some to Elliott next door, who – if the racket he's making is anything to go by – appears to be engaging in a colossal amount of DIY. Perhaps I'll ask him to fill in the marks I've made in the kitchen walls these last few years, the fist-sized dents I've created while venting my frustration with Moo. Elliott doesn't look the type to ask awkward questions, make assumptions, or go gossiping to the neighbours. Yes, flapjacks it shall be!

\* \* \*

Barnaby loved my flapjacks. Even in the weeks and months following Harvey's death, when he must have been missing his father dreadfully (and his mother too, I suppose, because Moo was so blotto so much of the time, she was practically *in absentia*), he'd perk up visibly whenever I put a plate of flapjacks in front of him.

'Feeling better, Barney?' I'd ask.

He'd nod and smile awkwardly, mouth and cheeks bulging like an adorable little hamster.

'Made with love,' I'd add with a wink.

He'd usually slink off to his room after that.

In those days, Barnaby spent most of his time alone. Perfectly normal adolescent behaviour, I believe, and understandable for a grieving child who needed time to process his thoughts and feelings. Yet, as the months wore on, the time he spent alone increased, and when he started secondary school, I hardly saw him at all. Yes, looking back, I am certain that the first year of secondary was when Barnaby's mental problems really began. True, he had always been a sensitive child, rather mature for his years and out of step with the other children – something of a loner, I think. He'd always preferred his own company, or that of adults, which I attributed to his superior intelligence. But around the age of twelve – just over a year after Harvey's death – there were additional signs that Things Were Not Quite Right.

He would mutter incomprehensibly to himself, a running

commentary that I could not decipher, delivered to an unseen audience. On entering or leaving a room, he would tap the walls lightly with his fingertips and blink his eyes repeatedly. Moo – usually huddled on the sofa nursing a gin and tonic, and wearing the same stained velour jogging suit as the day before, seemed oblivious to her son's odd habits, just as she was oblivious to everything else. But I was afraid that other people, particularly his peers, would notice – and be less than kind. Barney had suffered enough from bullying at primary school. Heaven forbid that he should endure the same at secondary too.

An opportunity to talk to Barney's teachers arose during the spring term of his first year. It was parents' evening, and Moo was in no condition to attend. She had taken to her bed, from where she listened to the wireless pretty much constantly – Radio 4 mainly (she said she found the shipping forecast particularly soothing), with a little Radio 2 thrown in on the rare occasions when she felt more upbeat. I would take her meals and drinks on a tray, and permitted Barney to visit his mother once a day – assuming she wasn't too 'sleepy' to see him. Once a week, she might take a shower if she was sober enough, sometimes requiring my assistance if she was too weak to be left by herself. Yes, dignity had left the building, I'm afraid. It really was a strange time. In fact, now that I think about it, it was a mini version of my caring for Moo these last years! A foretaste of what was to come – a dress rehearsal, if you like.

So, it was down to Yours Truly to attend Barney's first parents' evening, with Moo's permission, of course. She had penned a note (dictated by me) that I could show his class teachers: 'I, Muriel Hinchcliffe, mother of Barnaby Hinchcliffe of Form 1HD, give permission for Ruth Donne to act on my behalf, and discuss my son's educational progress with his class teachers', etc, etc.

Barnaby accompanied me, dressed smartly in his uniform. I felt ridiculously proud to be with him. He had grown significantly in stature – was quite the young man these days – and his jawline and nose had strengthened, giving him a dignified, masculine profile. His hair had darkened, too – no longer a vibrant copper, but a rich auburn that befitted his more mature appearance. He was going to be even better looking than his father, and every bit as charismatic.

However, the charisma, I realized, as we did the rounds, was proving rather elusive. According to his maths, science, and French teachers, Barnaby was a bright, hard-working, rather quiet student, who did exactly what was expected of him, but very little more. He was always polite, punctual, and appeared to get on well with his peers, but if there was anything to mark him out from the crowd, it had yet to make itself known.

'He has lots of friends,' his form tutor assured me. 'I never see Barnaby on his own.'

'Really?' I said. 'He's so quiet at home! Isn't that right, Barnaby? And I think a little lonely too, because I've caught him talking to himself.'

Barnaby blushed. 'Auntie Roo!'

His form tutor, a young woman with bleached, cropped hair, shook her head dismissively. 'No talking to himself here, or at least nothing I or my colleagues have noticed, because they'd tell me if they had. Barnaby is doing just fine, which I think is a credit to him, actually, considering the challenging time he's had at home.'

'Of course,' I said, '*you* might think that is the case. But I've been quite worried about him – oh, Barney, don't look at me like that! You're very quiet, and I'd hardly ever see you if it wasn't for mealtimes.'

The tutor laughed (I did not take to her – her earrings were large discs of red plastic and far too big for her face). 'I think,' she said, 'you'll find that most boys can be lured out of their lairs with food at this age. Adolescents are notorious for leading a double life. Very rarely the same child presents at school the way they do at home.' She cocked her head to one side and grinned. 'Isn't that right, Barney?'

Barnaby shrugged and looked away.

Finally, his English teacher gave me what I wanted. She saw what I saw – and more.

'Barnaby is a very interesting and gifted young man,' she enthused, gazing appreciatively at him over her half-moon spectacles. (It was such a relief to finally speak to someone closer to me in age!)

'I'm very glad you think so,' I replied.

Barnaby shrugged and looked away.

'His creative writing is well ahead of his peers,' she added, 'as is his appreciation and interpretation of literary works. He has a very insightful mind. I would like to show you some of his essays, if I may. But I wonder if Barnaby could do me a favour in the meantime?'

Barnaby stared down at his shoes. 'Yeah,' he mumbled. 'Okay.'

She handed him a printed letter. From my brief perusal as

the paper fluttered between them, it appeared to be a permission slip regarding a school trip to see *A Midsummer Night's Dream* at the National Theatre.

'I've run out of copies,' the teacher said, 'and need to hand these out to the rest of the parents tonight. You know where the photocopier is, Barnaby?'

He nodded.

'Then I'd like twenty copies, please. Don't worry, I won't be telling your auntie anything bad about you in your absence. I'll just be showing her some of your work.'

Barnaby shrugged, took the letter, and unfolded himself from his chair. I watched him saunter down the corridor and out of sight before I spoke.

'Well, that was a little unorthodox!' I chuckled uneasily. 'I'm not sure how I feel about you getting Barnaby to do your administrative—'

'I wanted to talk to you alone.' The teacher removed her spectacles and raised an eyebrow at me. 'Barnaby's work is of a very high standard, as I've already said, but its content disturbs me.'

'Disturbs you? How?'

She flicked through an exercise book, smoothed over one page, and took a deep breath. 'Barnaby,' she said carefully, 'writes repeatedly about a "presence" in his house that feeds off its inhabitants. Does that mean anything to you?'

I shook my head.

'In a poem he composed at the start of the school year,' she continued, 'the presence was a bloated tick living inside his head, drinking from the blood vessels that feed his brain. In a short story he wrote at the beginning of this term, the presence was a wolf living in the cellar, stealing Barnaby's Weetabix, riding his BMX bike, and playing darts with its wolf-like friends. That was quite a humorous story, actually, and didn't concern me too much at the time. But yesterday, he wrote this . . .' She slid his exercise book towards me. 'Another story about "the presence", which now appears to be a bear-like creature living in the spare room, intent on killing his mother. From the hints that Barnaby has dropped to his form tutor, his mother is poorly, I believe?' The teacher cleared her throat. 'I mean, *mentally* poorly?'

'Well,' I said quietly, 'Barnaby's mother is still grieving for her husband. Grieving very badly.'

'And how does this affect Barnaby?'

'He doesn't really say.'

'Well, I'd suggest he's saying rather a lot here. Look, in this paragraph he describes how the bear washes and feeds his mother, and offers her love and succour. But the bear is highly controlling, and permits Barnaby to visit his mother just once a day. And the food the bear offers – while delicious – is pumped full of poison. Then at night, when the household is asleep, the bear – a highly intelligent bear, it would seem – fixes a cannula and a line into his mother's arm, to remove the poisoned blood and replace it with fresh. But the damage has already been done, and when his mother dies suddenly and is given a post-mortem, there is no evidence of poison and the bear gets off scot-free.' She exhaled loudly, shaking her head. 'A marvellous imagination, and he is wonderfully versatile – he's written some lovely romantic poetry – but golly, what on earth am I supposed to make of *that*?'

# The thing in the cellar

Moo is still engrossed in her scrapbook, so I have decided to venture into the cellar in search of rats.

I admit I am rather scared.

Not because I am afraid of rats. I find them quite appealing, actually, with their pointy faces and beady eyes. No, I am wary of whatever sick, ridiculous trick my mind will play on me next, and cellars are such fertile ground for that sort of thing. *Don't do it – don't go into the cellar!* we cry to the B-movie actress about to get her head lopped off by a subterranean axe-wielding loon. But venture into the cellar I must. I have to do it, for Moo's sake.

Besides, I need to satisfy myself that there is really nothing down there; that I really have left no stone unturned in searching this house from bottom to top. And as I turn on the cellar light, I can see straight away that there is no intruder lurking down there – 'down there' being an unremarkable brick-walled space with a sloping timber ceiling. The uneven concrete floor is covered in parts with moth-eaten rugs; the walls are crumbling in places – but that's only to be expected in a house of this age.

Yes, the cellar looks the same as ever, everything neatly piled and stacked, leaving nowhere at all for someone to hide. At my side is Barnaby's bike, next to the mini trampoline he used to bounce on when he was small. Muriel's old Singer sewing machine is just over there, on the oak chest of drawers that belonged to Harvey's mother, propping up several boxes containing Christmas decorations, photograph albums, and ornaments from my own mother's flat. Resting against the far wall are a hatstand, three broken garden chairs, and a bronze standard lamp with a mustard pom-pom-fringed shade. A dartboard hangs above the chairs, a remnant from the days when Barney and I played the occasional tournament together (I always let him win, of course).

I crouch down to examine the wall between us and the Americans-Next-Door, and can plainly see the arch linking their cellar with ours. A barrier of sorts has been erected from their side: a piece of tarpaulin that, I am sure, was not there before, a barrier that exists purely to protect their property from ours, as though we are the source of the rat infestation. The damned cheek of the pair of them! Yes, blame the two ancient biddies living next door, because everyone knows that the mad old bats will be living in filth, eating from bins, and lolling around in their own excrement. Is that how our neighbours see me and Moo – pest-harbouring hermits?

I resolve not to share my flapjacks with Mr American and his uptight wife, but decide to give the cellar a proper once-over anyway, just to be on the safe side. God knows what I'm looking for. Telltale droppings, or a nest, I suppose, and I spend several minutes tentatively opening boxes and drawers. I also spend rather too long wheeling Barnaby's bicycle back and forth over the cellar floor, finding the repetitive, bumpy motion strangely comforting.

Finally, I peer under the trampoline.

Coiled against the wall is a thick piece of rope, approximately two feet in length, and frayed at both ends.

I kneel down and draw it out, realizing at once that while it is not the rope I imagined I saw the day before last – fashioned into a noose and hanging from Moo's light fitting – it is a much shorter section cut, I think, from the exact same piece. The colour and width and twisting of fibres is similar, but that is because rope is rope, is it not? Once you've seen one length, you've seen them all. And anyway, why shouldn't there be rope in the cellar? It's probably been here for years. Maybe Harvey used it to tow his Jaguar, or perhaps it is even older than that. Harvey, Moo, and I used plenty of rope when we did our smash-and-grab on Heath House, using it to secure Moo's Persian rug to the roof of our van. Maybe Barnaby found a piece years later and played with it, pretending it was a snake, or using it to bind imaginary adversaries while playing down here. Perhaps it is part of the length that he used when he hanged—

Oh God. Not that.

\* \* \*

I should have listened to Barnaby's English teacher. I believe she saw the tragic discord brewing in that poor child's brain. I, alas, did not. I saw a sensitive, imaginative boy with a very high intellect, because I saw only what I wanted to see. When it comes to our children – the children we love – don't we all?

And I did not want to rock the boat. I did not want Moo even more distressed. So, I reported back to her that Barney was doing marvellously well. And she, in spite of being three sheets to the wind, was delighted to hear it. I poured her another drink as I gave my debriefing, while Barnaby's favourite band, The Smiths, jangled miserably through the ceiling above us.

'So, the boy's doing okay, against all odds,' Moo murmured, from her supine position on the sofa. 'Oh, Roo, I owe you so much. And I wish I was a better mother, really I do. But I'm always so tired, so lacking in energy – everything seems so far away all the time.' She picked up the empty mug from the hostess trolley at her side, and waved it at me. 'Make me another coffee, will you, dear?'

'Of course.' I beamed. 'I'll add this tot of whisky too. One Irish coffee coming up.'

She sat up suddenly. 'No,' she said.

'No? What do you mean, no?'

'No. Thank you. A straight coffee, if you please.'

I stared down at the bottle of whisky I was holding and sniffed it – force of habit, I suppose. I've always loved the smell. 'Are you sure?' I said. 'It's Glenfiddich.'

Moo looked at me in a peculiar way. 'Do you care for me, Ruth?' she asked quietly.

'Oh, Moo!' I replied. 'Do you need to ask?'

'Yes,' she said. 'I think I do.'

'I care for you,' I cried, 'more than words can say!'

'Then stop giving me booze. Please.'

'What do you mean?'

She smiled. 'Just as I said. Please don't give me any more booze.'

I didn't care for her tone at all, bright and breezy on the

surface, but with a deeply unpleasant undertone. 'Well,' I said, 'I like that! You make it sound as if I force you to drink!'

'I didn't say that,' she said. 'I take full responsibility for my habit, Ruth. But I'd like you to help me cut down.'

'Well, that goes without saying, of course!'

She cocked her head to one side. 'Does it?'

'Moo, I really don't like what you're implying.'

She smiled woozily. She was, I reminded myself, very drunk after all, and I really shouldn't take anything said in the moment to heart. 'Darling Roo,' she slurred, 'I am not implying anything. You like to make me happy, that's all. You like me to feel better. Isn't that right?'

Tears were pricking my eyes – awkward, astringent, angry tears. 'Yes. Yes, I do. Is that a crime?'

'Well, sometimes making people feel better by giving them things that aren't good for them isn't the right thing to do, is it? Barnaby says—'

'Barnaby? *He* thinks I'm getting you drunk?'

'He's said nothing of the sort. But Barnaby and I had a little heart-to-heart this morning, when you were having your bath, and he told me a few home truths, that's all. He's already lost one parent, he doesn't want to lose me too. And I've been rather selfish in all of this, thinking just of myself, drowning my sorrows . . .'

I felt hot and cold all at once. A thin trickle of sweat slid down my back towards my waistband. I tried to air myself by tugging at the open neck of my blouse.

'You're very red,' Moo said. 'Are you feeling all right?'

'I'm overheating,' I muttered.

Moo nodded knowingly. 'Hot flush,' she said. 'It'll be The

Change, my dear. Going through it myself, on top of everything else. Ghastly process – Mother Nature's such a bitch! But giving up the booze will help us both, don't you think? So, do the decent thing, Ruth, and take that bottle into the kitchen and pour it down the sink. And let's have . . . oh, I know! Even better than coffee, a chamomile tea!'

Directly above us, Barnaby yanked up the volume on his hi-fi. Morrissey's mellifluous vocals mocked me through the ceiling – something about being miserable. And drunk. I forced a smile.

'Two chamomile teas,' I muttered, 'Coming up.'

# Some musings while I wait for the flapjacks to bake

Hate is such an ugly emotion, and so misunderstood. Hate, my mother always said, is not the opposite of love at all. No, hate is passion. Hate means that you feel something, that the object of your loathing is worthy of your angst. No, the opposite of love, my mother believed, was ice-cold indifference.

I do hate Moo at times, but I have never felt indifferent towards her. Moo is a part of me, and I of her, and casting her out of my life would be like losing a part of myself. But now that I stop and consider that statement – losing a part of myself – I can't help but wonder, well, who the hell am I? Do any of us know who we truly are? Or do we just, over time, become the people that the people around us expect us to be? Yes, most of us drift into a role, I think. A role we'd not necessarily choose for ourselves, but one assigned to us by others – considerably more powerful others, who mould us to match their own selfish needs.

And I should know that better than anyone, because that's what happened to me.

Because, somehow, somewhere, between my showdown with Moo over the tot of Glenfiddich and my eventual eviction from her home (a period of around two and a half years), my role in the Hinchcliffe household morphed from that of much-loved family friend to that of an unpaid skivvy.

I had also started drinking, mainly in my room, by myself, after everyone else had gone to bed (and, in Moo's case, not always on her own). Because, having weaned herself off the booze, Moo had taken up exercise and adopted a healthy eating plan, thereby regaining her looks and her figure, and the attention of several middle-aged businessmen, including the repugnant Frank Keen.

Oh, yes, by 1989, she was having the time of her life, was Moo. Frank – evidently head over heels in love, and desperate to butter her up – had employed Moo as the agony aunt for *Venus Blue*, which by now was established on the magazine stands as a grubbier version of *Cosmo*. Thus, 'tragic ex-model and socialite' Muriel Hinchcliffe became a celebrity of sorts all over again, appearing on daytime television shows to answer such pressing dilemmas of our time as: 'Will he know if I fake it?' and 'Should I dare going bare down there?'

How Barnaby stood his mother's behaviour, I will never know. Yet not only did he stand for it, he seemed to positively revel in her inappropriate ways, actively encouraging her to date Frank Keen, beaming at the pair of them when they emerged at breakfast after spending the night together, laughing uproariously at his mother's advice in *Venus Blue*, quoting her smutty pearls of wisdom from the downmarket tabloids . . . Dear God, it was excruciating. I spent the best part of my final months under that roof not knowing where to look, so I kept my head down instead, beavering away at the cooking and cleaning, minding my own bloody beeswax, until I could retreat to my room at bedtime, bottle of Smirnoff and twenty Silk Cut firmly in hand.

My own journalistic work had dried up completely. I'm not sure why. It's a cyclical thing, I suppose – my style of writing and editing was out of favour for a while, and when word gets out that a commissioning editor has had to spike your articles once or twice, well . . . it takes quite some time and a lot of hard work to get back into the swing of things, I can tell you. Not that I was in much of a hurry. I had a long-standing tenant renting my maisonette and, in spite of the stress and frustration of living with Moo, Barney, and Frank, I needed the company. I also suspected that, outward appearances notwithstanding, Moo's mental health was fragile, and that the fabric of the new life she'd woven for herself could all too easily fall apart with the slightest tug of a loose thread.

In the end, it was Frank who evicted me. With an offer I couldn't refuse.

I heard the oily git's approach before I actually saw him. I was in the back garden at the time, deadheading a hydrangea.

'Munchkin!' he cried. 'Put down your secateurs. I have news. Great news!'

It was a stifling August afternoon, and I was exceedingly sweaty, though my choice of outfit didn't help. Alcohol and the approaching menopause had conspired to slap several pounds on my belly, and I'd taken to dressing for comfort and ease, wearing voluminous T-shirts teamed with Lycra cycling shorts. Cycling shorts were *de rigueur* among the youngsters back then, who wore them to raves, the pub and the like. I didn't go to raves. Barney, on the other hand, did, and found my clothing hilarious. I allowed him to tease me, of course. Had I not, I daresay he'd have had no reason to speak to me at all.

I froze the moment I heard Frank's voice. He had never sought me out before; I had been all but invisible to him during his clumsy courtship of Moo. He'd want something, I knew that for sure. So, I put down my secateurs as instructed, and waited, feeling suddenly conscious of my attire – until Frank's squat, portly figure waddled into sight. He was wearing Muriel's dressing gown: apricot silk with a fluted hem and a delicate waterfall neckline.

'Frank!' I cried, forcing a smile. 'Gosh, what a delightful surprise.'

'Well, it's not really, is it, Munchkin?' he said. 'You only saw me half an hour ago, at breakfast.' He touched my arm lightly, entreating me to move further away from the house. His voice lowered. 'Let's drop the pretence, Ruth. I quite like you, but you can't stand me.'

'You like me?' I asked, oddly flattered.

'I do,' he said. 'But you don't like me.'

'Does it matter?' I sighed, edging my way back towards the secateurs I'd stuck, tail-up, in the earth next to the hydrangea. 'Is that all you have to say? Because, if it is, I've a rambling rose that needs curtailing.'

He shook his head. 'Look. Your living arrangement here – it made sense, of course, after Harvey's death, and you've been the most marvellous friend to Moo. She couldn't have got through it without you. But now . . .'

He shuffled his feet awkwardly, folding his arms over Moo's waterfall neckline, exposing the few grey hairs scattered sparsely over his barrel-like chest. I looked down, mortified, only to see that he was wearing Barney's 'fun' Christmas slippers: large, furry monster feet with curved claw toes.

'But now,' he continued, 'Moo's moved on, as has Barney. But you, Ruth, you haven't moved on at all. You're stuck, Munchkin, thoroughly stuck. And therefore' – he cleared his throat – 'you should move out. For your own good.'

'And yours!' I exploded.

He shook his head again. 'Forget me for a moment, Ruth. Yes, I'm a selfish bastard, and I'd love to have Muriel all to myself, but she's made it perfectly clear that she does not love me, and never will. No one can replace Harvey, she says, and she doesn't want Barney to feel second best to any man that comes along. So, I have to respect that. This is just a bit of fun for us, apparently – well, for her mainly. I'd marry Muriel in an instant if she'd have me, but she won't, so fun it is,' he added miserably. 'Look, I'm doing this for you, Ruth. Well, for Moo, actually, because she worries about you. We all do.'

'How very kind of you,' I snarled.

'Not at all. Now, I know that you can't move back into your maisonette just like that – you've a tenant. And it would be bloody hard, anyway, rattling around in that place all by your-self, with nothing to keep you occupied.'

'Oh, do go on, Frank. You're making me feel so much better about myself!'

'Which is why,' he said, ignoring my sarcasm, 'I am offering you a job that you can't refuse. Well, you could refuse it, but you really shouldn't, because it's right up your street and very well paid, and if you don't take it . . .'

I managed to raise an eyebrow, even though the tears had started to fall, and the rest of my face was about to follow. 'And if I don't take it, then what?'

'Ruth,' he said, 'for the love of God, just take it, will you?

I've bought a smallish media group that covers the Midlands and Wales. Local papers, that sort of thing. I'd like you to be the Women's Editor of *South Wales Weekly*. Marvellous team you'd be working with – young and vibrant, just the tonic for someone like you. We'll put you up in a hotel until you find a place of your own, and you'll have plenty of company, because half the team are having to relocate and will be staying in the same place. Bloody hell, Ruth, you'll have a ball! Four-star hotel, all expenses paid, in Cardiff. It'll be like living in university halls all over again, but this time with money!'

'Cardiff? You're sending me to Wales?'

'It's either that or Wolverhampton.'

'To live in a bloody hotel?'

'It's a Trusthouse Forte!'

'And if I don't? What then?'

'We'll have to insist you leave Moo's house,' he said quietly. 'You're a good friend and a top-notch journalist, Ruth, not a bloody housekeeper. For the love of God, get some self-respect. And some decent bloody clothes.'

And with that, he turned on his claw-footed heel and padded back into the house.

I agreed to leave, of course. What choice did I have? I wasn't wanted, and that was that, though I was going to make damn sure I was needed, and my loss would be desperately felt by them all. I wasn't going to make it easy, oh no. And so, for the next three weeks, I barely said a word, refused to eat or drink with them, all the while upping my domestic duties considerably: scrubbing the paintwork, disinfecting the floors, shampooing the carpets and curtains, working into the early hours as noisily and abrasively as I possibly could.

'Congratulations, Munchkin,' Frank said, passing me on the stairs one day, while I was busy cleaning the fretwork between the bannisters with a toothbrush. He winked at me. 'You're treating us to a veritable smorgasbord of passive-aggressive cleaning techniques.'

The day before my departure, Moo came to my room to 'sort things out'.

'I've gone along with your behaviour these last few weeks,' she said indignantly, 'because I thought you'd come round eventually, see why this is for the best, and that we only love and want what's right for you. But I see you're as bloody-minded as ever. So, I've come to wish you luck, Ruth, and to let you know that when you're ready to behave like a grown-up, I'll be here for you.'

'You might be here for me,' I retorted, 'but I'll be on the other side of the Severn bloody Bridge.'

'There are trains, buses, cars,' she replied. 'Telephones and letter writing. That's how normal friends keep in touch and conduct their relationships. They do not need to live on top of one another.'

'I do not live on top of you,' I said. 'I live along the landing, and I help around the house because you need me. Who,' I enquired, 'will do your washing and cleaning now?'

'Barney and I will do it ourselves,' she said. 'I'm not a child. And I can always employ a cleaner—'

'Do you know,' I said, cutting her off, 'how to operate a Hoover?'

She laughed. 'Roo, you could teach a rhesus monkey to operate a Hoover!'

'Or how to make an Irish stew?'

'I have an A grade in O-level Domestic Science. Of course I can make an Irish stew.'

'Then why,' I cried, 'have you never made one for me?'

'Because,' she sighed, 'you always get to the kitchen first.'

'So, all this is my fault?'

But she was already halfway down the stairs. 'It's everybody's fault,' she was saying. 'Mine, yours, Harvey's, your mother's. *My* mother's. Christ, what a mess.'

I'm not proud of what I did next. But she made me do it, dragging my mother and Harvey into our argument – blaming everyone but herself! And so, I approached her later that evening, when Frank and Barney were downstairs, watching the television. I'd completed my packing, and had been waiting on my bed for quite some time, surrounded by cases and boxes, listening out for Moo's approach between bouts of hysterical sobbing. Moo's nightly routine was predictable by then: around 8 p.m. or thereabouts, she would retire to her room for an hour or so, until Frank came to join her. I have no idea what she did in that time. Attend to her bits with her feminine wipes? Cry? Pray? Throw up?

Finally, I heard her mounting the stairs, humming an indefinable tune to herself, her wedge-heeled mules slapping against her heels with each step. As soon as I was sure Frank hadn't followed, I made my way across the landing and knocked lightly at her door.

'Oh, Frank,' she cried, 'be a patient bunny, there's a dear! I haven't had a chance to—'

'It's me,' I said. 'I want a word.'

Silence.

'I come in peace,' I added.

The door eased open, and Moo's flushed face appeared through the crack. She smoothed a curl from her bouffant hairdo, thereby exposing her eyes, which were framed by lashes coated in layers and layers of bright blue mascara. She and the lashes visibly bristled. I jumped back a little.

'Yes?' she snapped.

'I've come to apologize.'

The door opened wider, exposing Moo's cream silk negligee – low-cut, with see-through panels of lace positioned here and there, hovering just about on the right side of decency.

'You'd better come in,' she said.

'No,' I replied shakily, 'I won't. It's not the right time. We'll talk in the morning. I just wanted to say, I know I've been an idiot, and . . .' I started to cry. 'All I ask is that Barney spends some time with me tomorrow. Just ten minutes of his time. Just ten minutes when I can have him all to myself for one last time, and tell him how much he means to me before I catch my train.'

'Oh, Roo!'

She took a step forward to hug me, but I quickly backed away, painfully aware that just one touch, one second in her arms, would weaken my resolve and completely ruin my plan.

'Not now,' I said hoarsely. 'I can't bear it just now. Tomorrow.'

She nodded sympathetically. 'Tomorrow,' she repeated. 'You'll see, Ruth. It'll all seem so much better after a good night's sleep.'

I woke the following morning to the foulest weather. An Atlantic depression had ushered in a late summer storm, just in time for the August bank holiday weekend. The rain lashed, the wind moaned, and my bloody taxi turned up half an hour early, putting my intended ten-minute chat with Barney and my entire plan in jeopardy.

'We can have a lovely weekend together, once you've found somewhere permanent to live,' Moo chirped brightly, helping me into my raincoat. 'Frank and I will drive down with your boxes, we'll leave Frank to unpack them, and you and I will go out for dinner and drinks. We'll make a proper occasion of it! What do you think?'

I gave a watery smile. 'I think this wasn't how I expected our parting to be,' I said, watching the flat-capped driver merrily sling my cases into his boot. 'My own fault.' I shrugged. 'If I hadn't been such a stupid cow these last few weeks . . .'

'Nonsense,' Moo said. 'You were hurt, that's all. We should all have been more sensitive. Which reminds me . . .' She bustled to the foot of the stairs. 'Frank? Barney? Ruth's going! The taxi's early!'

No reply.

She had the good grace, at least, to look embarrassed. 'Gosh, I'm so sorry, Ruth. I don't know where they are. I suppose they weren't expecting you to leave for another . . . oh, here comes Barney!'

My boy. My darling, flame-haired boy! Too grown-up now for his Auntie Roo, but my darling boy nevertheless, lolloping down the road towards me, all arms and legs and attitude, a can of Coke in one hand, an empty newspaper bag dangling at his side.

'Of course!' Roo exclaimed. 'He's just finished his paper round. Barney? Barney, hurry up – Auntie Roo's leaving!'

Barney swaggered up the steps, giving a brief wave as he passed. 'See ya then,' he said.

'Is that it?' Moo scowled, sidestepping in front of him to thwart his progress towards the stairs. 'After everything Auntie Roo has done for us? After how she cooked and cared for you – and that's it? *See ya?*'

I saw my chance.

'It's all right, Barney.' I gently patted his arm. 'I understand, you've outgrown me, which is exactly what should have happened.' I smiled at them both through a haze of tears. 'You're a man now. My work is done.'

Barney, baffled, stared at his mother. 'What's she talking about?' he said.

'She's basically saying that she's given years of her life to bring you up, not that you've bloody noticed or cared! Oh, Roo – we've taken you so much for granted!'

'The pleasure,' I whispered, 'was mine. All mine. Don't feel bad. I don't want that.'

'Okay,' Barney said. 'Mum, can I have a shower?'

'No!' Moo exploded. 'You bloody well cannot! You will stand here and say goodbye to Auntie Roo, and thank her!'

Barney looked helplessly from his mother to me, and back again.

'Well, come on,' Moo said. 'Thank her!'

'It's all right, Moo.' I dabbed at my eyes with a tissue. 'Just seeing Barney this one last time is enough. Really, it is. It'll make the long, long journey to Cardiff so much easier, knowing I've had a few final seconds with him.'

Barney shrugged. 'Okay. Thank you, Auntie Roo.' He turned to his mother. 'Now, can I have a shower?'

Moo raised an eyebrow at me. 'Do you think he deserves a shower, Roo?'

The taxi driver was waving at me to get a move on. 'I really can't get involved with this,' I said. 'I have to go.'

'Well,' Moo huffed. 'This is no way for Barney to say goodbye to you after all you've done for him. So, Barney, you're getting in that taxi with Auntie Roo to Paddington, and when you get there, you can help unload her cases from the cab, and put them on the train. And you will *wait* until the train leaves, before you come home to me – by Tube. You can use the Underground for once, instead of swanning around in taxis, or being driven everywhere by me or Frank. If you're grown-up enough to be so cool and casual with your Auntie Roo, you're big enough to travel halfway across London to see her off safely. Okay?'

So, I had him all to myself for forty-five glorious minutes. He was as miserable as sin, of course, and I didn't help matters by wittering on and on. I was both excited and terrified, you see – my plan had worked very much better than expected. Barney was my captive audience for considerably longer than ten minutes, and there was so much I needed to say to him.

The Friday morning rush hour wasn't fully underway, and the taxi made swift progress through Muswell Hill and Highgate, the force of wind against our wheels bearing aloft the first fallen leaves of early autumn. A few game specimens clung wetly to the windscreen, until the driver, cursing loudly, obliterated them with his wipers, but after several minutes of this and Barney's brooding silence, I could bear the tension no longer, and launched into a cheery commentary on everything we passed. There was Waterlow Park! Did Barney remember Waterlow Park? Such a pretty place, Waterlow Park . . .

'Can you stop saying Waterlow Park?' Barney growled, staring sideways out of his window as a bank of Victorian terraced houses slipped smoothly by.

'Sorry,' I said. 'I just remember the happy times we had there. The picnics we had, just you and me, when Mummy and Daddy were too busy with work. Remember the picnics, Barney? They were on very different days to this one, though.' I shuddered. 'So cold and wet today. It's like autumn.'

'That's because it is nearly autumn.'

'But the days of our picnics . . . well, the sun always shone so brightly, didn't it, Barney? The sky was always so blue. And I'd roll out the tartan blanket, and we'd have sausage rolls and lemonade, and play hide-and-seek in the bushes, and take a turn around the lake and—'

'I don't remember.'

'I do,' I said quietly. 'And the trips to Highgate Cemetery. You loved the cemetery, Barney. You said it meant you could visit the stone angels, that they were all your friends.'

'I don't remember.'

'After Daddy died,' I ventured, 'you stopped asking me to take you there. Why was that?'

He stared at me. 'Why do you think?' he asked coldly. 'Because it was a cemetery. And my father was dead.'

'You never talk about Daddy,' I said. 'Do you miss him?'

'Yes, I bloody miss him,' he mumbled. 'Can we drop it, Auntie Roo?'

'Of course.'

Neither of us uttered another word as the taxi made its progress through Belsize Park and Chalk Farm, though my mind was whirling the whole way, desperate to work out how to say what needed to be said. And then, when we reached Marylebone Road, which was pretty much stationary with traffic, the taxi came to a standstill outside Madame Tussaud's. In spite of the weather and early hour, a ridiculously long queue had already formed, snaking along the pavement – a queue in which Harvey and I had stood, in similar weather, over twenty years before.

'When your father and I were first married,' I blurted, 'we came to Madame Tussaud's. On our honeymoon. We had a stay-at-home honeymoon, because we couldn't afford anything else.'

Barney's eyes swivelled uneasily from the brightly coloured anoraks and umbrellas milling around outside his window, and settled briefly on my face.

'You know, of course, that I was married to your daddy before he married Mummy,' I said.

He nodded, swiftly returning his gaze to the poster-paint scene outside his window.

'And you've never been curious,' I asked, 'as to what happened between the three of us?'

He shrugged.

'Your parents never explained anything to you?'

He shrugged again. 'None of my business.'

'Oh, but it is your business!' I cried. 'Had it not been for *my* sacrifice, you would never have been born!'

He looked at me, startled. 'Sacrifice?'

'Barney,' I said, patting his knee, 'your daddy and I loved

245

each other very much. But he loved the idea of having a baby very much more. And it turned out that your mummy loved Daddy too, and so she agreed to go along with it.'

'What do you mean?' he said. 'Go along with what?'

I reached forward, drawing across the glass that separated the driver's cab from our seats in the back. Not that there was any danger of the driver deliberately eavesdropping. He was far too busy guffawing at the inane radio chit-chat to be interested in anything I had to say. But the delicate subject matter was for Barney's ears only.

'I couldn't have babies, my darling,' I said. 'Daddy and I were very happy together, but I couldn't have babies, you see. And he so desperately wanted one. Oh, he'd have done anything at all to have you, so . . .'

'So?'

'So he decided, with my blessing, to leave me for your mummy. And she was' – I blinked through tears – 'the most marvellous wife to Daddy. Even though she struggled so much with, well . . . with . . .'

'Struggled with what?' Barney asked, alarmed.

'With *you*, darling. Motherhood didn't come naturally to her, which you've probably realized by now. And now you understand why, because Mummy would never have chosen to have you, if Daddy hadn't persuaded her. Daddy did his best with you when you were very small, because Mummy struggled so much.' I sighed. 'And I couldn't bear to think of her struggling, so I moved just around the corner, so that I could help out. But I helped out a little too well in the end, and Mummy got very sad, and they decided it was better if you went away to school.'

He shook his head. 'No, that wasn't how it was! They were busy with Dad's business, Mrs Donne was going batty, you were getting – I overheard them saying – you were drinking too much, you were getting *obsessed*, you had an *unhealthy interest* in me . . .'

I cocked my head to one side. 'Is that really what you overheard?'

He nodded. 'Yes! That's how it was! You were weird! You kept stroking me, holding me too tightly!'

'But, darling, it was so hard for me – when Daddy kept complaining to me that Mummy wasn't interested in you.'

'She was! She was!'

'Oh, Barney . . . think! Think back on how much time we spent together, you and I. Think! Was Mummy there for you at all? Or was she always *busy*?'

'I don't remember. I can't remember!'

'She wasn't around much at all, was she, darling? But *I* was. And that's the wonderful thing. You sort of had *two* mummies. A birth mummy and a proper mummy. Me!'

'I want to get out of the cab.' Barney's trembling fingers fiddled with the door lock. 'I don't feel well.'

I clamped my hand over his. 'Barney,' I said firmly, 'I'm very sorry, but you need to stay. You need to know the truth about Mummy and her weaknesses, especially now that she'll be marrying Frank.'

'What?'

'She's going to marry Frank!' I chuckled. 'He's asked her. Oh, yes. And it's just a matter of time before she says yes. A man like that, with all that money – he's perfect for her. Absolutely perfect. And she won't have much time for you

247

any more, I'm afraid, with all the high living and partying she'll be doing with Frank. But I daresay they'll be able to afford an altogether better calibre of boarding school for you this time around. Eton, perhaps?'

He was breathing heavily now. 'So you're saying,' he said weakly, 'that Mum only had me because you couldn't, and the two of you went along with it because you both loved Dad?'

I nodded. 'That's pretty much it. And it explains so very much – you know, her drinking, her depression, her distance from you . . .'

'SHE WAS NOT – IS NOT – DISTANT FROM ME!'

The driver, I noticed, had turned off his radio.

'She sent you off to boarding school aged six,' I said quietly. 'I never forgave her for that, though I did try to understand. Mummy is a very fragile woman. Anything could set her off drinking again, including you confronting her with any of what I've just told you. But you're a mature young man with very broad shoulders, and I'm sure you can keep it to yourself.'

He shook his head. 'I don't believe any of this.'

'Believe what you like, my darling,' I said. 'But when the truth hits, when Frank gets his feet under the table, when they casually mention packing you off to boarding school, think about what I've told you. And always remember that Auntie Roo loves you very much indeed, and is always on your side.'

Five days after my arrival in Cardiff, Moo telephoned my hotel room, begging for advice.

'I can't do anything with the boy!' she wailed. 'God knows

what's been wrong with him the last few days. He's hardly said a word to me, or Frank. He's sullen, withdrawn, not his usual self at all!'

'Drugs,' I replied. 'Mood swings, secretiveness . . . classic symptoms.'

'Drugs?'

'Ecstasy, Moo. Ecstasy. All the London youth are taking it. Very dangerous drug. The ups are ups, but the downs are something else, so I understand. There have been lots of deaths. Haven't you heard about it in the news? It's the drug of choice at raves, and we both know how much Barney loves his weekend raves.'

'Well, I've heard of it, obviously, but I never thought for a moment that Barney . . . Oh God, Roo, what am I going to do?'

'Personally,' I said, 'I'd get Barney out of London and away from all that druggie stuff as quickly as possible.'

'But how? The boy needs an education!'

There was silence as the penny dropped.

'Oh, Roo, you don't suppose boarding school is the answer? I can afford it now that I'm working again – I'm sure Frank would chip in too. And Barney was so happy boarding when he was younger. What do you think?'

I sighed. 'Does it matter what I think? It's what Barney thinks that's important. Look, why don't you and Frank sit him down, and gently suggest his going away to school? See how he reacts.'

Next news, Frank Keen was yesterday's news.

He and Moo, it transpired, had mentioned boarding school to Barney over dinner that evening, but Barney 'completely flipped' at the suggestion, throwing a chair at Frank with such force that it broke his jaw in two places.

'Frank's keeping his distance for now,' Moo sobbed in a late-night telephone call a few days later. 'For Barney's sake, we're keeping it just-good-friends. I think I misread Barney completely – he's nowhere near over his father. I'd suggest counselling if I thought he'd speak to a stranger, but he's closed down completely and refuses to have anything at all to do with me. Oh, Roo. I wish you were here!'

# The Jiffy-Kwik confessional

The cellar door has been firmly rebolted. Moo does not know I have been down there, thank God, because the questioning would be intolerable. Why the cellar? What was I looking for? Rats? Rats! Dear God, she hates rats! Though not as much as she must hate me just now. What a day this is proving to be.

You see, I made the mistake of popping into the dining room a few minutes ago, just to check on her mood. *Quelle surprise*, her earlier angst had completely disappeared, and she was in an altogether sunnier frame of mind.

'I'm suddenly feeling so much better, Roo,' she said, beaming. 'I'm sure that everything will be all right. And – consider this – no funny faxes for forty-eight hours!' She smoothed another photograph into her album, daintily patting it into place with the pads of her fingers. 'Kate Porter must have got bored. Besides, what can she actually *do* to me? We're perfectly safe in this house.' She frowned. 'Then again, perhaps she means to cause me mental rather than physical harm. What do you say to that, Roo?'

'I think,' I mused, staring over her shoulder, 'we'll cross that bridge when we come to it – if we ever do.' The photograph,

I slowly realized, was jarringly familiar. 'Moo, where did that picture come from? Where did you find it?'

I did not mean to snap at her, but the photograph was of me as a baby, sitting on my mother's lap. Mother seems so happy to be with me, presenting me proudly to the world with an ease in her smile, a light in her eyes, that I cannot recall seeing in real life. She looks almost pretty, as do I, though my face is partly obscured because I am gnawing on her pearl necklace, holding it up to my mouth in a plump, proprietorial hand.

'You stole that from me!' I cried. 'It's one of the pictures that vanished years ago, when you had the house redecorated . . . It was you, wasn't it? Not the cleaners or decorators at all, but you who took my . . . my . . . personal effects!'

'I did no such thing,' Moo scoffed, slapping one hand over the photo, as though to protect it from my gaze. 'This is *mine*. It is in *my* collection, because the photograph is of *me*. Sitting on your mother – *my Auntie Vi's* – lap.'

'*My mother's* lap. And the baby is me, not you!'

'Oh, come on, Roo!' She pointed at the photograph, poking my podgy infant face with her index finger. 'That can't be you!'

'Why on earth not?'

'Well.' She fixed me with a challenging stare. 'It's far too pretty a baby, don't you think?'

I lost my temper then. 'Fuck you, Muriel Hinchcliffe,' I said. 'Fuck you, fuck you. At least my mother didn't abandon me. At least my mother loved me enough not to drink herself to death, at least she clothed and cared for me, and I had a father who loved me too, not a father who screwed any old slut, who couldn't wait to send me away, who couldn't bear me in his sight . . .'

When I finally ran out of steam, she said, without looking up, 'Feeling better now?'

I stormed out of the house just now without saying a word. Moo can feed and clean up after herself, for once. She can bloody starve and fester in her own filth, I don't care. I don't give a shit any more. I should have stopped giving a shit years ago, after she had me dispatched to Cardiff. Because it was all her idea, I am sure of it. It was etched all over Barnaby's face when he waved me off on the train at Paddington – utterly bereft, the poor boy was, saying goodbye to his Auntie Roo, the only person in the whole world who actually gave a damn about him! Oh, how my heart broke as I watched him shuffle across the station concourse towards the Underground, hands in pockets, head bowed, a shadow of the carefree, swaggering youth of just one hour before.

There I go again, reliving the past. Torturing myself with thoughts of my darling boy, but it's ever so hard when there are reminders of him everywhere. This biscuit tin that I'm carrying, for instance: an old McVitie's tin stuffed to the brim with his favourite flapjacks. A peace offering that I'm taking to Ray, though baked with love, as ever, for Barney.

I admit I have a soft spot for Ray. He's such an uncompli-cated, happy fellow, and handsome too, in a cuddly sort of way. In my younger days, I am certain I'd have made a play for him. Making a play for much younger men, after all, made my five years at *South Wales Weekly* bordering on bearable. Being so far away from Moo and Barney, having no meaningful intimacy with anyone at all . . . well. Sex suddenly became incredibly important to me, and I was quite insatiable for a while: stalking the Cardiff bars and discotheques with my editorial team in tow, taking them out on expenses for 'bonding exercises'.

Speaking of bonding exercises, I can see that Mrs Number 73 is engaging in some quality time with that thoroughly miserable toddler of hers. There she is, the ridiculous creature, standing at her window, bouncing demon-child on her hip and encouraging him to blow a kiss and wave at passers-by. The glass, I realize, before turning my head so we don't make eye contact, is plastered with unpleasant smears – probably from demon-child's snotty little fingers. Barney never had snotty fingers. I made sure his nose was always clean, and taught him how to blow it as soon as he had the co-ordination to hold a hanky up to his face, which, naturally, was very early on. He was always such a *forward* child.

The Jiffy-Kwik Convenience Store is empty save for Ray, who is seated on the raised platform behind his counter, bald head buried in a tabloid newspaper. In one hairy-knuckled hand he grips a Jaffa cake, in the other a mug of strong-smelling coffee.

'Ray?' I venture.

He looks up, alarmed, flicking away the crumbs that have fallen down the front of his overalls. For a split second, his face falls. I must have offended him more than I realized.

'Miss Donne, you have caught me with my hand in the till, so to speak,' he says, jamming the Jaffa cake into his mouth and shoving the rest of the packet under the counter. He grins, eyes and cheeks bulging. 'You remind me of a London bus,' he adds, mouth full.

'I'm sorry?'

'I don't see you for weeks,' he says, wiping his lips with the back of his hand, 'and then you visit my store three times in one day!'

'Oh yes.' I chuckle. 'I see what you mean. Yes, very good, Ray.'

He folds his paper, slides it off to one side. 'Now,' he says, leaning over his counter, 'what can I do for you?' He lowers his voice to add, 'I have a bottle of cut-price Tanqueray, if you're interested?'

'Another time I'd be delighted. But I've come on important business. I have come' – I take a deep breath – 'to apologize. For being so rude a couple of hours ago. For being so dismissive of Moo – Mrs Hinchcliffe. You, very kindly,' I add, struggling to keep my voice on an even keel, 'put a lovely note in my bag that made me ashamed of my behaviour. And so, in the spirit of one good turn deserving another, I have baked you some flapjacks!'

I thrust the tin towards him, prising open the lid to give him a sniff of the syrupy aroma.

'Flapjacks?' Ray recoils with a frown.

'Don't you like them?'

'I like them,' he says apologetically, 'but they don't like me. I have an allergy. To oats.'

Oh God. Why must everything I do turn to shit?

'You're crying!' Ray exclaims. 'Oh, Miss Donne, I am so sorry! I didn't mean to hurt your feelings.'

'No, no. You haven't. I just wanted to put things right between us, that's all. And, as usual, I cock everything up!'

'But you don't have to put things right with me. I wasn't

offended, just puzzled, Miss Donne. You have not cocked-up on my account.'

I sniff. 'But why,' I ask, replacing the lid on the tin, 'were you puzzled, Ray?'

'You seemed very cross when you were talking about Mrs Hinchcliffe. And, at first, I couldn't understand why.'

'Well, yes. I *was* cross.'

'And why might that be, do you think?'

'Well,' I say, 'I suppose because sometimes it feels as though . . . well, everything always ends up being about Moo. Mrs Hinchcliffe. And it gets a bit wearing, after a while.'

Ray smiles triumphantly. 'That's what I thought,' he exclaims. 'You are jealous of her!'

'Don't say that!'

'But it's true, isn't it? And understandable, up to a point.'

'But jealousy is such an ugly emotion!'

'It is.' Ray nods. 'But it is also a very human emotion, Miss Donne, and you are only human.'

I give a weak smile. 'Well, I was the last time I checked.'

'Might I suggest,' Ray says gently, 'that you consider how Mrs Hinchcliffe's life has not always been so easy? She is chronically ill, yes? And she has suffered a lot over the years, I believe, with the loss of her husband and only son.'

'He was my husband first!' I explode.

'He was?'

'Yes, he was! *She* took him from me! And at least Moo had a baby. I couldn't have a baby! That's why *my* husband left *me* for *her*!'

Ray shakes his head. 'I'm sorry, I didn't realize, I—'

'So, yes, maybe I am a teensy bit resentful of Moo's success. Wouldn't you be?'

'Well, I—'

'Wouldn't you be, Ray?'

'Miss Donne, please . . .'

'Wouldn't you be? Wouldn't you? Wouldn't *you*—'

And then I register the panic on Ray's face. And the fact that the heel of my hand is hurting like hell. I look down. I have thumped a bloody great dent in the lid of my McVitie's tin.

'I'm sorry,' I whisper. 'I don't know what came over me. I'm sorry, so very sorry.'

'Here.' Ray takes my smarting hand in his, gently eases me up on to the platform behind his counter, and settles me down on a stool.

'I'm not proud of myself and my feelings,' I can hear myself saying. 'But I really am proud of Moo's writing and her MBE. It was wrong of me to mock it. She deserved her award. That's all I wanted to say to you, Ray. That in spite of all she'd been through, she still managed to be successful. Success that has always,' I add with a bitter laugh, 'completely eluded me. But she did it, she earned her MBE for . . .' The words stick in my throat for a moment. 'For services to literature. Not my choice of literature, you understand, but what she wrote she wrote very well. And, you know, she penned the first book within months of suffering the most appalling tragedy.'

'The death of her son?'

I nod. 'Yes. He hanged himself. But you know that, of course.'

Ray smiles apologetically. 'People talk.'

'Yes, they do. But I daresay they don't know the half of it, and what you've heard is mostly made up by the gossips. No one' – I take a deep breath – 'no one knows the truth about Barney but *me*.'

Ray raises an eyebrow. 'You? You know more about his death than his own mother?'

'I know things. Terrible things.'

'Perhaps it would help,' Ray gently suggests, 'if you got it all off your chest, Miss Donne? If you told someone what really happened? Perhaps you could tell me the truth.'

*The truth.*

But what was the truth of it all? How much truth do I recall? How many gaps have I filled over the years with my own inventions, interpretations? How much have I omitted, obfuscated, obliterated from my mind? The pain of it all. Oh God, the pain. The guilt. The responsibility.

'Only if you want,' Ray adds, lifting a cautionary hand. 'I don't want to pry. But whatever you tell me will, of course, be in the strictest confidence.' He grins. 'We shopkeepers have our ethics, Miss Donne. We have a code of conduct, you know.'

He takes both of my hands in his. It is so nice to have someone's full attention for once, to feel so cared for. Special. I inhale deeply, steeling myself.

'Would some wine help?' Ray asks.

I shake my head. 'Best not.'

'Or a Jaffa cake?'

'No, but you go ahead, Ray.'

He shrugs. 'I've had quite enough for one day. Now, talk and I will listen. I am not here to judge, remember.'

What do I have to lose? And what might I gain from Ray's sympathy? I briefly stroke the hairs on his knuckles. My heart is beating fast. 'All right,' I say. 'Here goes. I'll start with Barney. What can I tell you about Barney? Well, I can tell you he'd not been right for years. I should never have left them, never have left him and Muriel by themselves. I went to work in Cardiff, you see. A job offer I couldn't refuse.'

'You are a highly intelligent woman,' Ray says. 'You mustn't punish yourself for indulging your ambitions.'

I shuffle awkwardly in my seat. 'It was a little more complicated than that. But anyway, after I left London, the relationship between Moo and Barney soured. I . . . I . . . don't know all the details – I hardly saw them during that time, because I was busy and miles away, and Moo was up to her neck in being a celebrity agony aunt, and Barney was always somewhere else – both physically and mentally, it seems, because according to Moo he spent as little time as he possibly could at home.' I shrug. 'That's teens for you, of course. They're programmed to jump the mother ship, but with Barney there was so much extra baggage he was carrying. Anyway, somehow he muddled through school, and did well enough to study English literature at a very good university.' I can't help beaming proudly. 'Oxford, in fact.'

'I know it well,' Ray smiles. 'My son is there, reading psychology.'

'Well,' I sigh, 'I hope he's having a better time of it there than Barney did. I think he was a fish out of water at first, because Moo said he phoned her rather more than she expected – nightly, at first – which was odd, because he'd been so distant from her for so very long. I think Moo was pleased that he needed her after all, and that he seemed to be building bridges. He even telephoned me once or twice. But then he met a woman. An older woman. Stephanie.'

'And did Stephanie make him happy?'

'Yes, she did, for a while. But it was all a bit sordid, because she was one of the cleaning ladies in his hall of residence, and Moo wasn't backward in coming forward with her disapproval of their relationship. Then Stephanie got pregnant and Barney, being Barney, did the decent thing and married her – quietly and discreetly, in a registry office. Neither I nor his mother attended. We were not' – my voice is starting to rise a little, and I struggle to squash it – 'invited.' I take another deep breath. 'Which, of course, was Barney's decision, and Moo and I respected that.'

'It must have hurt your feelings, though.'

'Yes, it did. But he was content, or so we thought, and that was all that mattered. They had a little honeymoon, in Cornwall, I think, and a few months later the baby – a girl – was born. And then it all went wrong.'

I pause, because I cannot speak. The tears are starting to fall.

'You don't need to go on if you don't want to.'

'Oh, but I do! Because what happened next – it was all my fault! I moved back to London, because I was made redundant just after Stephanie got pregnant, which was actually a blessing in disguise, because I'd never settled in Cardiff. Living in hotels and rented flats for years . . . well, it took its toll on my health and my finances, and I had to sell my only asset – my maisonette – to cover my debts, so I was broke and homeless too. Moo was rattling around that big house all by herself, so she let me move back in with her, until I sorted myself out.' I smile ruefully. 'We're both still waiting for that to happen, actually. But then Stephanie threw Barney out . . .'

'Slow down,' Ray says. 'Slow down, Miss Donne, I'm finding it hard to keep up with you.'

'Stephanie threw Barney out after Courtney was born,' I continue, 'because he'd gone to pieces. He would have nothing to do with the baby. Oh, not because he didn't love the baby – he loved her far too much, you see, and was terrified of doing something wrong, of hurting her, of killing her. He said he didn't trust himself, that he was too young for all of this, that Courtney was in danger from him, and that all three of them – him, Stephanie, and the baby – were better off dead. So Stephanie said that for everyone's safety, he had to move back in with us until he was better. And Barney agreed to that, because it meant the baby would be miles away from him and protected.'

Ray frowns. 'He became very mentally unwell, it sounds to me. It seems as though he was suffering from a very severe depression. Some sort of male post-natal depression. My son says—'

'Yes! Yes!' I cry. 'That was it, exactly! Only we didn't know it back then. We thought . . . we thought he was being weak and silly. We didn't understand, you see, the way that people understand these things now.'

'And you and Mrs Hinchcliffe looked after him?'

'Yes, we did. We did our best. We tried to be sympathetic. But he wouldn't speak to either of us. He stayed in his room for weeks on end. I've no idea what he was doing in there – his coursework, I suppose. I could hear him on his typewriter, tapping away into the early hours. We'd take him food and drink and leave it outside his door. It was like having . . .' My voice is starting to rise again. 'It was like having a ghost in the house. Stephanie came to visit occasionally, with Courtney, on condition that Moo and I stayed in the room with them, you know, in case things got out of hand. But it turned out that wasn't necessary, because he'd refuse to see them anyway, which was very painful for all concerned. And this went on for months. But then, one day, Barney came out of his room – just like that. He was dressed and washed, and seemed very much better. Moo was out of the house at the time, at some sort of agony aunt award ceremony – God, the irony – so it was me he came to see. I was in the kitchen, making lunch for us both – Heinz tomato soup, in mugs, with ham and tomato sandwiches, and flapjacks to follow. And out of the blue, he started to *talk* to me – more than he had in years! More than he had since he was a child. And I was so excited, so delighted, after being rejected by him for so long. He'd chosen *me* to open his heart to, Ray! Can you imagine how that felt?'

'I think I can.'

'And he said to me: Auntie Roo, he said, I think I might be ready to go back to Stephanie and the baby now. I don't think I'll harm the baby. I know I love her, and that she'll be perfectly safe with me. He insisted he was much, much better. He kept saying, I can deal with everything, now, Auntie Roo. Things seem very much clearer. Don't you think I can deal with it, Auntie Roo? Don't you think I can cope with being a dad? And I said, well, I'm not sure, Barney. You couldn't cope before, and . . . and . . . I was honestly trying to do the right thing, I was trying to be helpful, I promise, Ray, though I also didn't want him to leave me either, because it felt as though he'd only just found me again, and I couldn't bring myself to let him go – but anyway, I said, well, it's in your blood and your genes, I'm afraid, not being a very good parent, because your mother and father weren't good with you. It's true, Ray, they were neglectful! I pretty much brought that child up by myself! And then I told him he needed to be absolutely sure that he was ready to go back to Stephanie, so he didn't damage the baby the way . . . the way that *he'd* been damaged. Did I do wrong, Ray? Tell me, did I do wrong?'

'I don't know,' Ray says quietly.

'But I *didn't* do anything wrong. I couldn't have done anything wrong, Ray, because after our chat he was very much better! He seemed, for the next week or so, to have more energy somehow. He tidied his room, ate his meals with us – in silence, mostly – but at least he was with us. He even finished his dissertation – on Daphne du Maurier, I think it was – and posted it off to his university tutor. And Moo and I thought, well, Barney's turned a corner! He's turned a corner at last! And then . . . and then Moo found him, early one morning, a week or so after he came to see me in the kitchen. He was hanging from the light fitting, in the front room. He'd tied a rope around the flex, and . . . and . . . Moo woke me up with her screaming. I went downstairs and found them both.'

Ray exhales loudly. For a moment, I can't speak.

'You might think it odd that we still live in that house,' I whisper. 'Or that we still sit in that room, which we do – day in, day out – though we never talk about the fact that he hanged himself just above where we sit. We never think of it like that. We find it comforting, I think. Neither of us can bear to leave him, you see. We can't bear the thought of leaving him, hanging there, all by himself.'

I start to cry.

'I am so very sorry,' Ray murmurs, turning to stare out of the window at a passing bus. 'How awful,' he says. 'How tragic. What a terrible turn of events.'

'What was he thinking, Ray? I wish I knew what made him do it, especially after he seemed so much better. He gave no indication of what he was planning. He left no note for Stephanie, though he did leave one for Moo.'

'And what did he say in that?'

'I don't know.' I shake my head. 'Moo refuses to tell me – or Stephanie – anything about its contents. She did once tell me, during a row, that he did what he did because he was "tired of being frightened, and was under the influence" of something. Though of what, she wouldn't say. Drugs, I suppose.'

# I try to put things right

'If you want my advice, you should have a heart-to-heart with Mrs Hinchcliffe while you still can,' Ray said just now, before I left the shop. 'You cannot change the past, so make the present better. Go home and do what you can to make things right between the two of you. Do something nice for your friend, before it's too late.'

'Too late for what?' I asked.

'Well, too late for whatever might befall you – not today or tomorrow, but maybe next year or the year after that. None of us knows what lies ahead, so let's make today okay and keep our friends close to us while we still can. Yes?'

I could tell I was beginning to bore Ray, because he'd taken to rearranging the cigarettes on the shelves behind his counter, exchanging the row of Marlboro Lights for the Silk Cut Extra on the shelf below, and vice versa.

'You're right,' I said, taking the hint. 'You are absolutely right, Ray, and very wise indeed. Thank you. For everything.'

Ray raised his hand in salutation, but didn't turn to look at me. 'No problem, Miss Donne,' he said. 'No problem at all.'

*

'I'm home!' I cry, slamming the door. 'Moo? I'm back. I'm so sorry that lunch will be late. I had a few errands to run.'

Silence.

So, I am to be punished with being ignored, I suppose. Well, what did I expect? Moo is a master of psychological warfare at the best of times, and the last few days have not exactly been the easiest between us. But I have resolved to change all that. I fake a smile, before popping my head around the dining room door, fully expecting to see Moo's pious face glaring back at me.

'Moo?'

No sign of her. Her scrapbook is still on the dining room table, though: a green, leather-bound tome that, on closer inspection, is embossed with a fancy swirled pattern around its edges. I owned something similar once, where I kept cuttings of my journalism, short stories and the like. And one or two of the better poems I wrote about Harvey, expressing my eternal guilt and regret . . . .

'Moo?' I stroke the cover with trembling fingers, bracing myself to open it. 'Moo?'

A voice behind me speaks coldly. 'There you are. At last.'

I turn to see Moo in her wheelchair, wedged in the dining room doorway.

'Oh!' I exclaim. 'You took me by surprise. I didn't hear you coming.'

'Evidently not,' she replies, tight-lipped, and more than a little breathless. She is, I realize, flushed. Is Moo coming down with something?

'I was in the study, because this' – she lifts a wilting hand to reveal a sheet of paper – 'arrived just now. So, is this what you're up to while you're out and about? Popping into one of your little friends' houses to send more threatening faxes?'

'I have done no such thing!' I cry. 'You can phone Ray at the Jiffy-Kwik Convenience Store and check on me, if you like. I took these to him,' I add, shaking the McVitie's tin at her, 'because he's been such a good friend to me. Which is more than can be said for—'

'Oh, dear God. Have some self-respect, you ridiculous creature! Chasing shopkeepers and bribing them for sexual favours with home-made bakes. Do you have no shame?'

'Don't be disgusting! He's a very kind man. He actually' – I'm aware that my voice is escalating, and I check myself because I don't want Elliott or Mr and Mrs American-Next-Door to hear me – 'told me to be kinder to you. Not that you deserve it. You use me, you abuse me—'

'I do nothing of the sort,' Moo snorts. 'I give you board and lodging, free of charge. What more do you want?'

'I want to be treated with kindness and respect, with some acknowledgement of everything I do for you!'

'Oh, come on, Ruth,' she says with a chortle. 'Let's drop the pretence. Your caring for me has nothing to do with self-sacrifice, or altruism. We both know that. We're both after what we can get from this relationship. It's all we have left.'

'This *friendship*,' I correct her. 'We're *friends*, Moo. Very best friends.'

'Are we?' she says wearily. 'I'm not sure what or who I am any more. Well, apparently, I'm the nemesis of Kate Porter, and my days are numbered, it seems, because if you didn't send this fax, she did. She's up to her old tricks again.' She thrusts the fax at me. 'Take a look at what she's written this time.'

I know exactly what you did and now I'm going to make you pay

The countdown begins: 7 p.m. this evening

The Ivy

'The Ivy?' I say. 'What the hell does she mean, *The Ivy*? Is this a ridiculous moniker she's given herself? Poison bloody Ivy? Well, that does it. That takes the biscuit. She's gone too far this time, and I'm calling the police.'

'You'll do no such thing!'

'Then I'll tell the neighbours. There's a rather nice American man and his English wife living next door, or Elliott – Joanna's fancy man – on the other side. We'll explain what's happened, and ask them for help. They might be able to track Porter down from the fax number – get an address, or something like that. It's worth a try, surely? They can use their phones and computers, and do some sleuthing on the internet! And then they'll find Kate Porter and warn her off!'

Something flits across Moo's face. Panic? Fury? I can't make it out.

'No!' she cries, snatching the fax from my hand. 'Not that! I don't want anyone else involved. I will not have anyone in this house!'

'But why not? Outside help is what we need! And you know, Moo, I've been thinking. We *can* make some changes around here, after all. You know, structural changes. I'll ask Elliott – Joanna says he's very handy – if he could widen the door into the kitchen, and then we can be together even more. What do you think?'

'But you always said,' Moo replies, wide-eyed, 'that the builder you'd consulted believed it was impossible!'

'Well, maybe he was wrong,' I mutter. 'I'm sure there are materials that good, professional builders can use to strengthen the supporting wall. We need to broaden our horizons, Moo!'

I'm feeling suddenly energized, and rather emboldened. 'We need to get you back into the outside world. If we widen the kitchen door, that means you can get into the garden! And while we're at it, why don't we have a ramp built over the front steps? Then I can take you for walks in your wheelchair! Wouldn't that be fun?'

'No!' Moo cries, aghast. 'It would not be fun! I don't want fun! I don't want to be outside!'

'But I DO! This situation – your illness – how long has it lasted? Twenty years! And how many more? We're not living, Moo, we're existing. This is a living death! It isn't good for either of us, your being shut away like this. We need people, space, variety! We both need air! We've been suffocating in this house – it's . . . it's *diseased*. We need fresh air, we need to breathe!'

'You're being ridiculously melodramatic.' Moo begins her retreat, wheeling her chair backwards into the hallway. 'It's a stupid fax from a stupid woman, who means to cause us mental – not physical – harm, and you are letting her win. I do not want the police involved. I do not want the neighbours here. But I would like my luncheon before suppertime, if that's quite all right with you. I shall be,' she adds imperiously, 'waiting in the living room. And at some point today, I would like a pedicure, if you please. And a foot massage. That is,' she hisses, 'if you're not too busy flirting with the local shop-keepers.'

# Early evening, following a lengthy afternoon nap

I wake with a start, one thought in my head, a very important thought indeed:

*There were no nitrazepam left in my mother's medicine chest when I made Moo her lunch.*

None. The bottle had vanished.

I'd promised myself that this would be the final time I'd drug her. I wasn't even doing it for myself – no, it was for Moo's benefit, for a change. I was simply going to pop a couple of nitrazepam into her soup to keep her quiet, while I summoned help from Elliott or Mr American-Next-Door. My plan was this: while Moo was asleep, I'd get the men busy on their phones or laptops tracking down Kate Porter, then phone Porter myself and shake her up with a very stern warning. Once Moo was awake, I'd confront her with my *fait accompli*. *All sorted!* I'd crow. *See what I've done for you, Moo? See what a wonderful friend I am? Can't do without me, can you, Moo? You can't bloody do without me!*

I should have known my plan would go tits up. The omens were terrible from the start. We were completely out of tomato soup and had to settle for oxtail instead; the accompanying bread was hard and stale, the butter off, and the organic ham fatty, dried and curled around its edges. And then, just as I started heating the soup in a saucepan, and was about to reach under the sink for Mother's medicine chest, the telephone rang in the study next door.

This did not concern me at first. We are often disturbed by the telephone, cold-callers usually, cheerily enquiring after my or Moo's health following an unspecified 'accident', and offering free legal advice. We generally leave the phone to ring out, reasoning that if the call is urgent, the caller will try again soon enough.

On this occasion, however, Moo was clearly still very cross with me, and keen to assert her authority, because she hollered from the living room:

'For God's sake, will you get that, Ruth? It's getting on my nerves!'

I thought it wise to do as I was told, and hurried into the study.

As I lifted the receiver, I realized Moo had left a shopping list next to her typewriter, written in her (often illegible) hand. *Sellotape, pen, scissors, glue sticks, bananas, chocolate digestive biscuits, paracetamol* – and she'd written something else that I couldn't make out; *armadillos*, I thought it said, which made me chuckle to myself, briefly shifting my attention from the garbling at the other end of the phone.

But the voice, I slowly realized . . . there was something odd about the voice. Muffled and warbly, as though the person on the other end was underwater. Or underground.

'Hello?' I said. 'Who is this?'

'It's me.' The female voice was clearer now, but echoey. Familiar too, though I couldn't put my finger on why.

'Who is this?' I said again.

'It's me,' the voice cried, part-relieved, part-distressed. 'I'm back. I'm here. Where are you? Why can't I see you?'

'I'm sorry,' I replied. 'I think you have the wrong number.'

'No, don't say that! I've been waiting so long, so long to speak to you – to *anyone*. It's dark down here. And I'm cold. So very cold.'

I was starting to feel annoyed and a little unnerved. Funny faxes are one thing, funny phone calls entirely another. They are altogether more personal, taking increased effort and front on the perpetrator's part. 'Look,' I said, 'I don't know who you are, but if you're Kate Porter and responsible for—'

'No, no,' the voice wailed. 'My name is Fiona and I'm in a tunnel and the lights have gone out. The train has stopped, but I can't feel my legs. Where are you? Why won't you come to me? Why did you leave us, Ruth? Why did you leave us? Why did you leave us, Ruth, why did you—'

The phone slipped from my hand, falling onto the desk with a *clack*.

'Roo?'

I spun round. Moo was in the doorway, staring at me quizzically. She manoeuvred herself beside me. 'Roo?' she repeated, gently touching my arm. 'Who's on the phone? What's happened? You're as white as a sheet!'

'Someone,' I blubbered. 'That voice . . .'

Moo picked up the receiver and held it to her ear, listening keenly.

'I'm going to be sick,' I said, bolting for the kitchen, reaching the sink just in time.

There was not too much in the way of vomit, because I had

not eaten for several hours, though the stench of simmering oxtail soup made me retch repeatedly. By the time I was done, there was only a little bile left to bring up. I shuddered at its bitterness against my tongue.

Moo was calling from the study next door. 'Roo? Roo, where are you?'

'In the kitchen.' I sniffed, wiping my mouth with my apron.

'Come here.'

'No. I don't want to.'

'I insist. Come here, at once!'

I did as I was told.

Moo was holding the telephone receiver aloft. 'Listen,' she said gently.

'No,' I said. 'I don't want to. Please don't make me.'

'For goodness' sake, Roo, listen,' she said. 'Go on. Tell me what you hear.'

I stooped down, allowing her to hold the receiver up to my ear.

At the other end, an automated female voice was intoning:

'There is a PPI reclaim waiting for you worth £4,689, with a £150 admin fee to process the reclaim. Press one to give your bank details, press two to speak to one of our advisors, or three to repeat this message.'

I briefly abandoned the lunch preparations to have a cigarette on the back step. I don't normally smoke so close to the house, because Moo is a non-smoking zealot with an addiction of her own – nagging me to give up my habit. But this was an emergency. The phone call had thoroughly shaken me up, and I think I was muttering to myself – some gibberish about Fiona Hart falling apart, cut into pieces under a train – when Puss crawled out from under the shrubbery, looking the worse for wear. He made straight for my feet, mewling pitifully. I leant over and picked him up, poor sack of bones that he was.

I nuzzled his head. 'What's that you said, Puss? That I'm losing the plot? Sadly, I suspect you're right.'

The cat started kneading my lap with his paws, the way cats do. 'Old habits die hard,' I said, flicking my ash onto the patio with one hand, tickling Puss's notched ear with the other. 'And speaking of habits, what I'd like to know is where I've put the bloody nitrazepam. What the hell have I done with the bottle, Puss? Am I losing my mind, like my mother? Losing things, forgetting things, seeing things, hearing things – like Fiona Hart's voice, just now?'

'When's my lunch coming?' Moo bellowed from the study.

'In a moment!'

'It's gone three o'clock! And put that damned cigarette out. I can smell it, you know.'

I sighed.

I put Puss down on the patio, where he remained in his crouched position, too tired to move.

'Try and eat something, there's a good boy,' I said. 'You'll waste away, if you're not careful.'

Moo and I ate most of our lunch in silence.

'Penny for them, Roo?'

'Hmm?'

'Your thoughts. You're looking rather worried, dear.'

Moo had already polished off the bread and ham, and was now sniffing at her untouched mug of oxtail soup like a pernickety toddler. I felt a pre-emptive wave of rage, fully anticipating a querulous eruption of *I don't like it! I hate oxtail soup! Take it away, at once!*

'I have a headache,' I said, cradling my own mug in my hands, blowing on the contents to cool them down – a habit Moo deplores, yet for once she didn't reprimand me.

'I'm sorry,' she said. 'I've not been very kind to you lately, have I? It's been a most peculiar few days. The atmosphere . . .' She smacked her lips, trying to find the right words. 'The atmosphere has been heavy, that's it. Oppressive. We need a decent thunderstorm.' She nodded sagely to herself.

'We had one,' I replied, 'only three days ago. Remember? Just after I gave you your pedicure. Just after you said you were going to die in seventy-two hours' time.'

'Oh, yes,' she said with a little laugh. 'So I did. I was having a case of the dooms that day, wasn't I? Well, there's no sign of this old bat popping her clogs just yet. In fact, so confident am I of my postponed demise, I challenge you, Ruth Donne, to a tournament of Scrabble this evening. Best of three. What do you say? It'll make you feel better, I'm sure. Now, finish your soup, there's a good girl. Come on, drink up. Just a few more mouthfuls left. It's nourishing. Comforting.'

What could I say? 'All right,' I replied, downing the meaty dregs in one, struggling not to gag.

'Well, you could sound a little more enthusiastic!'

'I don't feel well,' I said, placing the empty mug on the hostess trolley at my side. 'I've been feeling unwell for a few days now, as I tried to tell you this morning. I believe, I really do believe I need to see a doctor, Moo. My memory, you know. My mind. Things are not right with me at all.'

'Nonsense!' Moo laughed. 'You have the memory of an elephant!'

And that's all this particular elephant can remember, until it woke up three and a half hours later.

I had been dreaming. Such a delicious dream at first, because it was just me and Barney and Harvey, the three of us in the dining room on a winter's day. God, it was achingly lovely. I was ironing one of Harvey's shirts, with my board set up in the bay window, the warm, fragrant steam from the iron misting up the glass. Even so, I could see that it was snowing outside: thick, slowly falling flakes that smothered the parked cars, blurring the boundary between kerb and road with undulating mounds of white. The wireless was playing Christmas songs, and Barney – a little five-year-old Barney, a pre-boarding school Barney, with ruddy chops and bright auburn hair – was sitting at the table, chewing on a slice of toast and playing Monopoly with his father. We were laughing, because Harvey's metal boot was in jail, while Barney's boat was visiting, when Barney looked up and smiled at me and said, 'Mummy, please may I have a drink?'

I looked around for Moo. But Moo wasn't there. And I must have looked confused, because Harvey rose from his chair to stand beside me, looping his arm around my waist, whispering in my ear – *Darling*, he said, *darling, are you feeling all right?*

And I knew then. I knew! He was talking to me – *me*! *I* was his darling, was Harvey's darling, was Barnaby's mummy – his own darling mummy – and that meant that everything turned out all right in the end. That this, this gloriously cosy tableau, with George Michael crooning 'Last Christmas' on the wireless, was *real*, the only reality that mattered, while the other real, the shitty reality I'd had to endure for decades, did not exist at all, but had simply been a dream. A very bad dream.

But then I heard her. My mother. Her voice booming from somewhere deep inside the house:

'RUTH!'

And I turned to Harvey for help, but he'd already pulled away from me, was sucking frantically on his inhaler, bent double over the dining room table, gasping and wheezing.

My mother's voice again –

'RUTH!'

And I shouted: *Barney!* But he didn't look up, because he was staring at the Monopoly board and whimpering, *Mummy, I need a drink, Mummy, I need a drink, my throat is so tight, there's something tight around my neck and I can't breathe . . .*

Mother's voice was edging closer. She was directly beneath me now, in the cellar, ready to burst through the floorboards and catch me out.

'RUTH DONNE, WHATEVER HAVE YOU DONE? LOOK AT YOURSELF, YOU RIDICULOUS CHILD! WHATEVER HAVE YOU DONE?'

And I looked down at myself, like she told me to, and I was wearing a blue organza skirt – the skirt of my favourite party dress, but plastered in iron-shaped holes exposing my nakedness from the waist down. And Harvey and Barney had stopped wheezing and choking, and were now pointing and jeering at me, laughing at my grotesqueness, my awkwardness, my uselessness, asking me what had I done, whatever had I done with my life, and I heard my mother's voice again –

'RUTH!'

And I knew from her tone – RUTH! RUTH! – that I was in for it this time, that I was in for the hiding of my life, in public, in front of Harvey and Barney, and the shame and pain of it all would kill me, finish me off once and for all.

I ran to the dining room door. It was shut – a big red cross, like the one on Mother's medicine chest, painted at its centre – and I hauled it open, launching myself into the hallway, sliding over the parquet flooring in my stockinged feet, only for another door to block my way. And I pulled at that door too, only to face sequential doors, each painted with the same red cross, each progressively heavier and harder to open, the parquet flooring slipperier and slipperier and harder to navigate beneath my feet, and my mother's voice, edging nearer –

'RUTH, YOU EVIL CHILD! WHAT HAVE YOU DONE? SHALL I TELL YOU WHAT YOU'VE DONE, RUTH? YOU PLAGUE, YOU CANCER, YOU CURSE!'

I woke up then, gasping for air, opposite Moo's wheelchair. My cheeks were wet, my arms aching with the hauling of multitudinous imaginary doors.

And then I thought – the nitrazepam. What had I done with all the nitrazepam?

And then I realized that Moo wasn't there. That her wheelchair was empty.

And if she wasn't in her wheelchair, then where the hell was Moo?

# She's gone

'Moo?'

I stand at the foot of the stairs, call out again: 'Moo?'

But the whole house is silent. And –

Oh.

The seat of the stairlift is here, at my side. At ground-floor level.

So, Moo must still be downstairs, lying on the damn floor somewhere, collapsed in a heap, unconscious, crawling around on all fours in a dither, or slithering around on her belly, like a snake, like the snake in the grass that she is –

'MOO!'

Maybe she's crawled into the kitchen? Yes, that must be it, the one part of the house off limits to her –

'MOO!'

– but she's not in the kitchen, no sign of her there –

'MOO!'

*And I can still see her, in my mind's eye, twenty-three years ago, bent over the kitchen sink clutching her belly – wounded she was, broken in two, this ex-mother of one – while I rock back and forth on my heels at her side, moaning Barney – oh, Barney! How could you? How could you? And she looks up at me, a string of vomit hanging from her trembling lips, and she says – he left me a letter, Ruth. He told me it all, yes, he did. Said that he had to do what he did, because of somebody's thoughts, words, and deeds, but mostly because of their words, because he was influenced by their words. Oh, Ruth, whatever have you done?*

And she's not in the study, either –

*Get out of my study, she's shouting, get out of my study, you cancer, you curse! Just leave me alone, Ruth, leave me alone! I have writing to do that's no business of yours. Yes, writing to do, because I can write too, and these words are all that I have left now that Barney is gone – my Barney, my Barney! So leave me alone, Ruth, leave me alone, and no, I don't want another cup of chamomile tea, just leave me alone with my grief and my words, and your deeds, and clean the house for me, cook my meals for me, clean me, care for me, feed me. Clean up the mess you've made, Ruth, clean up your mess . . .*

– she's not in the dining room, either –

'MOOOOO!'

*I've been very busy, haven't I, Ruth? So busy with my grief. But look at what else I've been up to these last few months, while you've been cleaning, and both of us grieving, both of us mouthing, Oh Barney! Oh Barney! into the night, where you remain, but I've opened my eyes to the light at last, and now I have these novels. Look, aren't I clever, Ruth? Aren't I so clever? Look, books that I've written, Ruth. Books that I've written! But what have you done with your life, Ruth? Whatever have you done?*

And now I'm back in the living room, gripping the arms of Moo's wheelchair in a panic, a frenzy, wishing they were her damned wrists I was holding, because I am so angry with her, so angry with her for scaring me like this –

'MOO! WHERE THE BLOODY HELL ARE YOU?'

*She's swanning around in her favourite kaftan, draped over that stupid chaise longue of hers, hugging that pom-pom cushion and looking ever so pleased with herself. Trilling away like a tropical bird, preening her plumage and saying, Ooooh, look, Ruth! Look at these letters, so many offers from literary agents, coming out of my ears! Whatever shall I do, Ruth? Who shall I choose? And now I'll be richer than ever before and, she says, I will need you, Ruth. Need you more than ever to cook for me, clean for me, keep everything clean for me, Ruth, keep yourself clean for me, keep your nose clean . . .*

\* \* \*

I remember.

I remember she said the most peculiar thing to me then, the day she bagged herself an agent. She was reading the letter from Ridley & Pumbridge Literary Representation, for the umpteenth bloody time, and then she looked up and addressed me with the strangest smile on her face.

'*Oft have I heard grief softens the mind, and makes it fearful and degenerate. Think, therefore, and cease to weep.* You see, Ruth, I had to do it. I had to find a way to earn more money, so that we could survive.'

'Well, congratulations,' I replied. 'It would appear your writing is a great success, though I'm not entirely sure why you feel the need to quote Shakespeare at me in such an imperious manner. And, as for needing to make more money, well, surely that's unnecessary. I thought you were quite comfortably off in that department.'

'For now.' She nodded. 'For now. But that money won't last forever. And I have to think of the future, Ruth. There's a good few years ahead of us yet.' She bit her lip. 'I will need to keep you in the manner to which you have become accustomed.'

I wasn't sure what to say to that. I mean, she really didn't need to *keep* me at all, and I had half a mind to tell her so, while the other half wanted to ask what the bloody hell she meant by my being *accustomed* to a manner of something or other, especially as my purpose at that point amounted to little more than that of an unpaid skivvy. She was talking nonsense, of course, and given all she'd been through was probably quite unstable. So I resolved to keep my trap shut. And yet, I couldn't help asking –

'What about the Shakespeare?'

'Hmmmm?'

'*Henry the Sixth, Part Two*,' I said. 'That speech by Queen Margaret. What a very odd thing to quote at me. And you quoted it wrongly too. It's "think therefore *on revenge*, and cease to weep".'

'Is it?' Moo replied. 'I don't remember the revenge bit. I always thought that quote was about grief. You know, about not giving in to it, not allowing it to weaken you. And I think this' – she waved the agent's letter at me – 'proves that my mind has not been softened by grief, in any shape or form.'

I shook my head. 'You're wrong,' I said. 'That quote is about revenge, not grief.'

'Is it? Well, I suppose it must be, if you say so. You're the one with the English literature degree, after all. I'm just a dried-up ex-model who used to demonstrate hostess trolleys at Selfridges, remember?'

\* \* \*

'MOO!'

I'm out on the street now, screaming and shouting, whirling my arms like a lunatic. I feel as though I'm floating above myself, watching myself, directing myself, telling myself that Moo must have made it out of the house somehow. But where has she gone? How has she gone? And why has she done this to me?

'ELLIOTT!'

I pound on Joanna-Next-Door's window. 'ELLIOTT!'

No reply. I shield my eyes, pressing my forehead against the glass.

Joanna's front room is completely empty. Of everything: furniture, carpets, light fittings, even the mantelpiece. Gone. That magnificent Edwardian black-marble mantelpiece, ripped from the wall – such an act of violation! – leaving great chunks of plaster littering the floorboards with decades of dust, muck, and rot.

This must be a dream.

I stare down at my fists. They are red and they hurt. Not a dream. This is real.

'Elliott?' I whimper.

But Elliott isn't here any more. Elliott has left the building. Elliott has vanished, having ripped out Joanna's mantelpiece, her claw-footed bath, her carpets, her heart.

Oh God! What if Moo saw what Elliott and Jonathan Hayes were up to? What if they crept into our house, and took her away to silence her while I was asleep?

I hobble down the steps. What next? Mr American-Next-Door – I'll try him. Maybe he's seen or heard something. Adam. That's his name – Adam, Adam, Adam . . .

'ADAM?' I shriek through his letterbox. 'ADAAAAM! ADAAAAM!'

But Mrs American comes to the door.

'Adam,' I grunt, clutching my chest. My heart hurts. I can't breathe. 'Adam,' I sputter. 'I need Adam.'

'Adam's not available.' Mrs American frowns down at me. She is still wearing that khaki dress she had on this morning. There are no dark patches of sweat under her arms, though I am aware of the sharp, allium stench of BO drifting up from my own. The smell of fear.

And then she makes that gesture again. The one she made at the Jiffy-Kwik Convenience Store that passed me by at the time, but must have tucked itself away in my subconscious: that smoothing of a stray tendril of hair behind a delicate, shell-like ear that reminds me of –

'Fiona Hart!' I whimper.

'No,' she replies, puzzled. 'Rebecca. My name is Rebecca.'

'You're just like her,' I can hear myself saying. 'So very like her. And your age – you must be . . . oh God. You're her daughter! The baby she left behind!'

Mrs American glances nervously over her shoulder. 'Adam!' she cries. 'Adam, I need you *now*!'

My mind is working furiously, whirling, skittering over the last few days.

'You broke into my house, didn't you?' I whisper. 'Through the cellar door, and you've been doing things to get back at me, for what happened to *her* . . . to your mother!'

Mrs American's mouth opens wide. She shuts it again, then opens it wide, gasping like a fish – a dying fish, a lying fish.

'I knew,' I'm saying, 'I knew there was something odd about you the moment we met!'

'ADAM!'

'You've been trying to send me mad, haven't you? You came into my house, and you took the nitrazepam tablets out of Mummy's medicine chest, and you move Moo's wheelchair around, and play with her stairlift, hang ropes from my light fittings, send funny faxes, and make telephone calls! You come into the house through the cellar, you force the door open, because you're young and you're strong, and you bolt it again, and let yourself out through the front door when no one's downstairs . . . oh!'

I am exultant! I AM NOT GOING MAD.

'ADAM!'

'It was you!' I cry. 'It was you all along! So where is she?' I pump my elbows at my sides, preparing to force myself past her. 'What have you done with Moo?'

Mr American hurtles down the stairs, a large white towel knotted around his waist.

'What's going on?' he asks breathlessly. 'Ruth, what's the matter? What's going on?'

But *she* interrupts before I can speak.

'Ruth thinks I am someone else,' she says quietly. 'I think Ruth might not be very well.'

'I am perfectly well!' I exclaim. 'I feel better now than I have done in days! And so, if you will excuse me, I have the police to telephone.'

'But why?' Adam asks, perplexed. 'Why must you call the police?'

'Because your wife is an imposter!' I cry. 'She is the daughter of Fiona Hart!'

'My wife is the daughter,' Adam says, 'of Lord and Lady Henry Twill of Maldon Farm, Wiltshire.'

'The *adopted* daughter!' I correct him. 'Your wife is the birth child of Fiona Hart!'

'Ruth,' *she* says (gazing at me with 'concern' in her eyes, the artful bitch), 'Ruth, my parents *are* my birth parents. Look, I have photos to prove it.'

She produces a mobile phone from the pocket of her dress, swipes at the screen with her finger. 'This is me, Mummy and Daddy, and my twin sister, Verity, at her wedding, three years ago.'

'And you're not seeing double.' Adam laughs nervously. 'Verity is Rebecca's identical twin.'

I look at the photograph. It's true. The heads of the bride and chief bridesmaid could be interchangeable, no doubt about it.

'Fraud!' I cry. 'You've faked the photo, knowing I'd want to see evidence!'

'Okay,' Adam says carefully. 'I'll go and get the magazine.'

'*I'll* go and get the magazine,' his wife says, eyeing me warily. 'I know where it is.'

She backs away from the door, before scurrying into the house.

'Ruth.' Adam gently takes my hand. 'Ruth, you're shaking. You're not well. Please, let me call someone. A doctor, perhaps?'

'I am as sane,' I reply, snatching my hand away, 'as bootlaces. Don't patronize me.'

His wife reappears, holding a publication – *Wiltshire Life*, it says on the cover, above a photograph of a large spotted pig gazing wistfully at the camera. She flips the magazine open.

'Here,' she says.

It is the same photograph as the one on her phone, but this time fronting an article:

## *MIDSUMMER JOY AT MALDON FARM*

### By Marie Swift

Lord and Lady Henry Twill had double cause to celebrate at the wedding of their daughter, Verity, to local landowner, Mark Steele. Verity's identical twin sister, Rebecca, had announced her betrothal to American businessman, Adam Zucker, just two weeks before.

'We are so delighted,' Lord Twill told us, 'that both girls have found such happiness. As many in our community know, they did not have the easiest start in life, as my wife gave birth to them two months prematurely. The girls spent the first ten weeks of their life in the Special Care Baby Unit at Swindon General Hospital, and it was touch and go at times. In view of our indebtedness to the unit, the happy couple have requested donations to Swindon SCBU in lieu of wedding gifts.'

*Should Wiltshire Life readers like to contribute to the fund, please contact Marie Swift at the usual email address.*

# Oh, Ruth Donne. Whatever have you done?

Adam and Rebecca were remarkably decent following my outburst on their doorstep. There aren't many people, I suspect, who'd be so forgiving of such disgraceful behaviour from a neighbour, and I found their empathy humbling – truly I did. I made a mental note not to make snap judgements about people in future, though I suppose it's a little late for that now.

They even offered me a cup of tea which, of course, I declined. However, I did accept their insistence on accompanying me home.

'There must be,' Rebecca said, as she ushered me through the front door, 'a rational explanation for where Mrs Hinchcliffe is. Did you check upstairs, Ruth?'

'No,' I replied, 'I didn't. But that was because Moo can't possibly have got up there, because her wheelchair was in the living room, and the stairlift at ground level. She hasn't the strength to get far without either. Oh, this is a nightmare!'

Adam bellowed up the stairs: 'MRS HINCHCLIFFE!'

Inexplicably, Moo's voice warbled from her bedroom.

'Who's there? Who are you? What do you want? I have no valuables in the house, you know!'

'Don't panic, Mrs Hinchcliffe!' Adam yelled back. 'It's Adam from next door. Everything's fine. We've got Ruth with us, but she's a little upset. Shall we bring her up to you?'

Silence.

'I said,' Adam repeated, 'shall we come up, Mrs Hinchcliffe? Are you all right? Do you need some assistance?'

'No, no.'

Moo – damn her! – sounded vaguely amused. 'I am quite all right, thank you,' she trilled, 'but I'm not really in a fit state for polite company. It's best that Ruth comes up alone.'

'I'll go up,' I said quietly. 'I need to see her. To talk to her. To find out how . . .' I waved my hand at the stairlift. 'How on earth she managed to make it up there. Moo' – I raised my voice – 'I'm coming up!'

'Well, bring the pom-pom cushion from the living room, there's a dear, so I can rest my feet on it while you paint my toenails. And do hurry up. *The Archers* is due to start any second.'

'It's something that we do,' I muttered. 'Something that we've always done. For years. She listens to *The Archers* while I paint her toenails.'

'We should go,' Rebecca said, touching her husband's arm. 'We're meant to be meeting your dad at Heathrow, and if we leave now we might just make it. Stay there, Ruth. I'll get the cushion, and then you can go up to Mrs Hinchcliffe.'

'It's in that room on the left.' I made a limp motion with my hand. 'Gosh, your father, Adam. I'd forgotten he was coming. I'm so sorry. I've held you up.'

'Not at all,' he replied.

'And he sounds such an interesting man,' I garbled, increasingly mortified at the fuss I'd created, and the absolute fool I'd made of myself. 'A Vietnam veteran, no less.'

Rebecca emerged from the living room, gliding over the parquet flooring, her sundress billowing around her. She was bearing the pom-pom cushion at arm's length, a look of distaste wrestling with the breezy smile she was struggling to maintain.

'Is this the one?' she said. 'It's very . . . distinctive.'

'Yes,' I replied. 'It is. Moo's taste, of course. Well, thank you both, and apologies for my behaviour just now.'

'Not at all,' Adam said again. 'You're clearly under a lot of stress.'

I stood at the top of the steps, clutching the cushion to my breast, as he and Rebecca made their descent, and gave me a little wave from the pavement.

'We'll call round in a few days to see how you are,' Rebecca said.

I nodded. 'That would be nice.'

And I shut the door, my cheeks and eyes burning, acutely aware that the Americans-Next-Door had not repeated their earlier request that I meet Mr American's father.


'There you are!'

Moo, resplendent in a cream silk nightie, was tucked up in bed, her white hair hanging limply over her shoulders. She had reapplied her make-up with a particularly heavy hand: rouged cheeks and lips, pencilled brows, eyes lined with thick black kohl, which struck me as odd, because it was almost her bedtime, and she was usually such a stickler for removing her *maquillage* before sleep.

'Stop gawping at me, Ruth. *The Archers* will be starting any second, and you haven't even started on my feet.'

'The varnish on your toenails,' I said slowly, 'gets awfully chipped, even though you never walk anywhere.'

'And whose fault is that?' she snapped. 'If you will insist on only applying the one coat!'

I shook my head. 'Two,' I said. 'I always apply two. And they usually last for more than three days, but this time—'

'Shhhhh! It's started. Shula's having a crisis.'

We were silent for a while, Moo listening keenly to *The Archers*, while I pretended to busy myself selecting wads of cotton wool and nail polish remover from her bedside table. But I felt sick to my stomach, and my head was whirling with half-formed thoughts. Something Was Not Right, had not been right for a very long time. Had been wrong, terribly wrong, and I had not seen it. Had not wanted to see it. Had been far too frightened, too desperate, too lonely, to see it.

I sat down on the bed, picked up the cushion and held it up to my chest. For what? Comfort? Protection? The familiar stink of her feet?

'I don't understand,' I said. 'There is so much, Moo, which I don't understand.'

'Then shut up and listen,' she hissed. 'If you keep on talking through it, you'll never get a handle on who's who. Ambridge is a very complex—'

'You had been downstairs with me,' I said slowly, 'eating lunch. Then I fell asleep. And then I woke up. And your wheelchair was there, but you weren't. Where were you, Moo?'

She stared at me. 'Up here,' she replied.

'How did you get here?'

'I flew,' she said, with a giggle.

'Moo, please don't.'

'I used the stairlift, of course!' she said indignantly. 'I wheeled myself over to the stairlift like I sometimes have to, when you're asleep, or too lazy, or drunk, or drugged.'

I shook my head. 'I'm never drugged. I never take drugs.'

She smiled coquettishly. 'If you say so, dear.'

'I do say so. I admit I drink, but I never take—'

'Oh, do shut up. I want to listen to my programme in peace. And you haven't even started removing the old varnish.'

I tried again. 'Your wheelchair was – still is – in the living room, Moo. I saw it. I felt it.'

'Shhhhhh!'

'I know what I saw! I'll go down there now and check it's still there.'

'Shhhhhh!'

'It's you, isn't it?' I whispered. 'Playing jokes, sending me mad, it's you . . . it's been you all along. There's nothing wrong with you. You can walk, you've been able to walk for the last twenty years. I'm not going mad, it's you, it's you—'

She slammed her fist on the bedside table with alarming force. I jumped.

'Can I not,' she growled, 'listen to my programme in peace, Ruth, without you wittering on at me? What must I do to make you shut up? All right, I'll admit it – I'll say whatever you like, if you'll just stop droning on! So, here goes . . . I'm not wheelchair-bound at all. No, this has all been an elaborate plan expertly executed by me, because I get a thrill from pretending I'm partially paralysed, just so I can watch you debase yourself cooking and cleaning and wiping up my piss and shit. Then, when you're out and about, I keep myself fit and trim by jogging on my treadmill, and I move things around the house to keep you on your toes. And why might I be doing this? Hmmmm, now, let me see. Oh, yes. I'm doing it to punish you, because I've loathed and resented you for years, for ruining my life. And I've been able to feed and house us both, because my elaborate ruse was bankrolled by royalties from *The Camelford Chronicles*, which, as we both know by now, weren't written by me, because I'm too much of an airhead to write anything of note. No, they were penned by Barney before he hanged himself, and I found them in his room and passed them off as my own, thus defrauding my very own granddaughter of her rightful inheritance. And all to make you pay. Yes, of course, I'd deny myself any life worth living, simply so I could watch you crawl at my feet on your hands and knees.' Her voice had dropped to a whisper by now. 'Because you're the centre of the damned universe, Ruth, or at least the centre of *my* damned universe, which has been more like a hell since losing Harvey and Barney, because of *you*, and the clumsy, cack-handed disaster you are—'

'What – what do you mean? Is all this true?'

'Oh, for God's sake.' She leant across the bed and turned up the volume on the wireless. 'Whatever I say, you'll create your own narrative anyway. I've told you what you wanted to hear. Just shut up and leave me alone.'

'But I only want to hear the truth!'

'Shhhhhh!'

'Stop shushing me!' I was thumping her now with the cushion. I didn't mean to, though, I really didn't mean to.

'TELL ME THE TRUTH!' I think I was shouting. 'TELL ME THE TRUTH, MOO! TELL ME THE TRUTH!'

'SHHHHHHH!'

'DON'T SHUSH ME! TELL ME THE TRUTH, BITCH.'

'You want the truth?'

And she was laughing at me, rolling side to side in the bed, dodging the cushion and laughing. 'I'll give you the truth, you ugly bitch,' she was saying, 'I'll give you truth that you've never been loved, that nobody loved you, ever ever ever, not Harvey, not Barney, not even your mother. They all loved me, me, yes me, yes me. Your stupid mother couldn't love her own daughter, stupid disgusting old woman, who nobody loved. But she loved me, oh she loved me all right, Ruth, fawning all over me, pawing all over me—'

'LIAR!'

'Not lies, Ruth. The truth, Ruth. Shall I tell you what she asked me to do for her, Ruth, what you never saw, because you were so stupid—'

'YOU'RE A DISGUSTING LIAR!'

'You're just like your mother, just like your mother, just like your mother.'

'SICK BITCH!'

I did it then.

I pressed the cushion over her face and held it there, and I must have climbed onto her chest with my knees on her elbows to press down harder, and I was saying over and over again, how dare you, how dare you, and how she wriggled and thrashed at first, and I laughed and pressed down even harder, and now I was the one with the power, the one crowing and jeering, you bitch, you bitch, you took everything, you took it all, yes you did, you took it all from me, everything from me, but you won't take this, you won't take Mother from me . . .

\*

When I pulled the cushion away from her face, Muriel's mouth was agape.

Dribbling.

Eyes wide. Terrible. White.

Dead as a doornail she was.

And *The Archers* music had started, oh yes –

*Dah de dah de dah de dahhhhhhhh*

Exactly seventy-two hours since I'd last heard it play.

# Thursday, 4 July 2019

*One week later*

# Independence Day

They will be having a party next door this evening. Mr American warned me this morning, when I was making my way back from the postbox. He was standing outside Number 73, with his wife and another young couple similarly dressed in shorts and loose-fitting shirts, whom I did not recognize. They were clearly discussing something important, because there was lots of urgent whispering with equally urgent hand gestures. I tried to pass by unnoticed, but Mrs American called after me.

'Ruth! How are you? We're so sorry we haven't popped by, but we've been so busy with Adam's dad. Oh, and apologies if you've noticed any strange smells.' She grimaced. 'Poison solved our rat problem, but at a rather unpleasant price, I'm afraid.'

'It's good to see you, Ruth!' Mr American beckoned me over. 'Come and say hi to Lucy and Jeremy. They live at Number 71. Lucy and Jeremy, this is Ruth – she lives at Number 76, with Mrs Hinchcliffe. Ruth's her carer.'

'Oh!' The Lucy woman eyed me with interest. She had bleached blonde hair, horn-rimmed spectacles, and was wearing large hooped earrings. She was, I suspected, one of those women who tries to look sexy and intelligent, but fails miserably at both. 'God, Muriel Hinchcliffe – my mum loved her

299

books back in the day! Didn't she end up in a wheelchair or something? Oh shit, I'm sorry . . .'

I nodded stiffly, firmly rooted about six feet away from them all. I didn't want them to smell me, you see, because I've been in such a pickle these last few days, I haven't felt inclined to attend to my ablutions.

'No problem,' I said, smiling. 'I'll keep my distance, though, if you don't mind. I have a touch of the flu, and I'd hate for you to catch it.'

'Oh, I'm so sorry!' Mrs American said. 'What about Mrs Hinchcliffe?'

'She's not very well either.'

'Oh dear! Perhaps we should pop over.'

'Not necessary.' I smiled. 'I have it all under control.' I patted my shopping basket. 'Paracetamol, whisky. It's all I need.'

'Well, if you're sure.'

'Yes, I'm sure.'

Mr American cleared his throat. 'Please, call if you need anything, Ruth,' he said earnestly. 'Anything at all.' He was feeling guilty, I suspect, for having neglected me these last few days, because his long, slim toes kept curling and uncurling beneath the brown leather strap of his Birkenstock sandals. 'We were just saying to Lucy and Jeremy here that we should all try to be better neighbours. You know, after what happened . . .' He cocked his head towards Number 73. 'And right under our noses!'

'Shocking,' Mrs American said. 'Slavery! In this day and age!'

'Slavery?' I replied, inwardly kicking myself. Being drawn into a conversation was the last thing I needed.

'Yes, right here! At Number 73. Poor Linh – that pretty Vietnamese girl – and her brother.'

'Linh? Her brother?' I said, confused. 'That toddler she was always lugging around?'

'No, no!' Mr American frowned. 'Linh's brother is two years older than her. No, the toddler belonged to the Lamberts. You know the Lamberts. They own the Lyttle Shop on Lyttleton Road.'

'And, it turns out, several nail bars in north London,' the Lucy woman added.

'I'm lost,' I said. 'I'm sorry. My head is a bit fuzzy. Please excuse me. I'll catch up with you another time.'

'The Lamberts,' Mrs American interjected, 'own Number 73, though they live in a much grander house on Palace Avenue. Come on, Ruth, you must know the Lamberts – such pillars of the community! He's on the council, she's always flouncing around, chairing some local committee or other. Jesus, to think I actually voted for him!'

'And she's a school governor!' The Lucy woman sniffed and pushed her spectacles further up her nose. 'She even had the cheek to lecture Sheba's class on the importance of being kind! Hypocrites, the pair of them.'

'And they'd have carried on the way they were' – Mrs American sighed, gazing at her husband adoringly – 'if it wasn't for Adam's dad.'

Everyone turned and beamed at Mr American. 'One of the few upsides of being a Vietnam veteran,' he shrugged. 'And let's face it, there aren't that many – poor guy still has PTSD. My dad got chatting to Linh a few days ago, Ruth. He decided to learn Vietnamese after the war, by way of atonement . . .'

At this, there was even more beaming and murmurs of approval from the rest of the group. 'And she told him everything. Told him she'd been trying to get someone to notice her for months. She and her brother were trafficked here, with about a dozen others. Some of the girls got dragged into working in the Lamberts' nail bars, but she got landed with the 'job' as an unpaid nanny for the Lamberts' youngest kid, who they kept away from their formal residence as much as possible, because he was a poor sleeper and a bit of a handful. The Lamberts, of course, were far too busy and important to deal with that kind of stuff themselves.'

'Poor little thing,' Mrs American said with feeling.

'Though it wasn't a job at all,' Mr American continued, 'because Linh wasn't paid. Oh, she had food and drink and shelter, and Mrs Lambert's designer cast-offs to wear, but what use is that when you're imprisoned with your brother on a weed farm in a country where you can't speak a word of the language?'

By now, my interest was well and truly piqued. 'Weed farm?'

'Oh, yes. Linh was downstairs tending to Lambert Junior, pretty much 24/7, while her brother was upstairs tending to hundreds of cannabis plants.' Mr American turned to the other man, and spread his palms entreatingly. 'How did we not know? I mean, looking back, the signs were there – those plantation shutters in the upstairs rooms were always closed, and when it snowed last winter, I said to Rebecca, didn't I, darling? I said, isn't it odd that Number 73's roof isn't covered in snow? They must keep the heating on all the time!'

'But it looked so normal from the outside!' Mrs American insisted. 'Even down to the damn petunias in the hanging baskets! God, we've been so stupid.'

I looked across at my own house, thinking – oh, but we're all stupid, Rebecca, my love. Because none of you have noticed a thing, have you? You have no idea of the horrors lying behind my bay window, gabled front door, and red-brick facade. You haven't a damn clue. And I half hoped that one of them might follow my gaze and look up, and wonder out loud why a blackening mass of bluebottles had gathered behind Muriel's bedroom window. But none of them did.

Instead, 'Oh,' Mr American said suddenly. 'Dad said Linh mentioned you. She said that her brother had tried to get the attention of an older lady across the road, who he saw in an upstairs window. He'd been threatened with a beating or worse if he ever opened the shutters, but a couple of weeks ago he did just that. He said that when he used to look through the gaps, he'd often see a woman walking on the spot in the bedroom opposite, and that while she was old, she had such a beautiful face that he was sure she'd be a beautiful person, too, and would help him. So, one day, he opened the shutters and waved to her, but she looked very cross and upset, and he never saw her again.'

He was talking about Moo, of course, and I nearly gave the game away.

'That wasn't me,' I said.

No one disputed this.

'Well, he must have imagined it.' Mr American shrugged. 'I guess you'd imagine all sorts of stuff, living in those conditions.'

'Yes,' I said, with some relief. 'I'm sure you would.'

And then, he invited me to his Independence Day party, which I politely declined. And the four of them started discussing something else – something about a band they all liked that was playing at Alexandra Palace the following week – and I quietly slipped away.

Back home, I hurried through the house to the garden. No sign of Puss, I hasten to add. I haven't seen him since my ding-dong with Moo, which is just as well, all things considered, because I've been a bit of a wreck these last few days. Mother has reappeared, however, taking up residence in the garden shed. She literally hangs out in Harvey's old hammock, and is out for the count most of the time – her cedarwood medicine chest at her side – but she wakes now and then to smile and gesture at me to climb into her lap. I've resisted so far, but have moved into the shed to be with her anyway, because the house was getting too much for me. The telephone wouldn't stop ringing, you see – all hours of the day and night, though the fax machine has remained dormant, thank God. No, ever since Kate Porter revealed her true intentions, two days after my bust-up with Moo, all has been quiet on that front. A parcel arrived, wrapped in brown paper and addressed in thick black marker pen. Inside was a hardcover book entitled *I Know Exactly What You Did and Now I'm Going to Make You Pay* (which hardly trips off the tongue, I know, but I believe convoluted titles are where it's at these days). Folded inside the front cover was a handwritten note:

*I am not surprised you ignored my faxed invitations to the launch of this book at The Ivy on Thursday evening. But I wanted to thank you both anyway. Thank you for getting me sacked from my job, which gave me the impetus to*

*write my first novel. And thank you both for the
inspiration that I took from poor Barney's account of your
truly appalling behaviour over the years. Behaviour now
immortalized in this tale of two bitter women so determined
to destroy one another that they unwittingly wreck the lives
of anyone unfortunate enough to get close to them.*
   *Yours, Kate Porter*

I have no intention of reading the book, of course. Not
my cup of tea at all.

For the first two nights after losing Moo, I sat in the chair beside
her bed. It seemed the natural thing to do, I suppose, to stay
close to her body, her hand in my own. But by the third night,
the death of her had permeated the whole room – not just the
bed, but the space all around it, which had grown in area
somehow, becoming all at once cold, forbidding, and dark. So
I returned to my own simple, bright room, with its unpretentious
furniture and paucity of knick-knacks. But that wasn't much
better. The death of her followed me there: the ice-cold touch
of her permanently on the tips of my fingers. And so I moved
down to the living room, where I tried to rest on the sofa. But
Harvey found me in the early hours – I couldn't see him, but
he found me – and I could hear him in the darkness, wheezing:
*Whatever have you done, Ruth? Whatever have you done?*
   I couldn't sleep in the study either. I tried to nap in Moo's
chair, but the telephone kept ringing and ringing, and I couldn't
bring myself to answer it, because – well. It could have been
any one of them, couldn't it? Harvey, Moo, Fiona, Barney. So
here I am in the shed, with Mother, and my Bag for Life and

its contents: twenty Silk Cut, a tube of Pringles, sixty paracetamol, and a bottle of Scotch. It's a pleasant enough evening for it, soft and balmy, with the sound of birdsong and someone mowing their lawn a few gardens down. Mr and Mrs American have lit their barbecue. I'd find the smell appetizing, were I not quite so sick at heart.

I've been a bit up and down these last few days. Down, because – well, you would be, wouldn't you. But the brief highs I've experienced! Oh, dazzling isn't the word for them. Sometimes, I want to hug myself with the satisfaction of it all, with the knowledge that I *mattered*. I mattered enough for Moo to ruin her own life in order to wreck my own, that she loved me and hated me so – that she *must* have loved me after all, because the opposite of love, my mother always said, wasn't hate, but ice-cold indifference; and the years of planning, the plotting, the Herculean efforts Moo went to just to piss me off were not indifference, not one little bit. No, they came from a place of *passion*. And to think of her jogging on that stupid treadmill, when I was out and about! Her bright blue eyes darting up and down the street, watching for my return. God, it makes me laugh and laugh and laugh and weep to think of the silly old bat, keeping fit for her crafty flits around the house when I was asleep, or drugged, or whatever.

Oh, she drugged me, of course, I know that now. Drugged me as much as I drugged her. *Touché*, as they say, as I'd say to her now, if only she was still with me. *Touché*, Moo. How many points might that word gain me during a game of Scrabble, I wonder? Is it even in the Oxford English Dictionary, being technically French? Fancy a game of Scrabble, Moo, and a cup of chamomile tea?

How frightened and sad she must have been when Linh's brother saw her on the treadmill that day. How sorry she must have felt that the game was up, or very soon would be.

Moo always loved playing games.

I have looked inside Mother's medicine chest and discovered the missing nitrazepam bottle (with several pills missing, of course) miraculously re-materialized. Moo must have replaced them just before I killed her, because she knew I'd kill her, of course; knew exactly which buttons to press. She wanted me to kill her, wanted to be with Harvey and Barney again. But more than anything else, she wanted for me to live on, to have a living death without her, burdened with the knowledge of what I'd done.

What was it she said that night, the night she asked me to kill her?

*At least I can always rely on you, Ruth, to be hopelessly predictable.*

She was right about that, of course she was. She was always right. About everything.

Oh Moo, I cannot live without you—

Moo, I cannot live without—

I cannot live.

There was a downpour last night. This morning, on my way to the postbox, the air was filled with the rich, earthy smell of fresh rain on parched ground. The fragrance has a name, you know – petrichor. Such a beautiful word to know and say, though I have never used it before in my life, and daresay I never will again. Petrichor, petrichor. It trips so easily off the tongue.

I was out and about, because I wanted to catch the post for

my letter to Stephanie and Courtney. I have also left a note for Joanna-Next-Door, who is due to return from her travels tomorrow. A simple note, though I think it tells her everything she needs to know:

> Dear Joanna,
> Thank you for everything. Call the police. I'm in the shed, Moo's in the bedroom. All rather unpleasant, I'm afraid, so please don't come in as it'll only upset you. Apologies for the inconvenience, and I'm awfully sorry about what Elliott's done, but I honestly didn't realize until it was too late. Please give my regards to your father.
> All best wishes, Ruth.

Poor Joanna. No amount of Pilates or yoga will help her through what she's about to endure.

My letter to Stephanie and Courtney is equally straight to the point. I tried and tried to explain myself, but, unusually for me, the words wouldn't come. In the end, I thought it better to direct the pair of them to the series of notebooks and journals I have continued to keep over the years, including this very notebook, which – rather poetically, I suppose – I have very nearly finished. I have only the final page to fill, which I will with some self-indulgent musings. Actually, I will attempt to explain my behaviour to Stephanie and Courtney after all. It's the least they both deserve.

Yes, I will do so now, while my head is still clear. Before the nitrazepam, paracetamol and half-bottle of Scotch I have just polished off take their full effect.

*Dear Stephanie and Courtney,*

*I know I have already apologized in my letter to you, but I would like to take my final few moments to explain myself. I am so sorry. Sorry for all of us, but most of all, I am sorry for you. Moo and I took from you both that which wasn't ours to take, so determined were we to hold on to each other and the only purpose in life we knew – a perpetual one-upmanship – much to the detriment of anyone unfortunate enough to know us.*

*But Moo and I did love each other. I am absolutely certain of that. I don't think two people ever loved or needed each other more, actually, because no one else loved us at all. Not our mothers or fathers, not even our husband – not really. Moo was prized for her looks, and as for me – well. The less said about me, the better.*

*But you, Courtney – oh, you are so lucky! Because you have a mother who loves you. A mother who loves you unconditionally – just as I know your father loved you too. Your mother is very proud of you, but (and this is crucial, Courtney) she loved you even when you were not easy to love; when you were not a source of pride, but of worry and disappointment. Please understand and appreciate the value of that. Unconditional love is the greatest gift a child could have, a gift worth a thousand times more than this house, which is yours now, of course, along with the royalties of* The Camelford Chronicles. *Your grandmother's solicitor, Mr Tonks, from Tonks, Waring and Hustwick solicitors, has his instructions, a copy of which you will find in the top drawer of your grandmother's desk.*

The Camelford Chronicles *will, I am sure, enjoy a resurgence in popularity once your father's identity as the true author comes to light, along with the disgraceful behaviour of his mother and her oldest friend. The downmarket newspapers love that sort of thing. I daresay you will find yourself famous for a while.*

*You will need help with all of this. Your mother is a sensible woman who loves you. Please listen to her advice.*

*Wishing you both every happiness (and God knows, you deserve it),*

*Ruth.*

A blast of wind blows the shed door open, ushering in the sound of laughter, popping corks and clinking glasses from Mr and Mrs Americans' party next door.

It's tempting to leave the shed for the garden, where I can observe my neighbours carousing from the safety of the shadows. But I am afraid of departing this place – my sanctuary these last few days – with the ghost of my mother, my booze, my pills and journals for comfort. It's always a risk, moving on. You never know whether what lies ahead is better or worse than whatever it is you're leaving behind.

But it's time.

I rise from my deckchair and stand on the threshold, where I linger a moment, staring into the darkness. Then Mr American releases the first of his Independence Day fireworks, and I step out, as the night sky above me erupts in a hail of dazzling stars.

# Acknowledgements

I have dreamed of writing and publishing a novel ever since I was a child. Without the help of the following people, my dream would not have come true. Thank you all, from the bottom of the heart of the six-year-old girl who cried to her mum that she'd never publish a book, 'because all the best stories have already been written'.

Thanks to the team at JULA, especially my amazing agent, the lovely Jo Unwin, for her wit, wisdom and unfailing support, and to Milly Reilly, for her patience and kindness.

Thank you to my publisher, Wayne Brookes, for his enthusiasm and expertise, and for falling in love with Moo and Roo in the first place. Thanks also to the rest of the talented Pan Mac editorial team, especially Marta Catalano, Kate Berens, Lucy Hale, Gillian Green and Ellah Mwale. Thank you, Kieryn Tyler, for the wonderful jacket design and Holly Sheldrake for your production expertise. Thank you to Natasha Tulett in marketing and Philippa McEwan in publicity. Thank you also to the sales team, especially Stuart Dwyer, Rebecca Kellaway and Claire Evans.

Thank you, David Llewelyn, for being Moo and Roo's champion. You are one in a million. Our next lunch is on me – no arguing this time.

A huge thank you to the marvellous folk who read the first draft of *The Final Hours* and laughed in all the right places: my sister-in-law, Rae Parkin, who read the entire manuscript on her phone – I'll never know how you managed it, but I'm so touched that you did; Jenny and Chris Smith, thank you for your friendship, advice, hand-holding and for being the best pub-quizzing teammates ever. Thank you, Belinda Lawley, for letting me blether on about submission processes during the Ally Pally parkruns.

Thank you, Mark Williams and Elaine Mitchell, for cheering and clapping me on and for being ace big brother and fab sister-in-law.

Thank you to the friends whose encouragement has spurred me on through the years, especially Isabel Sutherland (you always said I'd do it!), Cathy McDowell, Florence Barras (thank you for The Vineyard pep talks), Mark Borland, John and Caroline Hiscox (heroes, the pair of you), Helen Prangley, Sarah Carpenter, and Neil and Sue Margerison.

Thank you, Megan Wilson, my Form 1 English teacher at St Cyres Comprehensive School. You wrote in my end-of-year report that you expected me to write a novel one day, and I never forgot your words. It's taken forty-two years, but I was always tardy with my homework.

To my late parents, Barbara and Leighton Williams: thank you for nurturing my love of writing and for buying that Silver Reed typewriter for my twelfth Christmas. Best present EVER. I hope I've done you proud.

Finally, my immediate family: dear H and E, thank you just for being, and for the joy you both bring me on a daily basis. I love you, unconditionally.

And R. Thank you for keeping the faith, especially when I was rapidly losing faith in myself. Without your unwavering love and support, *The Final Hours of Muriel Hinchcliffe* would not have been written, and for that I can never, ever thank you enough.